Man Behind the Gun

OTHER FIVE STAR WESTERN TITLES BY LAURAN PAINE:

Tears of the Heart (1995); *Lockwood* (1996); *The White Bird* (1997); *The Grand Ones of San Ildefonso* (1997); *Cache Cañon* (1998); *The Killer Gun* (1998); *The Mustangers* (1999); *The Running Iron* (2000); *The Dark Trail* (2001); *Guns in the Desert* (2002); *Gathering Storm* (2003); *Night of the Comancheros* (2003); *Rain Valley* (2004); *Guns in Oregon* (2004); *Holding the Ace Card* (2005); *Feud on the Mesa* (2005); *Gunman* (2006); *The Plains of Laramie* (2006); *Halfmoon Ranch* (2007); *Man from Durango* (2007); *The Quiet Gun* (2008); *Patterson* (2008); *Hurd's Crossing* (2008); *Rangers of El Paso* (2009); *Sheriff of Hangtown* (2009); *Gunman's Moon* (2009); *Promise of Revenge* (2010); *Kansas Kid* (2010); *Guns of Thunder* (2010); *Iron Marshal* (2011); *Prairie Town* (2011); *The Last Gun* (2011)

Man Behind the Gun

A WESTERN DUO

Lauran Paine

FIVE STAR
A part of Gale, Cengage Learning

Detroit • New York • San Francisco • New Haven, Conn • Waterville, Maine • London

Five Star Publishing, a part of Gale, Cengage Learning.

Set in 11 pt. Plantin.

LIBRARY OF CONGRESS CATALOGING-IN-PUBLICATION DATA

Paine, Lauran.
Man behind the gun : a western duo / by Lauran Paine. — 1st ed.
p. cm.
ISBN 978-1-4328-2561-4 (hardcover) — ISBN 1-4328-2561-5 (hardcover)
I. Title.
PS3566.A34M24 2012
813'.54—dc23 2011047017

Published in 2012 in conjunction with Golden West Literary Agency.

Printed in Mexico
1 2 3 4 5 6 7 16 15 14 13 12

CONTENTS

★ ★ ★ ★ ★

Fort Morgan

★ ★ ★ ★ ★

I

Once they left the forested uplands and were crossing the grassland their route of travel was across an undulating landscape where part of the time they were in swales, and part of the time they were crossing low, thick land swells. Occasionally, in the swales, they encountered groves of trees that were flourishing and very dark green. Several times they came across creeks of clear water with scurrying trout minnows in their glassy depths, and where they crossed a mile-wide swale there was fresh evidence of a big hunt having been concluded here not very long before, maybe a day or two. From that point on they made it a point to study all the surrounding land each time they topped out over a land swell.

This was Blackfeet country and while there had been treaties in existence for some years now, meeting delegations of Indians in Washington or elsewhere was very often very different from meeting bands of armed Indians on their historic hunting ground.

The facts that the Blackfeet lived in a country surrounded by enemies and were only marginally more acceptable to other tribesmen than the Crows—who were disliked by everyone—made it additionally essential to ride cautiously.

The town was southwesterly. They could see roof tops, a few of which were metal and therefore reflected the leaden light of a sun that had been nearly obscured by gray overcast for two days now.

Sam Starr scratched and stood in his stirrups to gauge the distance yet to be covered, then sat down and said: "You fellers likely won't believe this, but I knew all along we'd make it."

The other two eyed Sam caustically. "The omens," one of them said, and shook his head.

Sam was unperturbed. He had been the subject of mild ridicule about things of this nature ever since he had joined up with Jack Pate and Roger Bemis. But Sam Starr, raised in a Brulé camp and in many ways more red man than white man, was unshakeable in some things.

He was a stalwart, powerful man with a bullet head and a neck as thick as an oak stump. He had a slightly hooked nose and a pair of shrewd, knowing blue eyes half hidden behind the perpetual squint of a man who had spent most of his life in wind and heat, cold and storm.

Sam was ageless. He had probably never looked young. He did not look young now. He was weathered, lined, loose and supple in his movements, and for all his faded, worn clothing, the ivory-stocked six-gun in its shiny old hip holster spoke volumes about Sam Starr, whatever his age was. He probably only had a general idea of his age himself.

He was also a wanted man.

Jack Pate had broken out of the grinding poverty of his earlier environment in one brilliant afternoon four years earlier. Jack had built a fire on a railroad track, had plundered the mail car, and had been running ever since. As Roger Bemis once said, when a man robbed the mail, he had the whole force of the national government after his hide, and that included the Army, the secret service, and every lawman between Canada and Mexico.

Jack was a tall, lean man with black hair and eyes to match. He had a wide, thin mouth and a noticeably wary kind of unique confidence. Four years after most newspapers had carried lurid stories of his robbery, he was still running loose. That would have made any outlaw feel some confidence.

Roger Bemis had gray around the temples, never rode anything but the fastest, most durable horses he could buy or steal, and in Montana as well as over in Idaho he had prices on his head for bullion robberies. He had an uncanny knack for knowing when stages would have a bullion box in the boot. Three times in a row he had scored, and each time the mining companies had hired private detectives to hunt Roger down. Once, two Pinkerton men nearly caught him in Cheyenne, but he escaped by jumping on a moving train heading south, and that was how he had met Jack Pate. In fact, they did not rob the train, they rode it all the way down to San Francisco, sitting in one poker session after another, and losing most of the time, then they had bought outfits in San Francisco and started north and east again.

Behind them, across the mountains beyond Blackfeet country, they had all three of them blown a bank's safe out the back wall in a town called Coffeyville. Now, having had no chance to spend any of the money, or any chance even to slow down until the last few days, they were heading toward that distant town with the tin roofs here and there, without any idea what the name of the place was, and only a very general idea of the territory they were passing through.

But they knew Indian sign and they had been encountering it for several days now. The money in their saddlebags would not be worth anything at all if they ran afoul of a hunting party out in this open country with no one to see what would happen, or who would ever afterward be able to find the three cleverly concealed graves.

Robbing banks, stages, railroad trains was a hazardous way to make a living, but intruding on Indian hunting grounds even in these latter days when there were treaties to cover just about everything including trespassing was something altogether different.

As Jack had dryly said when they emerged from the shelter of timber and forest gloom: "If we get across all that damned open country and find a town, it'll be because the Lord is watchin' over us."

Neither Sam nor Roger commented, but now, as they were getting closer to the town they had seen from thirty miles across the undulating country, Sam spat aside, straightened in the saddle, and smiled at his partners. "I always figured the Lord was against fellers like us . . . outlaws and what-not. It sure makes me feel a lot better knowin' He ain't entirely off us. But like I told you, the signs said we'd make it."

Roger, who had been watching something in the infinite distance for a while now, raised a gloved hand to point. "Your omens say anything about us maybe gettin' real close to a town and still not makin' it, Sam? Look yonder."

Eight or ten mounted Indians were sitting woodenly in a tight band upon a far land swell, gazing down where the three partners were riding. Two additional red men had left the men on the top-out and were loping easily on a curving, intercepting course, carbines balancing upon their thighs, heads up and watching.

Sam looked, spat again, figured the course of those intercepting horsemen and finally said: "They won't get us. Not just the two of them. Anyway, if they figured to get us, the whole blessed band of them would be strung out across our route. Too close to town, gents. They start a big fight out here and the folks in town'll hear the shootin' and them Indians'll have more trouble than they can handle."

It sounded very reassuring, but the intercepting horsemen were still angling to be on both sides of the three outlaws, and those other bucks were still sitting up there, waiting and watching. They could, depending upon their intentions and the circumstances that would develop shortly now, race down off that land swell and still form a line between the three partners and the town.

"Roger," Sam said, "you talk any Blackfeet?"

Bemis did not take his eyes off the two distant horsemen when he answered: "No. I have trouble enough with everyday English. How about you?"

Sam sighed. "Sioux. I can talk it in either Lakota or Dakota. I can talk a little Crow. But no Blackfeet."

Lanky Jack Pate said: "I get the feelin' those fellers don't want to talk anyway, and sure as hell as we bust out and run for it those other ones on the little hill are goin' to break out and try to cut us off from the town. You fellers care to know something? It's times like this that I wish I'd listened to my old granny . . . she always wanted me to be a soldier."

Roger grunted, speaking again without taking his eyes off the Indians. "Soldiers have run-ins like this all the time. Anyway, the pay is lousy and the suits they give a man are too thick and heavy."

The two racing broncos stopped, spoke briefly beyond gun range, then split up, one racing still farther southward, the other one turning eastward at a trot, clearly preparing himself to be in a position along the north side of the three outlaws where he could rake them, while his companion was covering more ground to be in a position along the south flank of the outlaws.

Pate watched, then said: "You know, if those damned idiots weren't always so pumped full of a notion to prove what great warriors they are, the whole batch would be tryin' to get us on both sides instead of just those two."

Roger tipped down his hat to shield his eyes better. "If I was to guess, I'd say these two are young warriors. The older fellers out there on that ridge figure to let these two greenhorns count their coup . . . if they can . . . and if they don't hack it, those other lads are going to cut us off and. . . ."

"Naw," scoffed Sam, who had been raised with the Sioux, after being orphaned by them in a wagon train raid thirty years earlier. "I already told you . . . too close to that town. They got at least one spokesman up there on that ridge, one gray head. He won't let it grow into no battle. Not here, but if they had caught us ten miles back. . . ." Sam drew a rigid forefinger across his unshaven gullet. Then he smiled. "And the biggest mistake these young bucks have made . . . they run their horses too long and too far, and we been just pokin' along. You fellers ready to outrun those braves, and make 'em look bad before their friends? Let's go!"

They drew carbines and flourished them as they also sank in the spurs and broke over into a belly-down race. Upon that distant land swell the seasoned men watched in disgust as their fellow tribesmen were easily outrun by three unshaven, heavily armed strangers.

II

They cooled out their horses for the last mile and a half. By the time they were on the outskirts of the town, there was no sign of the Indians back yonder. Sam chuckled about that. He had been correct about the seasoned warriors being disgusted with the lack of foresight of the two broncos who had worked their horses too hard in getting down there, and had nothing left to use in the pursuit. But Sam's amusement went a bit farther; he had said the omens promised safe arrival in this town. About omens he had been right before. Each time he became more unshakeable, so the occasional ridicule rolled off him like water off a duck's back.

Jack Pate, a man of deduction and observation, was still a ways out when he said: "They sometimes got a board nailed to a post with the town's name on it."

There was no sign, although at the upper end of the place where there was a big palisaded corral yard and a sod-roofed old log barn some faint lettering spelled out Fort Morgan.

But even before they got down that far Sam also noticed something else. "Damned place looks deserted," he said, and by the time they were entering town the other two noticed the same thing.

The roadway was empty of people, the stores were closed, a couple of foraging dogs were snuffling along the edge of the plank walk, and three horses, plus a top buggy with an old mare between the shafts, stood drowsing at the rack out front of the general store.

At the log jail house there was a black bow made of ribbon material on the door, and at the lower end of town, where the livery barn stood, a runny-eyed old boozer came forth with skeletal hands to take their horses as they piled off. He did not utter a sound, not even when they handed over an extra cartwheel for especially good care of their livestock.

They stood in the gray overcast, saddlebags over their shoulders, looking up the empty roadway. Sam said: "Maybe they got a bad sickness around here." Indian-like, this thought frightened him. Men and guns couldn't do it but fear of an epidemic certainly could.

They trooped up the plank walk in the direction of the boarding house, and found only one person, a thick-bodied, flat-faced full-blood who eyed them from dark eyes with muddy whites. She could have been a Sioux or a Blackfeet, but her features and build were wrong for that, so she must have been a Digger, one of those wandering Paiutes who turned up in places where Paiutes had never arrived as hunters or warriors, only as pariahs.

She showed them three rooms, accepted their money, and turned her back to head in the direction of the smell of cooking, without making a sound.

Sam said: "This place gives me the creeps." He raised his head at the muted sound of singing. It was a dolorous dirge, and Sam's back hair stood up.

Their horses were tuckered, they had put a lot of miles between themselves and the place of their latest depredation, and the three of them, durable though they were, needed rest and a few conveniences, so no one, not even Sam Starr, suggested that they ride on.

If the sun had been able to break through that dismal overcast, it might have helped.

They returned to the roadway. The singing was coming from over behind town somewhere. Sam led off in that direction, and, when they saw the crowd of somber humanity in the solid gloom of cottonwood trees, they also saw the iron fence and the neat rows of headboards and inscribed stones.

Someone was being buried. Judging by the size of the crowd he must have been a well-liked individual. Everyone from town including darkly attired, freshly-scrubbed children were over there, their backs to the three outlaws who stood, looking.

When the singing died away, a massive, shock-headed man who more nearly resembled a blacksmith than a preacher stepped up onto a horseshoe keg and began his oration. He recited one virtue after another, never mentioned a name, and in a booming voice that reached easily back where the three outlaws stood called alike on God and man to gaze upon this final resting place of a person who had not failed to touch beneficially the life of every human being gathered around today to give him a proper send-off.

Sam said: "I'm dry as a bone."

They meandered back through the crooked byways to the main thoroughfare and strode across to the saloon. Inside, reading a dog-eared old newspaper, a bald, round-faced man glanced up. "Is it over with?" he asked.

Jack leaned on the bar when he answered. "No, but soon now. They're to the place where he never did any wrong. How about a bottle and three glasses?"

When the bar man returned and placed glass in front of them, he said: "Well, y'know, he really was a fine man."

Roger was watching Jack fill their glasses when he said: "Must have been. The whole town's over there."

"I wouldn't say he never done no wrong," stated the bald bar man, "but I'd guess he done more right things."

Roger reached for his glass. "How come you aren't over there?"

The bar man answered slowly. "I got a business to mind. But then, that's only part of it. He was a decent man . . . I wouldn't never say different. On the other hand he's given me fits over the years on Saturday nights when I got to make my profit for the week. He wouldn't tolerate no drunks, and before a fight could get started, he was on 'em like a rash. But I got to be fair . . . he done an awful lot of good around here. Out on the range, too. He could track like an Indian, fight like a catamount, and I'll tell you one thing for a fact, we ain't had no robberies nor killings around Fort Morgan since he was appointed town marshal, to replace old Steve Morse, who died pretty much the same way . . . one day old Steve was fit as a fiddle, and the next day he got down, stopped eatin', and within a week was dead as a stone."

The three outlaws were gazing directly at the bald bar man. Jack Pate said: "He was the law, this feller they're buryin' out yonder?"

"Yep. Been township lawman for four years. Nearly five years. Then, couple months back, he commenced to ail. Went downhill awful fast and died day before yesterday. There's an old cuss down at Potts's livery barn who can paint folks . . . when he's sober and don't have the shakes. They're going to take up a collection and have him paint a likeness of Marshal Houston to hang in the fire hall up the road across from the stage company corral yard."

Sam downed his whiskey and reached with a big, scarred hand for the bottle. Roger and Jack continued to gaze at their informant across the bar. Jack said: "Who've they picked to succeed the marshal?"

The bald bar man shrugged. "No one. There's been talk. They say old Alec Griffith, who was a lawman years before he got into the cattle business, turned 'em down, and some range riders was in here last Saturday night and they told me someone from the town council was out talkin' around at the ranches, lookin' for someone. No luck." The bar man made a sweep of the bar top with his sour bar rag, then glanced up. "Say, wouldn't be that by some chance one of you fellers could have been a deputy somewhere? The pay is good, you can keep a horse free at the livery barn, and the jail house ain't a bad place. Warm in winter and cool in summertime."

Sam grimaced over his second drink, pushed the little glass away, and blew out a big ragged breath.

Jack and Roger were wryly eyeing the bar man. Jack smiled a little. "Just riders passing through, mister," he replied to the bar man. "Don't know a blessed thing about keeping the law."

The bar man may not have been very hopeful anyway because, as he scooped up their silver coins, he said: "Yeah. Well, I guess it's not really the best job in the world anyway. I guess someone'll come along. But for a fact we have darned little law-breakin' in the Fort Morgan country, so I guess we'll get along. But folks are sure goin' to miss Clement Houston. Me, too . . . but not on Saturday nights I won't."

The outlaws returned to the roadway. Here and there people were drifting back from the cemetery, heading for home where they could change out of their Sunday clothes. Impatient children ran ahead like sheep, yelping back and forth. Attending a funeral where someone was nailed into a box, invisible to young eyes whose only real concern was with what could be seen, had simply been a thoroughly tiring and boring affair.

Sam rolled a smoke. "Nice town," he averred, lit up, and leaned on the log wall at his back watching people come out from between buildings and around byway corners. "Fort Morgan . . . nice town, gents. No marshal. One of the nicest towns I ever seen."

They ate at the solitary café in town. The café man was a garrulous former stager run to fat and age. But there was one thing to be said in favor of someone running a café in a cow town who had formerly been in a profession where men missed a lot of meals: when he spread a meal before a man, there was an awful lot of it.

Sam Starr could outeat almost any two men he had ever known, including Jack and Roger, but they gave excellent accounts of themselves because they also belonged to a profession where meals were frequently interrupted, or missed altogether, sometimes for a day or two at a time.

The former stage driver's name was Paul Benson. He had in his youth been a range man but had been hired on as a temporary replacement driver once, and had been following staging for the ensuing twenty-five years. There was very little of the country between Council Bluffs and Tombstone he did not know by the yard. He was also a man who saw the best in folks. While Starr, Pate, and Bemis were stuffing themselves, Paul Benson told them of the virtues of the deceased town marshal, and, unlike the bar man who still had a little deep-down resentment, Benson could not think of a single vice Clem Houston had possessed.

When this got to be too much for Sam, and he said—"He

should have sprouted wings."—Benson looked down his nose at Starr while answering. "Wings might get you up in the air, but a good head screwed on right down here on earth is a hell of a lot more desirable, and Clem Houston had one of the best heads I ever run across."

Properly admonished, Sam went back to his meal.

Jack and Roger were less likely to make snap judgments than Sam Starr was. Nevertheless when they were out in the early evening, down near the livery barn where they had looked in on their livestock, Jack echoed something Sam had said that morning.

"Yes sir, gents, I do believe this here is a real nice town. Friendly and . . . safe . . . now that they buried this lawman of theirs and don't have a replacement for him. Maybe we'd ought to sort of settle in for a week or two."

The way Roger saw it, a stroke of such good fortune probably only occurred once, maybe at the very most, twice, in a man's lifetime. The lawman was in his grave today; the town was a considerable distance from anywhere, surrounded by the hunting ground of Blackfeet who would discourage a lot of incoming traffic; there was no railroad or telegraph at Fort Morgan; the three of them were total strangers to everyone in this area—and they each had plenty of money in their saddlebags.

He made these points quietly, while the three of them were loafing out front of the livery barn near a huge old scarred and unkempt cottonwood tree. He concluded by making a valid summary.

"A situation like this, gents, is what folks like us work toward and run a lot of risks for. Sit back, get plenty of rest and grub, poker, a warm saloon. Not a damned thing to worry about."

"Until they pick a new lawman," Jack Pate said dryly.

They crossed over, strolling in the direction of the saloon, each of them losing their inherent wariness a little at a time. Sam bought them three stogies from the bald bar man, got a greasy deck of cards and a bottle, and settled with his partners in a corner where a round old rickety table was suitable for a poker session.

The saloon filled up gradually. A lot of the talk concerned Town Marshal Houston. Several range men came in late, and a pair of stagers, a driver and gun guard, arrived looking tired and dusty and dry as bone.

"Them damned Indians," Sam said during a shuffle, and swore mildly. "I'll tell you something about Indians. They couldn't have kept their country against even Mexicans, and I'll tell you why . . . they don't know how to fight."

Roger, about to deal cards, stopped moving and stared. Jack's broad brow slowly gathered into a frown of disbelief.

Sam was unaffected by any of this. "Really, gents. Let me tell you why they don't know how to fight. An Indian goes out lookin' for a coup. He don't fight alongside other broncos unless he absolutely has to. He fights as an individual. When he gets tired or thirsty or hungry, he just turns and rides away. Yeah, the last five, maybe ten years, they learned from watchin' soldiers, but by then it was too late. They was whipped to a frazzle."

Roger dealt the cards, picked his up, fanned them, and studied things for a moment, then raised his eyes to Sam. "You ever hear of a gent named Custer, Sam?"

Starr snorted. "I was in the Brulé camp. I seen more trinkets and hair come back from that fight than either of you fellers can even count." Sam smiled at Roger Bemis. "And, partner, that's the best example of how they didn't know how to fight. Couple hunnert soldiers and more'n five thousand Indians. It should have been a massacre. It wasn't. They wiped out old Turkey Neck and his troop, and never did get the forted up fellers on the hill, and the next day they commenced ridin' off to go huntin'." Sam wagged his head, dropped two cards, and called for replacements, then sweetened the pot with two silver dollars while Jack and Roger warily eyed him. Sam would bluff; he would use every trick he knew including that business of puffing out his cheeks, maybe even rolling up his eyes as though giving thanks, but he did not bluff often.

Jack threw in his cards and leaned to refill his glass. Roger teetered between raising and folding. It galled him that after so long a time he still did not know when Sam was bluffing. He swore and threw in his hand.

III

The most durable outlaws were horsemen. Anyone could ride a horse; all a person had to do was spread his legs and pull a horse under him, but a horseman was a lot more than a rider and Jack Pate not only specialized in horse stealing, he was also an excellent judge of horseflesh. He rode the best animals he could find. So did his partners, but Jack was a real purist when it came to cinching his saddle onto an animal, and he was good about caring for his horses. He rode nothing but the fastest, most durable, and breedy animals. His profession required nothing less, and he had been outriding pursuers for a lot of years, as had Sam and Roger, and, while they were equally sensitive to the needs of men in their line of work, they were not such inherent horsemen as Jack was.

In fact, after several days of easy living in Fort Morgan, Sam and Roger neglected to go down and look in on their animals, but Jack went down once each day, usually in the evening. He also rode out a few times to exercise his horse, leaving Sam and Roger at the porch of the boarding house or at the saloon.

One morning at the café he told them of sighting Indians the evening before, straggling westward, travois, dogs, horses, and noise.

Sam said: "Big hunt. It's the right time of year. Someone maybe saw an old mangy buffler and built it into a whole herd."

Some range men arrived in the early afternoon also to spread word of a big band of Indians crossing the range to the west. They said the cow outfits were detailing a few men to drift along and keep an eye on the Blackfeet.

No one anticipated trouble, nor in fact would there be any trouble. Not when the whole band was moving. There were always a few strong-hearts willing to issue a challenge, but older heads commanded when a clan was on the move. Perhaps a luckless old cow might stand her ground too long in their line of march, but no cowman made an issue of something like that, not if he had a lick of sense.

Nonetheless, some travelers, who arrived in Fort Morgan from the south and had heard the story of moving Indians, decided to lie over for a few days. The stage company's local supervisor advised it. Not, he said, because there was even a remote chance of danger, but just to keep folks from worrying too much.

That night Sam met one of the stage passengers at the bar, bought him a drink, and invited him to sit in on the nightly poker game with Jack and Roger.

The stranger was a traveling peddler who dealt mostly in hardware—plows, traps, and chain. He was a very good poker player. He cleaned the partners out and did it, as far as they could determine by intent scrutiny, without a single card up his sleeve.

Sam was a little disagreeable for the next two days. Nor did he invite anyone to join them at cards again. He had lost $11 to that traveling man, and, although he had bundles of greenbacks still in his saddlebags, it bothered him to be cleaned out. Like most men who played a lot of poker, Sam could not abide the suspicion that someone else was a whole lot better at cards than he was.

They went down to the livery barn, had their stalled horses turned out in corrals where they could exercise, then they watched that skeletal hostler at work on a piece of stretched canvas upon which he was sketching in the face of a craggy-looking man with direct, pale eyes and an iron jaw. The hostler worked between chores, and kept a bottle of rye whiskey under the stool he sat on at his painting.

When they returned to the roadway, Sam said: "I once knew an Indian who was better at it than that feller is. He could draw a man so good it sort of made you wonder about someone bein' able to do that, without havin' a spirit inside him."

Jack and Roger exchanged a glance, then the three of them headed for the café.

They had bought new britches and shirts at the general store, had bathed twice now in the last ten days at the shed out behind the barbershop, and the harness maker had re-soled their boots. Sam kept five or six stogies in his shirt pocket. He also carried the makings, and occasionally rolled a cigarette, but to Sam a cigar was the mark of distinction. A pocketful of cigars gave Sam Starr a feeling of complete affluence.

Those meandering Indians disappeared somewhere near the horizon where hulking mountains spread for hundreds of miles to the west and north. They gradually became less of a topic of conversation.

Several big cow outfits were working their ranges within a half dozen miles of town, so there were more range men in Fort Morgan for a week or so, before the range crews were shifted farther off.

There was talk along the bar, and throughout town as well, about a replacement for Marshal Houston. The range men laughed about that. What particularly amused them was the lack of success the town fathers were having, but, as Paul Benson confided to the three partners one night at his counter, the town fathers weren't really looking very hard any more. As long as Fort Morgan ran itself without a specific and definite need, the council saved a lawman's salary.

A grizzled old cowman named Griffith, Alec Griffith, arrived in town one high noon, went directly to the proprietor of the general store, and said in no uncertain terms that he had lost six head of his best using stock horses, and he wanted to know what the town fathers figured to do about it—about sending out a lawman.

The storekeeper, head of the council for this year, tried his placating best to alleviate Griffith's anger, and had very little success. He then convened the town council and relayed Griffith's words. One of the other members said that it was not technically up to the town to provide protection for the range; the cowmen did not contribute to the township fund, and, when Marshal Houston had been alive and had ridden out any number of times to enforce the law on the range, the cowmen had not only grumbled, they had occasionally said they were fully capable of handling anything that needed handling on the range.

It was the opinion of the town council, then, that while the search for a replacement for Clem Houston should continue, if any more complaining cowmen came to town, they were to be told the town was not going to be responsible for the range.

Fourteen more horses were stolen. Nine from one cow outfit, and five from an outfit that was at its marking ground, with the using stock inside a rope corral not more than thirty yards from where ten riders were bedded down, sleeping like logs.

People in town were disturbed, but in general agreed with the councilmen. Jack Pate was out front of the livery barn one evening and heard that grizzled, old, faded-looking cowman named Griffith tell a man Jack recognized as being the preacher at the cemetery that first day when the three partners had ridden into town that, if there was not going to be any law any more, the cowmen would revert to the methods they had used some years back before any lawmen had arrived in the country.

Jack relayed this to Sam and Roger at their nightly card game. He also said: "There always has to be some horse's rear end to stir things up."

"They're professionals, you can bet good money on that," stated Roger. "Five head taken right out of a rope corral at a marking ground."

"Indians," suggested Jack, and Sam stoutly shook his head. "No Indian I ever rode with would steal a few here and a few there in the same country. He'd round 'em all up and never even look back for two hunnert miles." Sam glanced over his cards at Jack. "White men steal horses like these fellers is doing."

Jack was quiet for a long while. He had not actually been bothered at the thought of professional horse thieves being in the country, but it did annoy him that Fort Morgan, which had been so quiet and peaceful up until now, was beginning to be stirred up.

Roger scooped in a $2 pot he had won as he said: "If they're professionals, Sam, they wouldn't keep it up. Not in the same area. Not with angry cowmen all around."

Sam knew better. "One last time, Roger. They figure to do it one last time . . . each night. It's hard to let go of something good when you got it in your fist."

Jack Pate said: "Yeah, and it's that one more time that gets 'em sunk in the ground with someone's lariat marks on their gullets."

Roger won four pots in a row. They broke up the game and

went over to string along the bar for a couple of rounds before heading to the boarding house for bed. A lot of time had passed. They not only felt at home in Fort Morgan, since nothing had happened to trouble them, they were also learning not to glance over their shoulders from time to time.

Out in the bland summertime night Sam yawned prodigiously, then grunted at his friends and went stalking over in the direction of the boarding house.

Roger and Jack had a smoke, first, then Roger also headed for his room. Jack finished his smoke, considered the flawless high sky with its rash of diamond-chip stars, listened to some talking cowboys out at the tie rack, then killed his quirly and turned southward in the direction of the livery barn.

An hour later Jack roused his partners, took them to his room that had not been visited since morning, sat them both down, and said: "We're cleaned out. That old bastard who's supposed to run the barn was passed-out drunk and the horses are gone."

Sam and Roger gazed steadily at Jack, neither of them speaking for a long while. They had both been asleep, and even now, when they were fully awake, things soaked in slowly.

"Those god-damn' cowmen and their talk! They've been getting raided for two weeks and what do they do . . . talk!" Jack pitched his hat onto the narrow little bed against the wall. "One more time?" he said bitterly, looking at Sam, whose earlier remark this had been. "Those bastards came right into town."

"Professionals," conceded Roger, and scratched inside his shirt with some vigor.

Jack was only interested in one thing. "We're afoot," he told the other two men. "That means we're sittin' ducks for the first posse man who pokes his nose around here lookin' for us."

Sam scoffed. "Hell, Jack, we been here for weeks. If there'd been anyone trailin' us, they sure as hell would have found this place by now . . . if they knew where it was, and if they figured we was here."

Roger stopped scratching. "God dammit, that horse was one of the best I ever rode. I don't like losing him any more'n I like the idea of being set afoot."

"There are plenty other horses," Sam stated, arising to go lean and look out the window. "What the hell time is it anyway? The roadway's plumb empty."

Neither Jack nor Roger answered so Sam turned, stretched, then went back to his chair and spoke the thought that his partners were wrestling with, as though it was the most natural thing in the world. "You want them horses back, gents, there's no law here to do it for us, so we got to do it ourselves."

He sank down, glanced from Jack to Roger, and yawned again, this time behind a paw of a hand.

Jack agreed. "It's not a matter for the law anyway. It's a matter for us fellers who own those horses to take care of. I never asked the law to look for a horse I'd lost."

Sam grinned from ear to ear. "You wouldn't dast ask anything like that." He slapped his oaken legs and stood up. "All right. I got to get my guns and hat, then I'll meet you fellers outside." At the doorway he stopped and looked back. "We sure better hide those saddlebags." Then he departed.

Jack and Roger parted. Sam had put it on the line for all three of them. Sam had not had one inkling of the irony. Jack and Roger had felt a little uncomfortable about this—outlaws hunting outlaws, horse thieves in pursuit of other horse thieves. Sam had blithely seen the matter in its totally realistic aspect—someone had stolen their horses, so the next thing to do, of course, was to get the horses back. To Sam Starr, there were no ironies.

When he met them out front in the utterly still town, booted carbine carelessly over one shoulder, hat crookedly atop his head, and that ivory-butted six-gun tied down, he smiled. "I was beginin' to get tired of just settin', anyway."

Roger did not smile. "That's good, because before we catch these fellers, we're likely to be sore in the feet and numb in the butt." He looked at Jack for confirmation of his thoughts. "Are there any horses at the livery barn that can keep up for maybe a week of hard use?"

Jack shrugged and led the way southward.

The hostler was still in exactly the position atop a pile of torn and discarded horse blankets he had been several hours earlier when, mouth open, face flushed, eyes closed, Jack had discovered that there had been a raid.

The full extent of the raid was not known until the three partners went in search of horses to ride. It had not only been their three horses that had been stolen, a number of empty stalls with ajar doors, and sagging-open corral gates out back indicated how thorough, and methodical, the rustlers had been.

Sam found a burly, short-backed buckskin, Jack came up with a ewe-necked, high-headed ory-eyed mare in heat, an animal that under normal circumstances he would never have deigned more than to glance at, and Roger found a pudding-footed combination Morgan horse, docile and friendly as a lamb, but bellied-up from too little exercise, and with a mouth of iron.

They left town with Jack savagely fighting the mare; she had taken a liking to Roger's Morgan horse, a long-time gelding who was not the least interested.

Jack estimated that the rustlers had a good three-hour start. He also surmised from experience, and his outlaw partners concurred, also from experience, that the thieves would stay to the open country as long as they could, or until daylight was close, in order to cover as many miles as possible and thus minimize peril from pursuit. Roger made one comment about this.

"If the cow outfits got riders out watching, they sure as hell will sound an alarm at anyone driving a big band of loose stock in the night."

It was a comforting thought, but an hour and a half later Jack put a dour look upon Bemis and said: "What watchers? We been out here across a lot of country for hours and haven't even heard anything."

It was true. It was also true, as Sam eventually pointed out while keeping a cautious distance from the mare, because she kicked now and then, that daylight would help, if not with a sighting, then at least with fresh tracks. No one could drive a band of shod horses overland without leaving a readable overlie.

IV

There were nuances to every trade. Jack made straight for the highest hill, but it was still too dark when they got there, so they had a smoke for breakfast and headed closer to the distant mountains and an hour and a half later were sitting upon a slope covered with scraggly lodgepole pines when they saw the dust.

It could have been cowmen moving a herd, so they waited to be certain it wasn't, then, satisfied at the swiftness of movement, went down off the slope on a diagonal course of interception. Cattle did not move that fast under normal conditions, but driven horses did.

Roger was skeptical of success, at least until nightfall or the following morning. But they were going to make the attempt, which was why they were out here.

Jack's silly mare was in a lather after three hours of riding through sunlight. She switched her tail, cakewalked, and watched Roger's pudding-footed Morgan out of the corner of her eye. From time to time she tried to sidle over to him, until Roger told Jack in an exasperated tone of voice to keep his damned mare away.

Jack obeyed, and eventually the mare seemed to be calmer. Maybe she was beginning to wear down. They covered a lot of miles with few periods for rest, which was what any pursuit boiled down to—a horse race with endurance as the determining factor.

Sam's short-backed buckskin was carrying easily a hundred pounds more than he should have been, but he had heart, he did not offer to sulk or play out, although by midafternoon he slogged along with his head down.

They had lost sight of the rising dust as soon as bright sunlight arrived, but they knew in which direction the horse thieves were riding because, in the boots of those men, they would have chosen the same direction.

They also watched the far-away mountains creep steadily closer, picked out a slot in the skyline where a pass existed, and decided the horse thieves knew of that pass and had probably been using it to trail out the other horses they had stolen.

When they halted in a lacy stand of willows along a creek late in the afternoon, they had the mountains close enough to make out distinctive big trees on the skyline, but distances were deceptive in air as clear as glass, so they estimated that they had perhaps six hours more of riding before they got to the base of that pass, and that, Sam said, was only going to help when they found the fresh shod-horse tracks, because they did not dare go charging up that pass behind the rustlers. He was not even sure whether the thieves would establish a watch over their back trail once they reached the mountains. But he thought by that time it would be close to evening, visibility would be limited, and the three of them could veer off and avoid detection.

They knew the mechanics of horse-stealing. They also knew the limited options that were available to any men, thieves or not, who were driving a bunch of loose horses.

Two hours onward they swung northward and kept among the breaks of the outlying foothills, moving slowly now and being careful to raise no dust with haste, or ride across open country.

The lay of the land helped. There were fringes of trees to be utilized as cover, hills and breaks and brushy areas. And—they were even more experienced at this sort of elusiveness than they were at stealing horses, so their progress toward that pass through the mountains was steady and secret.

The sun was still up there, but it had changed from golden to a shade of reddening duskiness, and it stood only a short way above the higher rims. Even after it sank, there would continue to be daylight for another couple of hours, this time of year, and Jack was banking on that.

Darkness came swiftly in the mountains. They halted once and watched tiny distant specks heading toward the funnel end of that cañon where the pass was. Roger said: "Six, seven miles."

Sam spat and lifted his hat to scratch, squinted eyes fixed on the distant movement. "They'd ought to stop soon," he announced. "There's not much point in stealin' a band of using horses, if you drive 'em so hard most of 'em play out. You stand to lose too much that way. Maybe there's a park up in there, a place with some grass and water where they figure to spend the night."

Jack spoke with fervent feeling. "I hope so. I'm gettin' hungry."

None of them had eaten since the day before, but, as Sam said offhandedly, they had been storing up fat for several weeks now; they could live on that for a few days if they had to.

From here on they rode purposefully and cautiously. When they came to the first hulking mountainside, they caught the unmistakable smell of horse sweat and dust. Sam smiled but neither of his partners did. Jack's silly mare seemed to have gone out of heat, but Roger kept an eye on her regardless. A kick in the shin was painful whether done by accident or on purpose, and he had never had any use for mares, had never trusted them.

Their horses were pretty well ridden down. Excepting the wiry mare they were not built or conditioned for this kind of endurance riding.

But having come this far, the men pushed them over against the slope where shadows hid them, and punched their way onward seeking a game trail. When they found it, the trail meandered southward in the general direction of the pass, and climbed a little as it went. Like most game trails made by four-legged animals, it did not press directly up the mountainside but achieved altitude a little at a time, which was better for the partners and their poorly-conditioned mounts.

The scent of horses grew stronger the closer they got to that broad slot in the mountains. This may have been the result of a very faint little breeze blowing into the faces of the three riders, or it may have been caused when the rustlers halted somewhere on ahead, up inside the darkening pass. In either case it was encouraging. After a hard day-long ride they were getting closer.

Sam tugged loose the thong of his ivory-stocked Colt. Roger and Jack had already done this. Jack's mare threw up her head to nicker and Jack reacted instantly with a diverting jerk of the reins. His partners looked from Jack to the mare, but said nothing. Jack had had no choice back at Fort Morgan so it wasn't his fault he was straddling a mare, but nonetheless if that silly animal whinnied, which she certainly would do sooner or later when the scent of the stolen horses was plainer, it would imperil all the riding the three partners had done since before sunup, by warning the horse thieves someone besides themselves was in the mountains.

Finally, with the dip in the dusky slopes southward indicating they were close to the pass, Jack wordlessly piled off, tied the mare to some underbrush, took down his carbine, and without a word started ahead on foot. It was the best way to prevent the mare from warning the rustlers. The other two did likewise, also drawing their carbines.

It was a long walk and Jack should have been too tired to undertake it, except that, after a full day in a saddle, walking was not a hardship, it was a relief, even to experienced riders.

They eventually heard horses. Darkness was coming in over the high peaks, but it was coming slowly, like molasses pouring down the side of a jar in wintertime; it advanced slowly. Inexorably but slowly. It would not reach the middle distance of the pass before Jack, Roger, and Sam got over there, but it would get down that far shortly afterward.

Sam's guess about there being a park up here was correct. It was fairly large; when they eventually halted in the final stand of trees to look at it, it seemed to be several hundred acres in size. The grass was tall and curing on the stem with heavy, full seed heads on each stalk. Animals grazing over this place would turn greasy fat if left here long enough.

There was a camp over where a number of willows shone paler green against the dark forest colors. A sputtery gust of white smoke lifted, to be followed by another, then a third and fourth little ragged gust of smoke.

Sam shook his head. No professional rustler would use punky wood like was happening over yonder. Bone-dry deadfall wood made no smoke. And even though the actual fire would be invisible from out across the eastward range, its smell would travel many miles. He said—"Greenhorns."—in scorn, but Roger thought differently. "They know where they are and that in another hour it'll be too dark in here for smoke to show. They're experienced, Sam. You see those horses?"

Sam saw them fanning out over the grass biting at everything close by, hungry as horses ever got.

"I'd guess they didn't lose any," announced Roger.

Sam could have argued that you didn't lose horses in open country anyway, but he merely grunted. They could not make out the number of men out there part way across the meadow. Sam thought it was only two but Roger thought he had seen three men.

They waited. When the trees farther back on across the meadow were becoming a blending shade of night color, they began a slow advance around the north side of the park until they were part of the molasses-slow advancing column of night.

Over there, closer to the area where the camp was, they made out only two men, and verified that this was the actual number by the two saddles, blankets, and bridles, and the pair of army-size saddlebags lying near the fire, which was now putting up a steady, thin spiral of gray smoke, the punky kindling having been consumed by this time.

Jack shook his head while watching the pair of horse thieves drinking watered whiskey from a pair of tin cups, smoking and sitting out, hatless and relaxed. He leaned toward Roger and said: "I was never that comfortable with a band of rustled stock around me."

Roger answered just as softly. "You never kept raidin' the same territory as long as those gents have."

Sam leaned on his carbine, wearing a little smile as he studied the horse thieves. There was no way of approaching them through that stirrup-high grass just yet. Sam was in no hurry anyway. He was satisfied about what was going to happen, pleased that they had been successful, and, when the smell of cooking came out to him, he had eating on his mind as a secondary goal.

Jack finally dropped to one knee and studied the route to the camp. Shadows were darkening behind him and off to his right.

He glanced up, bobbed his head, and struck out on all fours, but slowly and soundlessly. By the time he was close enough to catch an occasional word as the rustlers ate supper, full darkness had arrived, and except for the risk of noise, he could have made faster time.

There was not that much need for haste. The conclusion of the horse race was shortly to come about, one way or another, and even if there was trouble at the camp, the three crawling men had the advantage, not just of surprise, but of being prepared to shoot.

The starved horses cropping grass out a fair distance could be heard very plainly. It was the only sound except for some low and desultory talk at the campfire. There were a few weak stars overhead, but if there was to be a moon tonight it would have to appear later. There was no sign of it now.

Sam's nose wrinkled the closer he got to that cooking fire. They had made a meal of some kind of meat. As hungry as Sam was, it could have been horse and he still would have enjoyed it. He lacked the inhibitions of his partners. He had in fact been raised as much on horsemeat as other kinds.

Jack paused, raised his head slightly, studied the back of the nearest horse thief, studied the man opposite him at the fire, saw the bearded face, the greasy old misshapen hat, and the sloping, thick shoulders, then turned to see where his partners were.

Roger was ten feet behind and to one side. Sam was another ten feet on the opposite side. Jack caught their attention, gently nodded at them, and crawled another hundred feet, until he was so close he could hear water boiling in an open pan, then he waited.

Roger had crept closer, but northwesterly. Sam had also got closer, and he had slunk around to the southeast. Jack was directly behind the man whose back was to him. He saw the horse thief lean to make coffee from the boiling water, lean back, and reach with his free hand into the fry pan on three round rocks at the cooking fire. The man used a long-bladed clasp knife to spear his second piece of meat. Opposite him the other one said: "Not bad meat, considerin' it'd been in that icehouse maybe a year or so."

The man spearing meat said: "It ain't beef. Maybe it's elk. Don't taste like much else."

Jack saw the meat in mid-air poised on the tip of the clasp knife, the other hand holding a coffee cup. He arose up out of the grass as though he had come directly from the earth.

The man facing in his direction saw him at once. He was so stunned, he stopped chewing with his mouth half open. Both his eyes were sprung wide and both his hands, occupied at balancing a tin plate and holding the knife he was using as a fork, became motionless.

The man whose back was to Jack lowered his head to concentrate on cutting the meat in his tin plate. He had to put aside the coffee cup to do this. He was sawing away, completely oblivious, when Sam arose out of the grass in one direction and Roger came up to his full height in the opposite direction.

Not a sound was made and not a word was spoken until that paralyzed man turned his head slightly and saw the other two men with carbines pointing. In a soft, half-hoarse voice he said: "Alf . . . for Christ's sake don't move."

The outlaw in front of Jack Pate raised his head, both hands full, saw the expression on his friend's face, and gradually raised both shoulders, sitting very erect. Jack leaned and gently poked the man in the back between the shoulder blades with the cold tip of his Winchester. The horse thief's breath ran out in a shallow sigh.

Sam walked closer, kicked two booted carbines away, and disarmed the man with Jack Pate's Winchester against his back.

Roger walked around to come in from behind the second horse thief and disarm him.

Then Sam smiled, took the tin plate from the lap of the man Jack was standing behind, stepped back, and, by leaning his Winchester against his thigh, was able to start eating.

V

They did not ask their names and they did not ask where they had been taking the horses they had stolen in the Fort Morgan country. In fact each time one of the horse thieves offered to converse, he was growled into silence by the three partners.

Not until all the food had been eaten by the captors, all the coffee drunk, did Sam and Jack and Roger ease back and thoughtfully eye their unarmed prisoners.

The horse thieves were frightened. They had excellent reason to be. They did not know what kind of men they had around them, but they did know that in these mountains two gunshots would not be heard in the night, that there were a number of nearby little cañons where a pair of bodies could be rolled, and that the custom of cowmen was to exterminate horse thieves out of hand.

The very silence of their captors was menacing, as though they had already arrived at the decision that would determine what came next.

Sam rolled a smoke, lit it, then pulled the pair of saddlebags over and rummaged through them. He appropriated a fine gold watch with an engraved case.

Roger took the six-guns, and Jack Pate gathered the Winchesters. They still did not converse with their prisoners. Finally, fed and relaxed, Roger asked where the outlaws had been disposing of the horses they had been stealing.

The bearded outlaw answered promptly. "To a feller named Cantrell over through the mountains. He keeps a camp over there. We bring in the herds and he pays us."

"Regular organized system," said Roger, sounding almost as though he approved.

Sam was examining the handsome watch. "Where did you boys get this?" he asked, holding up the watch.

The bearded outlaw cleared his throat and shot a look at his partner. Sam was smiling, his habitually slitted eyes moving from man to man. When the answer was slow coming, Sam said: "From a stagecoach robbery. Right?"

The bearded man cleared his throat again. "Well . . . yes. But it wasn't nowhere around here. It was over in Idaho."

"You fellers keep busy," Sam said, and pocketed the watch.

Jack finished his coffee and his smoke, pitched away coffee grounds, put the cup aside, and said: "Take everything out of your pockets. Put it in front of you on the ground."

The bearded outlaw was beginning to frown a little. He looked from one captor to the next one and faintly frowned. He seemed to be arriving at a slow decision. He continued to scowl when he obeyed Jack Pate and put everything from his pockets in front of him where firelight shone off a clasp knife, some silver coins, a few rumpled greenbacks, a blue bandanna, and some matches in a circular-shaped little metal container.

His partner had roughly the same possessions except that he was also carrying a fiery green stone about two-thirds the size of a man's thumbnail. When the three partners leaned to watch firelight blaze and erupt in the depths of that green stone, Jack raised his eyes and said: "You pry that out of a ring or necklace?"

"Ring," muttered the outlaw, looking unhappy. "It's an emerald."

"From the same stage robbery?" asked Roger.

The outlaw nodded and regarded the emerald somewhat mournfully. Jack reached and hefted the stone, then dropped it into his shirt pocket. He said: "Your money belts, too."

It was a shot in the dark, but under the surprised glances of their captors each horse thief reached inside his shirt and pulled forth a belt with pouches in it.

Roger counted the money. There were $900 in greenbacks in one belt and $700 in the other belt. Sam silently puckered up to whistle. Then he looked with a little more respect at the prisoners. "You boys really *have* been busy."

Roger methodically counted out the money into three separate stacks while Jack addressed the prisoners.

"You got to leave the country. Cowmen have watchers on the range and folks are up in arms. It was foolish to keep raiding down there. You were bound to get caught when you kept it up. You're damned lucky it was us caught you and not someone else. We'll leave you tied. In the morning you can work loose. We'll take the horses back with us." He paused to accept one of the stacks of greenbacks from Roger, riffled it, then shoved it into a pocket. Now both the outlaws were eyeing their captors with expressions of suspicion.

"Damned lucky it was us," he reiterated with greater emphasis. "Don't come back to this country, gents. Next time it'll cost you a hell of a lot more when we run you down."

Sam methodically gathered the food and rolled it into a bundle using someone's spare shirt. They then left the speechless outlaws tied at wrist and ankle, went back for their horses, and, at about the same time the moon finally arrived, they got behind the stolen horses, eased them gently to the trail down out of the pass, and headed for home.

It turned cold an hour later, and got steadily colder as the night wore along. The stolen horses had managed to get half a feed back there on the hidden meadow, and they were leg weary from their previous run ahead of the men who had stolen them. They were perfectly content to be heading back in a familiar direction and slogged along unmindful of most night sounds.

Sam showed Roger his new watch. Roger looked at it, shook it, placed it to his ear, then shook it again before passing it back with his judgment. "It don't work."

Sam was not in the least upset. He could not read a watch anyway.

Jack counted the money he had pocketed back at the horse-thief camp. Roger watched, then said: "You and me got five hundred and fifty dollars. Sam got the rest. There's too much work splittin' it any finer'n that."

Jack nodded, satisfied, then he smiled, something he did not commonly do. "Those bastards back there," he said, ducking lower into the collar of his rider's jacket, "got to sit there all night and try to figure this out."

"They figured it," stated Sam. "They was watchin' the three of us like they finally was understandin' we wasn't goin' to lynch them, just clean 'em out." Sam chuckled. "Horse thieves gettin' robbed by other outlaws. That's funny as hell."

"They won't think so," Jack said, and yawned. "Damn, we earned it."

They did not have Fort Morgan in sight until shortly before daybreak when the sky had been turning a gun-metal shade of gray for an hour. Sam said: "What do we tell folks?"

Jack shrugged. "That we got back the horses and the outlaws escaped. Heard us comin' and got astride and fled into the mountains. They'll be satisfied with that. Gettin' back the horses is the main thing."

He was right. They corralled the animals, took care of the ones they had borrowed from the livery man, found the night hawk with a bad case of the shakes and sitting in the harness room with a rank old horse blanket wrapped around his shoulders, and walked forth into the new day.

It was still cold. For all the advancing gray daylight there would be no sunshine for another hour or so, but they saw a light sputter over at the café, and went over there. The café man let them in, yawning, asked what in hell had got them up so blessed early, and stared when they told him. He had not known any horses had been stolen from town, but, after reflection while he cooked their breakfast, he came along and said: "But I ain't too surprised. That worthless old cuss they keep down there at night . . . why, a man could steal every horse, all the harness, and half the saddles . . . he'd never know it."

They left the café just as the sun was rising, went up to the rooming house, and bedded down, replete but worn out. Nor did they appear again until late afternoon, by which time the entire town knew what had happened, that horses had been stolen and recovered.

Will Potts who owned the livery barn found the three partners over in front of the harness shop and effusively thanked them. It was a little embarrassing, but Will was a man of forthright sentiments. He even offered to give them a reward, which they refused.

Later, at the saloon, other men came over to express admiration. Several of them stood drinks for Sam, Roger, and Jack, but not until evening, out in front of the café after supper, did Carl Hanson, secretary of the town council, seek them out at their table in the saloon and offer them the town marshal's position.

Sam looked at Hanson as though the storekeeper had said something indecent. Roger stared directly at Jack with a hard twinkle in his eyes, and Jack told the storekeeper they weren't interested. He had to emphasize it three times before Hanson left. Then Sam said: "That son-of-a-bitch's got a lot of nerve."

They could have got drunk without paying a red cent, if they had cared to. Sam almost did, in fact. He could carry the least liquor of the trio, although it might normally be expected, being built and constituted as he was, Sam would be able to handle his share.

They finally left the saloon to saunter down to the livery barn. That skeletal night hawk saw them coming and reflected mixed emotions. They were in the runway to look at their own horses when he shuffled over and said: "The least you fellers could have done was wake me up. Mister Potts was sure mad. I didn't have no idea no livestock had been stole."

Sam said: "Wake you up? Partner, a cannon goin' off right beside you couldn't have done that."

The hostler sniffled, ran a soiled sleeve under his nose, and replied to Sam in a gently whining voice: "I got this condition, mister. Don't no medicine work on it, but now and then a wee dram of whiskey'll help it."

Sam said—"Sure."—in a sarcastic tone. "You got a condition for a fact, partner. Did you grain our horses?"

"Every morning and every night," averred the hostler. "Look in them feed boxes for yourselves."

They did, then they gave the hostler a silver cartwheel to continue his care of their animals, and went out front where Roger said: "A dollar in that gent's hand won't guarantee that our horses will get good care. It'll only guarantee that he'll head for the saloon as quick as he can."

It was true, but the hostler must have slipped out the back way, hastened up the alley, then cut through between two buildings to reach the main thoroughfare, because by the time the three partners got up in front of the jailhouse, which still had that black ribbon on the door, the hostler was scurrying on a diagonal course far ahead, over to the saloon. They saw him, recognized him, and said nothing.

Jack's summary of their rigorous manhunt came out in one sentence. "My butt is sore."

Roger nodded over that. "Bound to be. We been loafing here

for nigh onto a month now. A man gets soft awful fast, once he starts loafing."

Sam was neither sore, nor, after his day-long rest, very tired. He stepped to the edge of the plank walk to expectorate and remained out there as the sounds of a stagecoach entering town from the northeast held his attention.

The stage was behind a six-horse hitch and made its final approach slowly, trace chains slack and noisy. Several yardmen appeared with lanterns, and as soon as the coach halted, they were freeing the hitch to be taken into the yard and cared for, leaving the coach parked out front. It would be on the road again come sunup.

There were four passengers, all men and all stiff and sore from the ride. Sam eyed them with interest, but what especially caught his attention was the black, steel-bound box the whip leaned to hand down to the stationmaster. Sam said: "By God, they had a bullion box." He said it in an almost reverent tone of voice as his friends stepped up and also turned to look northward.

Roger softly said: "We're restin' Sam. No business talk while we're taking a vacation."

But Sam's professional concern had been aroused. "One driver, one gun guard, and four passengers . . . and a bullion box. By God, I've rode my tail numb to stop a coach that was carryin' a hell of a lot less."

Jack stood in watchful silence, lips pursed as he studied those four passengers, all heading for the saloon now, and the horses that were being driven into the yard after being released from the tongue. He finally said: "Roger, Fort Morgan's in the middle of nowhere. You just been through somethin' that ought to show you how slow these folks are at figurin' things out. Most of them didn't even know those horses had been rustled."

Roger turned. "Are you tired of this place?"

"No," replied Jack Pate slowly, and without looking away from that empty, parked coach up the roadway. "No, but we can't set around here forever."

VI

The raid was sudden. Unlike those horse thieves, the men who halted the southbound stagecoach five miles below town seemed to come from nowhere. There was no warning at all. They stopped the coach with two men on the ground and two remaining on horseback, covering the passengers, the driver, and gun guard with professional efficiency. They barely said ten words. The passengers were systematically robbed, all the guns were taken along with three mail sacks, and the stage was sent on its way.

It was not the custom for a stagecoach to break schedule when robbed, and head back to its last stop. The practice was to continue ahead and report the robbery at the next way station.

For this reason, along with a lack of any kind of inter-town communication system, the people up at Fort Morgan did not know the stage robbers had struck well within the township limits until the following day, and then they only heard the details when a pots-and-pans peddler drove his little wagon in from down south with plans to lay over for a few days to conduct his business.

Old Alec Griffith was in town the day that peddler arrived with his story of a stage robbery. Alec bitterly smiled. He was standing out front of the general store. When Carl Hanson came out, Alec turned and said: "This time it ain't up to the range men. This time it's up to you."

Sam's reaction when he heard the news was sudden anger. "Them sons-of-bitches," he told Jack. "Them lousy, connivin' no-good bums!"

It required no gift to understand that Sam's anger stemmed

from an idea he had been forming since the evening they had watched that bullion box being taken off the coach. What those stage robbers had done, in Sam's private view, was appropriate something that by all rights should have belonged to him—to all three of them. It was almost like being personally robbed.

Jack and Roger did not share Sam's indignation, but they were interested. From the standpoint of a professional Jack predicted that the people of Fort Morgan would react to this outrage about as they had to the theft of their horses.

Roger was inclined to agree. They were down at Paul Benson's café having breakfast the day after the robbery had first been talked about, listening to the café man telling another diner about the time down in New Mexico that he had watched a stage hold-up from a side hill a half mile away, and, when the diner asked why Paul had just sat up there, the café man's eyes got perfectly round.

"Didn't you know," Benson exclaimed, "that the most dangerous and killin'-minded outlaws is highwaymen? There was four of them fellers robbin' that coach and I wasn't goin' to go down there if the devil had been chasin' me. Them kind will shoot you just for the hell of it."

Outside on the plank walk Sam said: "By golly, I resent that."

Carl Hanson, the town blacksmith, the harness maker, and two other men came along with a purposeful stride, faces set in expressions of grim resolve.

Hanson said: "There you are. We been lookin' through town for you gents." He paused for a deep breath, then went on speaking. "We been talkin' things over, since you fellers brought back the stolen horses. Fort Morgan's got a crisis. We haven't been able to hire a replacement for the town marshal and we got an offer to make you men. You don't have to take Marshal Houston's job. We'll pay three hunnert dollars if you can catch those highwaymen. And that'll be over and above whatever price is on 'em by way of rewards. Three hunnert dollars. . . ."

Jack said: "Mister, you got a countryside full of cowboys who could do as much as we could, and for that kind of money most of them would sure do it."

One of the other councilmen said: "We don't have that much time. We're already a couple of days late. If we got to ride all over hell tryin' to recruit range riders, we might as well forget it."

Roger agreed with that. "You can't expect highwaymen to hang and rattle once they've raided a coach. Likely by now they're halfway over to Arizona. Personally I don't think we'd ought to take your money because I doubt like hell that we could even come close to those fellers."

"Four hundred," a man said gruffly from behind the partners. Alec Griffith, the cowman, was back there listening. He stepped closer. "I'll add a hundred to what these gents offered you boys, and I'll make my contribution payable just for you lads makin' the effort. If you don't catch 'em . . . well . . . it can't be helped." Griffith stepped to the edge of the plank walk, spat, shifted his cud, and stepped back. He eyed the townsmen with an unsmiling countenance. "I told you fellers two weeks ago to get a lawman. I might as well have been peein' against the tide."

The storekeeper made a little gesture with his hands. "We been trying."

Griffith was unimpressed. In his trade excuses did not mean a thing. "Not hard enough," he growled, and turned toward Sam, Roger, and Jack. "Five hundred, gents. Their three hundred and I'll sweeten the pot with two hundred. Just try your damnedest, because if you don't . . . if *someone* don't, this whole blasted countryside is goin' to be overrun. Word gets around." He jerked a thumb in the direction of the town councilmen. "By the time they hire another lawman, we'll all have been raided a dozen times."

Jack saw Sam's expression. $500 was a fortune. Moreover, Sam was still upset over someone else stopping that stagecoach. Sam was ready. Jack and Roger exchanged a glance and Roger shrugged. He was clearly not overwhelmed with enthusiasm, the money notwithstanding, but just as clearly he was ready if his partners were.

Jack answered Alec Griffith. "They got too big a head start. Even if we knew who they were, we likely wouldn't be able to catch them. But if you gents want to put up the money with no strings attached, we'll go."

The townsmen fidgeted. Their idea had been to pay a reward for the delivery of the outlaws. Old Griffith looked stonily at them. "You're going to louse things up again," he stated. "Whether these fellers run them bastards down or not, they'll make an attempt, and that's better'n anything else. You got to do something, otherwise, like I just said, we're going to be overrun with renegades."

Carl Hanson answered a trifle shortly. "We've been trying our damnedest, Alec." He faced Jack Pate. "All right. You get our three hundred and Mister Griffith's two hundred for doing your damnedest."

Jack nodded, then led his companions up to the saloon. They got a bottle, three glasses, and went to their table in a dingy corner. Sam said: "We got to find a map somewhere. This here is unknown country."

Roger was filling the glasses when he made his feelings known. "If they came a long way, hit that coach because they saw it out there, then my guess is that they made for a town. What we got to know is the shape their horses was in, how the men looked, and get some idea of where they'd go."

Jack nodded. "Where would you go?"

Roger picked up his little glass. "Depending on whether my horse was rode down or maybe needed new shoes, I'd likely head for a town." He dropped the whiskey straight down and blinked. "What did we do, the last time?"

"Came out here," responded Sam.

"And left a posse back a couple hundred miles," conceded Roger, "and kept right on riding until we figured we'd be plumb safe."

Sam reiterated his earlier statement. "We need a map."

Jack picked up his glass and sipped the whiskey, being quietly thoughtful. "What we need," he eventually told Sam, "is to get moving. Maybe we can pick up some sign out where they stopped the stage."

Sam agreed, then said something that indicated how his private thoughts were running. "How much did they take off the passengers? Didn't someone say there was a bullion box on that coach?"

Jack offered one of his rare smiles, and Sam, understanding what the smile implied, reached for his shot glass as he spoke again, defensively this time. "Well, hell, we let those horse thieves loose, after we cleaned 'em out, didn't we?"

Roger laughed and shoved up to his feet. "I'll fetch some grub from the store and meet you fellers in front of the livery barn." He was gazing at Sam Starr when he added: "Five hundred from these folks, and whatever we can loot off the highwaymen."

"Which by rights should belong to us anyway!" Sam exclaimed, also rising.

They paid the bar man for the amount of whiskey they had taken from the bottle, and walked out of the saloon to study the sky, the roadway, and the endless miles of open grassland southward, down in the direction where the robbery had occurred.

That alcoholic hostler was not down at the livery barn but Will Potts, the proprietor, was. He had already heard that the three men who had recovered the horses were now going after those stage robbers, and he was enthusiastic. So enthusiastic in fact that Sam, Roger, and Jack had to rig out their own animals while Potts talked a blue streak, offering advice, making suggestions, and finally wishing the three men good hunting.

They were a half mile below town when Roger said: "Fellers like that give me the trots."

It was not difficult to find the place where the hold-up had occurred because the coach had been wheeled to the side of the road before stopping. And there were plenty of tracks of shod horses. But there were also plenty of other shod-horse tracks on down the road, and over in the grasslands on both sides of the roadway. In fact, out where the grass was rankest, it was impossible to tell one set of marks from another, and to add to that someone had very recently driven a big band of cattle from west of the road across it to the range on the east side.

Sam finally said: "We'd have done better to ride a stage. Make better time, and they'd know where all the towns are."

Roger, who had been sitting his saddle studying the countryside, pointed westward. "They came from the east. That much we can figure from their sign. If it had been us fellers, we'd have kept right on going west. If there's a town out there somewhere. . . ." He looked at Sam. "What's your omens say? Let's head over in that direction for a few miles."

Sam did not have an opportunity to explain about his omens. They loped for several miles, then dropped down to a walk. Nothing changed, the land was like an ocean frozen in motion the way it rolled and undulated with mile-wide low places interspersed with land swells. There was no cover although they eventually saw tall trees where some cow outfit had its headquarters' buildings. Otherwise, they covered a lot of miles and eventually came upon another road, this one angling from the northwest in the general direction of a juncture with the road they had left far behind.

Sam squinted, then said: "There's a town up yonder somewhere. Roads don't exist where there ain't towns."

Roger was less salutary. "Yeah . . . ten, fifteen miles on we'll find a town. Probably the wrong one, and meanwhile those fellers'll be shoving their boot soles over a bar rung fifty miles in the opposite direction."

But they went up the roadway regardless of Roger's pessimism. Once, they encountered a high-wheeled old freight outfit, but the driver and swamper had seen no group of four riders over the past few days. That town on ahead, they said, was called Cedar Brake. It was about the size of Fort Morgan.

Jack was beginning to be influenced by Roger's pessimism, but, as he said, nightfall was close by and unless they wanted to sleep on the ground and eat tinned peaches for supper, they might just as well ride on. Then he lapsed into a long and thoughtful silence, leaving it up to Sam and Roger to peck at each other over their divergent notions on where those highwaymen had gone.

Cedar Brake was not as large as Fort Morgan, but in one respect it achieved an even greater eminence. Fort Morgan had one saloon. Cedar Brake had two of them, and one, the largest saloon, was also a café. Cedar Brake also had a livery barn where they put up their horses, paid for extra feed, and listened to the observation of the night man about a big storm being in the offing. They had been all day under a spotless sky so what the livery man had said went in one ear and out the other ear.

They ate at the saloon, then had a couple of drinks, and, when a large, florid man wearing a little star on his vest came in for a drink, they eyed him with interest. For once, in a manner of speaking, they were on his side of the law.

Even so, when Jack suggested striking up a conversation with the lawman, Sam abruptly recalled that he hadn't cleaned his horse's hoofs in the last day or two, and Roger said he'd hunt up the boarding house and arrange for three rooms.

Cedar Brake came to life after sundown. Range men loped in from the outlying country. Evidently the cow outfits over here had their home places much closer to town than had been the case around Fort Morgan.

Both the saloons seemed to be thriving. It no doubt helped that range men could ride to town every night. In fact that was probably what made it possible for a place the size of Cedar Brake to support two saloons in the first place.

Otherwise, though, the town closed up right at sundown, except for the livery barn that kept a lantern burning out front all night long.

Sam returned from the livery barn, located the rooming house, and found Roger on the front porch with his boots hooked over the railing, relaxing. They talked, watched night settle, speculated on the probable location of those highwaymen, and abandoned this topic when they saw Jack standing across the road in casual conversation with the large, florid lawman.

Sam spoke in disgust. "He won't know anything. You ever see one of those red-raced ones that didn't spend his time leanin' across someone's bar?"

Roger was making a smoke when he glanced up to answer. "I was always sort of partial to that kind myself."

Jack and the lawman parted, Jack strolling thoughtfully in the direction of the boarding-house porch, the lawman heading southward, in the direction of the second saloon.

VII

Jack sat down with a sigh, glanced at his partners, and said: "This has been a hell of a long day." Neither Roger or Sam commented. "And that town marshal wouldn't give a damn if the James gang rode in here and raided his whole town." Roger and Sam still sat silently.

Jack looked at Sam. "The horses get proper care?"

Sam nodded. "Plenty of hay and they been grained, watered, and cuffed. Jack, whenever you set down in that sort of mood . . . lookin' like a cat that's caught a bird . . . you got more to say."

Pate leaned back ignoring Sam's innuendo. "I figured all the time they'd head for a town," he said, and did not catch the glance exchanged by his partners. "Four riders arrived in Cedar Brake yesterday on worn-down horses, rested their livestock all day, and rode out last night." Jack glanced at Sam and Roger again. "The marshal saw them loafing at the lower end of town where they'd have a clean sweep of the range and the roadway."

"Watching their back trail," conceded Roger. "All right. I'll settle for these four." He sounded relieved that they had not been riding in the wrong direction, after all. "What else did that pillar of the law have to say?"

"The next town north of here is a place called Evansville. It's over against the foothills at the base of a pass called Turner's Gap. It's not much of a place . . . four, five stores. But it keeps going because of the pack and freighter trade through the mountains. West from here the next town is about eighty miles. Fort Stanhope. It's like Fort Morgan . . . what's left of an old Army post made over into a town. The lawman figures they'd head for Fort Stanhope."

Roger smoked and thought, and finally said: "That makes sense. What'd be the point of them heading north when they'd be paralleling the country where they raided that stagecoach?"

Sam leaned to expectorate over the porch railing into a geranium bed, then he leaned back to speak. "Wait a minute. Back yonder I told you fellers we needed a map, but, still and all, I got a pretty fair sense of direction. This place called

Evansville at the foot of a pass through those damned mountains has got to be about at this side of that pass where those horse thieves were heading when we overhauled them."

Roger and Jack listened, eyeing Sam Starr with the mild skepticism with which they usually regarded most of his pronouncements.

"Gents, I figure that old cowman back yonder . . . Mister Griffith . . . had things figured about right. The Fort Morgan country is bein' overrun by outlaws because by now it's got to be common knowledge all over the territory they got no law over there."

Roger looked pained. "What in hell are you trying to say, Sam?"

Starr edged his chair a little closer, his square-hewn, narrow-eyed face full of strong conviction. "I'm tryin' to tell you that those horse thieves said they had friends over on this side of the pass. The rustlers and their friends know there's no law at Fort Morgan. When they made a big sashay around Fort Morgan and come in from the east to hit that stagecoach, it looked like any decent band of highwaymen was workin' their way through the country. But then they didn't head south, they come back over here headin' north, toward this place called Evansville, which is where all them bastards . . . the horse thieves, and the feller they been sellin' stolen horses to . . . have a camp."

Sam stopped speaking. Roger and Jack were gazing silently at him. Eventually Roger turned in the opposite direction. "Jack . . . ?"

The tall, thin man offered no comment for a moment or two longer, then he said: "I don't know how you came to those conclusions, Sam."

Starr, believing he was being mildly derided, hitched his chair still closer to begin a vehement recapitulation of the process by which he had worked it out, but Jack stopped him with an upraised hand.

"It just damned well could be," he said to Roger, sounding puzzled and surprised. "Sam could damned well be right. One thing sure fits. Even if they'd been plumb strangers, they'd know that by ridin' north they'd be paralleling the same country they raided, and, if there was a posse out, they would be takin' one hell of a risk. But if they had friends up yonder and a safe hide-out. . . ."

Jack leaned back in his chair, Roger ground his cigarette underfoot on the porch, and Sam still leaned, watching them both for a clue as to what they were thinking.

Eventually Jack yawned and leaned to arise. "We ought to get an early start," he announced. "Try and at least get into the foothills or up alongside the pass before daylight, otherwise, if they're really up there, they're going to see us comin'."

Roger frowned as he arose to go inside to his room. "How big did you say Evansville was?"

Jack repeated what the town marshal had told him. "Four, five stores is all. Maybe altogether eight or ten buildings counting the ones folks live in. Why?"

"Because those horse thieves couldn't ride into a place with a passel of loose stock packing brands from the Fort Morgan country without folks over there figuring out what was happening. What I'm wondering, gents, is whether or not those storekeepers and what-not up at Evansville might not be friendly to horse thieves, and, if they are, us three riding in could plant us right in the middle of a whole nest of rattlesnakes."

Jack had yielded to an opinion of Sam Starr's this evening. It made it easier for him to accredit Roger's idea, so he said: "We'll ride in with our eyes open, and now we'd better get some sleep."

It was cold in the morning, colder than it had been for several weeks, and, as they rode bundled to the ears through star-mottled darkness, Sam predicted an early autumn and a hard winter. Neither of his friends commented. In July it was always safe to make one of those predictions because by the time winter arrived no one remembered.

The country turned lumpy in the darkness. There were more stands of timber in this upper territory than there were across the mountains around Fort Morgan. The farther they rode the colder it seemed to get. They had the mountains ahead and on their right. In this kind of country it always seemed to be colder, and to stay colder, probably because the sun abandoned the high slopes first and returned to it later the following day.

But the important thing was that they were nearly invisible as long as they had the brooding hills on their right as they rode up the roadway.

Roger pushed his head up a little, like a turtle, looked around, blew steam for a moment, then dourly said: "Five hundred dollars . . . it's not worth it."

Sam answered curtly: "The hell with the five hunnert. It's what those yokels taken off the stage I'm interested in."

Where the land finally broke into a series of cutbanks, brushy arroyos, and jutting headlands of the higher mountains, they left the road and kept working their way in and out among the breaks and timber stands. There was almost no possibility of anyone seeing them now, even if dawn had come. When they could dimly make out the break in the rims where that pass existed, Jack took the lead and, hugging a timbered side hill, using that break in the skyline as his pilot point, angled around until they all caught the rising scent of wood smoke in the sharp air.

From this point on they coursed in among the trees, found a decent game trail, and used it all the way to the top out overlooking a sudden big clearing that was nearly flat, and which looked to be at least a mile, maybe a mile and a half in size. It was one of those places a rider never expected to find in this kind of country.

At the east end of the clearing, the pass came forth between two widening slopes, one northward, the other one southward. There was a scattering of what appeared as random square wooden blocks down there, with a crooked roadway passing between most of them.

Jack said: "Evansville." Then he pointed over where the trail came down through that pass and said: "Turner's Gap. Sam, we don't need a map."

Starr said nothing. He was standing in his stirrups like an old-time bronco warrior, squinting hard through the gloom to understand the lay of the land. When he sat back, he reached to unbutton the topmost latch to his jacket, then he scratched a stubbled throat and jaw.

"If those fellers aren't down there. . . ." He ranged a look up across the bulwark of massive mountains northward. He spat, straightened up, and said: "Hell!"

They picked their way carefully. When dawn arrived, they were far enough down off the higher slope to make out the details of the village. Several dogs picked up their scent and started caterwauling. Sam muttered under his breath.

Where they came out was at the foot of the pass. If anyone had been looking in that direction, or if it had been possible to see that far in the feeble light, it would have seemed that Sam, Roger, and Jack had emerged from the pass.

They halted in some trees east of the village where an ice-water creek ran, glass-clear and so cold it hurt a man's teeth when he drank from it. Then they had a smoke for breakfast and Jack offered a plan. He would go in alone first, and, being a stranger in this hamlet, people would watch him, would probably be suspicious about him. He would wander around, get something to eat, take time caring for his horse, and keep the people watching, and while they were concentrating on him, Sam and Roger would scout up the area. Later, whenever Roger and Sam were satisfied, then the three of them would meet back here by the little creek in the trees, and discuss what was to be done.

Jack's primary objective would be to try and find something to support the idea that those stage robbers had been in Evansville, or might even still be there.

Sam had one misgiving. "If those horse thieves we robbed are around, they'll sure as hell recognize you. If they got friends like I figure they have, they'll sure be ornery, Jack."

Pate nodded. He had considered this possibility. "One thing those fellers know by now, is that we weren't lawmen. I'll gamble on that."

"You'll be gamblin' all right," Sam said dryly. "It's not going to matter at all to those fellers who we was. They're goin' to want their money back or someone's blood."

Jack left the other two just as the sun rose beyond the uppermost stand of spiky timber, and the sky began to pale out from dusty blue to pale pink. The cold remained, and probably would remain for another couple of hours. In a fold of the mountains like this, even in midsummer, nights were long and heat never became bothersome.

Sam worried. So did Roger but he kept it mostly to himself, whereas Sam spoke out. The two of them waited until Jack had disappeared among the log buildings, then mounted up and skirted up around to the northwest.

Smoke was rising arrow-straight from just about every stovepipe in the village. Roger sighed and shook his head thinking of the men snug and warm in lighted kitchens where some good women were cooking breakfast, maybe even smiling at their menfolk.

He said: "Sam, I think someday I'll get married."

Starr had been expecting almost anything but that. He screwed up his face, stared, then turned back to picking his way.

They encountered a place where villagers had turned out several milk cows. Two of the cows wore bells, and as a pair of wraith-like horsemen appeared, all the cows suddenly became not just intensely alert, but also ready to turn tail and run. Evidently horsemen coming forth from the trees was the least worry of those cows; this was also cougar and bear country, even this close to a village.

There were a few more distant log houses, generally with a few acres enclosed by split-rail fences where people lived who did not like being too close to other people. At one of these places Roger reined in at the fence, gazing over where several horses were cropping grass. He pointed. "You ever see a stump-puller or a clod-buster own an animal like that, Sam?"

The horse was powerfully muscled, about sixteen hands tall, with the fine head and eye of a thoroughbred, and he was young, perhaps no more than six or seven.

Sam leaned and said: "Race horse if I ever saw one, Roger. No, I never seen a horse like that belonging to a sodbuster."

They passed along, scouted up several more of those little outlying places, and a woman froze when she stepped out for an armload of kindling and saw them ride past. Sam and Roger lifted their hats.

Sam called over to her: "Goin' to be an early winter, ma'am!"

The woman straightened up a little, losing most of her sudden appearance of alarm. She called back in a musical voice: "I think you're right." Then she watched them pass, and finally turned back to the woodpile, satisfied they were simply a pair of local men.

It did not take long, slightly more than an hour, to reconnoiter Evansville. It turned out to be about what that Cedar Brake lawman had said it was. As Sam and Roger turned back in the direction of the ice-water creek near the mouth of Turner's Gap, they knew the area well enough. But they did not know, and this was now uppermost in their minds, about the occupants of the place.

That thoroughbred horse prompted Roger to a conclusion. "This darned place must be the end of the trail for horse thieves. I saw a lot of good horses in those little pastures. If I was to guess, I'd say these folks don't just make their living off the pack trains and freighters using that pass."

Sam summed it up succinctly. "Nest of rattlesnakes, Roger, and Jack's right down in the middle of them."

They reached the screening trees, off-saddled and hobbled their animals along the overgrown banks of the creek, and lay back in the rising heat to rest. Sam was snoring like an old boar hog in two minutes, but Roger did not close his eyes.

VIII

They did not have a constable at Evansville, but they had one of those insular, closed local societies in which strangers were under general surveillance from the time they rode in until they rode out.

The nearest Evansville had to a lawman was a large, graying man named Tom Burlingame who had a small smithy beside his cabin on the short main roadway, and who otherwise ran a pack outfit for supplying mines and other isolated enterprises in the mountains where only trails existed. He received word of Jack Pate's arrival in the village a short while after Jack had put up his horse and gone over to the café for breakfast.

When Jack emerged into the morning sunlight, Tom Burlingame was waiting, unsmiling, suspicious, and blunt. He nodded and said: "My name is Tom Burlingame. I'm the town blacksmith. I also act as sort of local lawman."

Jack stated his name and turned to glance up and down the roadway before continuing to speak. He had not anticipated such a swift or forthright encounter, but he had expected some kind of encounter so now he smiled at Burlingame as he said: "I buy horses and mules . . . when I can find decent ones. Do a little trading now and then."

"You been in this country before?" asked the blacksmith.

Jack's answer was casual, but cautious. "Not right here, no, but I been through the area down around Cedar Brake. That's where I heard about folks up here now and then having livestock for sale."

Tom Burlingame had been making a physical appraisal. Now he said: "There's usually a few horses or mules for sale hereabouts. But folks don't much keep poor animals. A man'd likely have to pay."

Jack agreed. "I don't handle second-rate animals, Mister Burlingame. I buy the best and sell the best. No spoiled horses or biting mules. I been selling to the same people, mostly cow outfits up north, for ten, twelve years. I can trail into their yards with a trading string, and be greeted like an old friend. That's how I built up my business."

Burlingame did not smile, even now, but Jack thought his attitude changed a little. He pointed. "See that corral across the road northward, the one with the new peeled poles? There's a feller over there named Craig. He usually has a few animals for sale. Morton Craig." Burlingame dropped his thick arm. "There are others around might sell you a horse or two. Mules . . . I got the best string in town and none of them are for sale. I pack a little now and then and need every one of them."

Jack considered Tom Burlingame. "Fact is, mules is mostly what I'm looking for this trip. You got the best string?"

"But not for sale, Mister Pate."

Jack did not relent. "Mister Burlingame, any animal is for sale. It takes a little more money to buy some than it does to buy others."

Burlingame seemed to agree with this even though he began shaking his head before he spoke again. "But the price could be damned awful high, sometimes, Mister Pate."

Jack smiled. "When there's a good market, Mister Burlingame, a man can pay a little better price."

The large, graying, unsmiling blacksmith pondered for a moment. "Well, I might have one mule I'd part with."

"Does he bite or kick?"

"No."

"Hard to catch, then, or bucks packs off?"

"The only thing I can fault him about, Mister Pate, is that he's sixteen hands high. I been hoisting pack boxes and other heavy loads onto him for three years. I prefer small mules, fourteen to fifteen hands. They're just as stout and a man don't have to strain every time he packs and unpacks."

"How much?" Jack asked.

Burlingame was no longer a suspicious townsman. He was now involved in something dear to the heart of every range man—a horse trade. He spat, considered two men across the way sitting on a wall bench, shifted his cud, and finally said: "Tell you what, Mister Pate. I'll fetch him around and tie him in front of the shop in a few minutes. You look him over and tell me what he's worth." Burlingame pointed northward across the road again. "Craig's home. You had ought to talk to him first."

Jack agreed and strolled past those two men on the bench and up to the log house with a new set of pole corrals out back. Tom Burlingame remained where he was, watching Jack for a moment longer, then he turned in the direction of his shop.

One of those seated men arose and headed over to intercept the blacksmith. The other one watched Jack stroll around back where the new corrals were, but, when Jack passed from sight, the man on the bench arose, also. He ambled in the same direction, found another place to sit, and pulled out a clasp knife to sit and whittle, his lean, bronzed face half hidden in hat brim shade.

Morton Craig turned out to be a wiry small man with lank gray hair, sharp features, and pale blue eyes. He was forking feed over the corral to several animals including two small mules, when Jack greeted him. Craig turned, studied Jack while leaning on the pitchfork, then responded with a little smile.

Jack explained who had sent him and why he was here. Morton Craig faced the eating animals and shrewdly squinted as he said: "Well, sir, Mister Pate, maybe you come to the right man. I got seven horses up for sale and four mules. I only got two of the mules in the corral right now, but I can fetch in the other ones right soon. I got 'em grazing west of town." He forked in another big bait of hay, leaned the fork aside, and stepped to the corral to lean there. "They're good animals. Broke, mostly sound, no bad habits that I know of. And because I got too many, I'm willing to thin down a little. Now you take that liver-chestnut mare yonder. She's only four, broke good, and she's dog gentle."

"Mostly," said Jack, eyeing the animals, "this trip I'm after good using mules."

Morton Craig was warming to his trade. "That big jack," he said, indicating another animal. "Bought him off a widow woman whose husband died recent, and he never used the mule for anything more'n hauling a stone boat with water barrels on it. Stout as they come and plumb friendly . . . for a mule."

Jack had been studying brands when he said: "What's that mark on his shoulder?"

Morton Craig leaned to squint. "Oh, that was put on him when he was a colt by some feller this widow woman's husband got him from." Craig rubbed an unshaven jaw. "I think it's an Arizona brand."

"Looks sound," Jack said.

Craig answered instantly and firmly. "There's not a bump on him and he's loose in the shoulders. As you can see, his back's never been scarred up. He's seven years old, right in his prime. Tell you what, Mister Pate, you can have him for . . . forty dollars on the barrelhead, and he's worth sixty any place you want to take him where folks needs sound good stout young mules."

Jack pursed his lips, wearing the expression of a man balancing a decision in his mind. He said: "How about that dappled mule?"

Craig smiled, showing tobacco-stained teeth. "Female," he announced. "But she's strong and willing. I got her off some fellers passing through a few weeks back. They was broke. She's five."

"Got faults has she, Mister Craig?"

The small, wiry man hung fire for just a second or two before answering. "Well, some folks just don't want no female mules. She's like any other mare . . . when she's comin' in she's flighty and cranky. But she's sound, Mister Pate, and, because I got her right cheap, I'll let you have her for twenty-five dollars."

Jack leaned back a little and turned toward Morton Craig. "She's cheap enough. Of course when I peddle her I'll have to sell her cheap."

"But you got a spread of maybe ten, fifteen dollars, Mister Pate," stated Morton Craig, smiling knowingly. "Tell you what . . . take the pair of them, and two more I'll fetch in for you to look at, and I'll make you a hell of a price on the lot."

Jack barely inclined his head. "When'll you have the other ones here at the corral?"

Morton Craig, sensing something worthwhile, answered quickly. "Hour. Hour and a half at the most. Just as soon as I can saddle her up, drink some coffee, and ride out where they're grazing, and ride back with 'em." He smiled genially. "You goin' to be around town for a spell?"

Jack shrugged. "For today anyway, Mister Craig. If I can get up a trading string by evening, I'll be heading out in the morning." He turned to gaze in at the mules as he added: "I never been up here before. A feller down in Cedar Brake told me you folks had animals to trade up here, mostly of pretty fair quality." He faced Morton Craig again. "I didn't see any horse ranches on the ride up."

Craig leaned to gaze at his animals as he said: "We're sort of on the freighter and trader route through the mountains. We get a lot of chances to pick up surplus critters." He turned back, facing Jack again. "Just about everyone in town trades a little. Mister Pate, it might damned well pay you to make a good contact here in Evansville, then, when you need a trading string, you wouldn't have to go all over hell buying an animal at a time."

Jack seemed to be considering this when he said: "I handle a lot of horses and mules, Mister Craig. Trail 'em north to Colorado and over into Utah. Do some peddling down along the border once in a while, too."

Craig's crafty look deepened. "Down along the border . . . well . . . folks aren't too particular about brands down there."

Jack conceded this. "They aren't for a fact. And neither am I, providing someone don't sell me horses from the same country where I go trailing through to do my peddling."

Morton Craig stood a moment in thought, then said: "Come back in a couple of hours, Mister Pate. I believe you and me are going to do some business." He smiled and nodded as Jack turned to go back around the side of the house to the dusty roadway.

Out front, a man sitting nearby was whittling. He did not so much as glance up as Jack cut diagonally across the road in the direction of the blacksmith's shop where a tall, big-boned, dolorous-faced mule was patiently standing tied to a stud ring deeply implanted into a tree trunk.

The blacksmith was smoking a foul little pipe and glanced up as Jack walked in. The shop was small, stained nearly black from years of forge smoke, and had that rank smell of most blacksmith shops.

Tom Burlingame gravely nodded, removed his pipe, and, while looking intently at Jack, said: "You do any good with Craig?"

Jack's answer was evasive. "Maybe. He's gone to fetch in some other mules. We'll meet again in a couple of hours. Is that your big mule out front?"

Burlingame strolled to the wide front opening of his shop and puffed his pipe a moment, staring at the mule out there. "Yeah, that's him. Strong as an oak tree." Burlingame plugged the little pipe back between his teeth, briefly puffed, then removed it to say: "Where did you say you came from, Mister Pate?"

Jack also stepped to the big opening to stand gazing at the mule. "I don't think I said, but I cover a lot of country with strings of trading stock. Originally I started out from Nebraska. Over around Council Bluffs."

Burlingame chewed his pipe for a moment before speaking again. "You been trading around over near Fort Morgan lately?"

Jack harkened to the little shrill warning deep inside his head. "I've traded over there a few times," he replied. "But I've done more business in better places."

"You got friends over there, have you, Mister Pate?"

The hidden alarm signal became more shrill. Jack turned. "Not particularly, Mister Burlingame. I try to make a friend or two wherever I go. It comes in handy when a man's trailing through. Saves time . . . local folks know who wants to buy or sell. I stand a few rounds now and then."

Burlingame stood watching his big mule and for a while he said nothing, then, as though inwardly shrugging something off, he pointed with his pipe stem. "You're welcome to climb on that mule if you want to try him. He rides pretty good. Or lead him around back where my packs are and load him." Burlingame turned, dead-level eyes fixed upon Jack. "As for making acquaintances, folks in Evansville are mostly friendly. You might even run into some fellers you've met before."

He let that lie between them a moment, then slowly turned. Back in the dingy gloom of the rear of the shop a man had stepped in from out back. He had evidently been standing back there for several minutes, perhaps listening. When Jack turned to follow the direction of Burlingame's glance and saw that man, his muscles tightened. It was one of those rustlers he, Sam, and Roger had robbed across the mountains in the dark.

Burlingame said: "This here is Mister Smith."

The horse thief walked a little closer, his eyes fixed on Jack's face. Jack smiled at him. "Glad to know you, Mister Smith."

Burlingame cut in right after those words to say: "Is this here one of them, Will?"

Will Smith stood staring, his body slightly stiff. "Like I told you, Tom, he looks like one of them, but it was damned dark. And there was two more. One of 'em wearin' a six-gun with an ivory grip. This gent sure looks like one of them."

Burlingame quietly said: "Go get Alf."

Will Smith nodded, stepped wide around Jack Pate, and hurried away. Tom Burlingame showed nothing in his face as he explained: "Some fellers was robbed on through the mountains a short while back, Mister Pate. You don't want to take offence, but Will thought you looked like one of them. He'll apologize if he was wrong." Burlingame stood there holding his little pipe, showing no particular animosity, and no fear. "I just ask that you understand. Folks got to be real careful nowadays. Hereabouts we make a point of bein' real careful."

Jack returned the older man's gaze without wavering, but he began to worry for fear someone might see Roger and Sam, and identify them, also. Or just see them, and report that there were two more strangers in the area, one with an ivory-handled Colt. Sam and that damned gun of his!

IX

The moment the man called Will Smith returned, Jack recognized the bearded companion he returned with. It was the second one of those horse thieves. It was in fact the man Sam had taken that broken pocket watch from.

They were both armed but Tom Burlingame did not have a weapon showing, nor did he act particularly anxious. His little pipe had died and now he was holding it in one big, scarred hand. He nodded in that grave way of his at the bearded horse thief, saying: "Howdy, Alf. This here is Mister Pate." Burlingame let that lie a moment before speaking again. "You ever see him before?"

Alf must have already discussed this matter with his partner and perhaps he had not been completely sure even before, because now, as he stood studying Jack, he said: "Sure looks like one of 'em, Tom. There was one of 'em I'd know anywhere. Stocky, squinty-eyed feller with an ivory handle to his six-gun. Kept grinning all the time they was cleaning us out. I'd know *that* one, even though it was dark."

Burlingame knocked dottle from his pipe and pocketed it. "Boys," he said mildly, "you're not bein' very helpful. Either you identify Mister Pate here as one of those renegades, or not. I can't do anything until you're sure one way or another."

Will Smith looked at his partner as though the decision would be up to Alf, but the longer they all stood there the less Alf seemed willing, or able, to accuse Jack directly. Nor did it require very much acuity for Jack to see the indecision. He moved boldly to reinforce it by saying: "Gents, you're both strangers to me. If I'd robbed anyone around here, I sure as hell wouldn't be standing here now, would I?"

"It didn't happen here," mumbled Alf. "It happened on the other side of the gap."

"The Fort Morgan side," stated Tom Burlingame, gazing at Jack. "And you said you'd been horse trading over there."

The crack of doubt seemed to be widening so Jack drove in another wedge. "Sure I traded over there. I also traded up around Green River, and over near Albuquerque, and before Fort Morgan, southeast in the bitterbrush country. I guess there probably were hold-ups in all those places while I was around 'em, but I sure as hell had nothing to do with them. Not those places, and not in this country."

Alf's gaze was clearly suspicious. Will Smith, possessing a mind of more clarity and less turgidity, finally flapped his arms and looked helplessly at Tom Burlingame. "He sure looks like he could have been one of them, but, like Alf says, the one we could identify easy was that squinty-eyed feller with the ivory gun grips."

Burlingame gazed at the pair of horse thieves, his stolid, thick features gradually assuming an expression of disgust. "Well now, what in hell am I supposed to do?" he asked sourly.

Will flapped again. "Let it go, I guess." He reddened a little under Burlingame's annoyed look. "I never said he more than looked like one of 'em, Tom, an' I told you it was damned dark when they rose up out of the grass and surprised us half to death."

Burlingame faced Jack. "This is a little embarrassing," he growled. "But I figure you can understand, Mister Pate. They lost a band of horses, a gold watch, a green stone, and their money belts."

Jack looked from the horse thieves to Tom Burlingame, and softly whistled, outwardly impressed at the amount of loss. "Gents, if I'd got that much off anyone, take my word for it, I'd maybe not lift a finger for a year. I sure as hell wouldn't be ridin' my tailbone sore trying to make up a fresh string of trading stock."

Alf continued to regard Jack from baleful, darkly suspicious eyes, but he said nothing. When his partner turned toward him, embarrassed and uncomfortable, Alf showed neither of those feelings, nor did he seem to be at all apologetic. Jack got the impression that Alf was still wavering, but now Tom Burlingame came reservedly to Pate's aid by saying: "All right, Will, this is how it's got to lie if you fellers can't do any better. Mister Pate, about this big mule. . . ."

They strolled over where the animal was still patiently standing. Over there, with the pair of horse thieves shuffling across in the direction of that wall bench again, Tom Burlingame sighed and shook his head. "Sorry to have put you through that, Mister Pate, but the fact is they was cleaned out pretty bad. I was sure they'd be able to call it one way or the other. Instead, they left me looking darned ridiculous."

Jack had sweat running under his shirt and it was not that warm a day, but he acted out his part to the very end by saying: "It was a little upsetting, Mister Burlingame, but, hell, it's done with. . . . About this big mule. Y'know, you're plumb right about him being awful tall."

The blacksmith glumly looked at his mule. "Tall, for a fact, but stout, Mister Pate. Strong as they come, young and without a blemish nor a bad habit."

"How much?"

"Well, sir, Mister Pate, it's not like I was offering you one of those little wring-tail jennies a man sees here and there. . . . Forty dollars."

"Thirty, Mister Burlingame."

"Thirty-five, Mister Pate."

Jack extended his hand. They clasped, pumped once, and let go. Burlingame pointed. "Yonder's some extra corrals. You can put him in down there until you've made up your string."

Jack counted out the money. Burlingame recounted it, folded it into a shirt pocket, and nodded. "You got a good mule," he told Jack. "If you buy others from Morton Craig, you can turn 'em all into those corrals yonder." Burlingame stood momentarily lost in thought, then he spoke again. "Mister Pate, I don't have any bill of sale for that mule. He's not branded, so I expect you don't really need one." They exchanged a look, then Jack studied his big mule before turning back to say: "I can get by without one." He then fished forth his makings, lowered his eyes as he went to work making a cigarette, and quietly said: "I'm not particular about bills of sale, Mister Burlingame. Sometimes I've made my own." He lit the smoke and held the blacksmith's gaze as he did so. "If I buy horses and mules in northern New Mexico, I don't trail over the line into Colorado to sell them. If I buy livestock near one place, I go at least three hundred miles before I commence trading them off."

Burlingame's gaze slid back to the big mule. His features were impassive. Eventually he said: "Well, I expect Craig'll be coming back directly." He looked squarely at Jack. "I think Evansville might turn out to be a place where you'll find just about whatever you want from time to time, Mister Pate. Now I got to get back to work."

Jack crossed to the vacant corrals with his big mule, got some hay for the beast, made sure the wooden water trough was full, then ambled back up to the Craig place and went out back to stand, silent and alone, beside the peeled-pole corral, looking in and not thinking about the corralled animals at all.

He had not pinned anyone down, but his feeling was that Burlingame, Craig, and probably just about everyone else in Evansville was in the rustled livestock business, which was interesting, but had no immediate bearing on why he was here.

He did not know, either, that those two horse thieves had robbed that stagecoach. If they had, then they'd had another pair of companions, and if Alf and Will, plus two additional renegades living here in Evansville became suspicious—which the pair of horse thieves seemed to be already, at least partially so—then Jack was in danger. But he had not expected to be safe or immediately accepted in this horse-thief's town. Nor had his nerve failed him during his test out front of the blacksmith's shop. His nerve did not fail him now as he leaned there, gazing unseeingly at the corralled horses and mules, carefully picking his mental way through the maze of doubt, suspicion, and misgiving that seemed to be steadily increasing all around him.

What he shortly had to do now was ride back to the point of rendezvous and palaver with Sam and Roger. But with perhaps two-thirds of the residents of Evansville taking an interest in him, he would have to make that ride under absolutely plausible circumstances.

He had evolved a plan a half hour before Morton Craig came slogging down the roadway with a number of led animals behind his personal mount. He wheeled in and Jack opened the corral gate for him, then leaned there studying each individual animal as they entered the corral.

Craig broadly smiled as he swung off to lead his mount outside to be tied and stripped. "There they be," he said to Jack Pate. "Sound as new money . . . none of them too old, stout, and usable right now."

Jack told of buying Tom Burlingame's big mule and Craig laughed. "You need a ladder to get anything onto his back. But he is sound and usable, for a fact." He finished caring for the horse, leaned on the corral gazing in, and continued to smile softly. "Mister Pate, I been thinking. Maybe you and me could get right well acquainted. I handle a fair amount of good, using animals. I'll be straightforward with you, and you peddle 'em. Maybe we'd both make a little money."

Jack had finished his examination of the fresh livestock and had selected a stocking-legged blood bay, a little aged but as handsome as a horse could be. He pointed to him and said: "How much are you askin' for the red horse?"

Craig's smile broadened. He spat amber, then said: "You got a good eye, Mister Pate. That there is a cuttin' and ropin' horse. He's smooth-mouthed but I'm here to tell you . . . try an' find even a wind puff on him. He don't have no blemishes and he's as nice a ridin' horse as there is in. . . ."

"How much, Mister Craig?"

"Well, sir. . . ." Craig spat to one side again before answering. "I can't let him go for no lower than fifty dollars. He's flashy and good."

"Thirty-five," said Jack, and turned to watch what he knew was coming.

First, Morton Craig's furry brows shot up like startled caterpillars, then his eyes reflected shock, disbelief, then anguish. He spat again, drew a soiled cuff across his mouth, and began dolorously wagging his head. "Mister Pate, you know better'n that. Just you look at that horse. Just look at him."

"He's smooth," said Jack. "Got to be maybe twelve years old."

"Nine," averred Craig stoutly, the age a horse lost his cups after which age was largely a matter of pure guesswork, and usually some lying. "Mister Pate . . . tell you what . . . let me rig him out. I want you to set on that animal. Just ride him down the road and back. You've never rode an easier-gaited horse in your life."

Jack had been leading up to just exactly this suggestion. But he had expected to make it. Now, he turned with a little smile. "All right," he agreed. "You ride along with me. We can dicker while we're riding."

Morton Craig moved swiftly and surely at saddling two horses, keeping up a running barrage of talk as he worked. Finally, as he handed Jack the reins, he said: "I tell you straight out, Mister Pate, I need a reliable partner. Well . . . not exactly a partner, y'see, but someone who can trail a string out, get shed of them, and come back for more. I need someone who can deal off a lot of horses and mules." As he swung across leather Craig added: "I had a couple fellers who helped out . . . not at peddlin' horses but at supplyin' me with 'em . . . and they got raided a week or so back and it plumb demoralized them. They're just settin' around now, mopin' and groanin'."

Jack studied Morton Craig's face. Evansville was a small place, but, even so, what Craig had just said did not have to apply to Alf and Will Smith. It could apply to them, though. If it did, Morton Craig also used the name of Cantrell. That was the name the horse thieves had mentioned when Jack and his partners caught them in their Turner's Gap camp.

Jack said—"This feels like a lot of horse under a man, for a fact."—and reined out of the yard with Craig at his side, pointing eastward through the upper end of town in the direction of a stand of trees to one side of the roadway, up close to the mouth of Turner's Gap.

"Mister Pate!" exclaimed Craig, urging his own mount up beside Jack. "That there horse is well worth sixty-five dollars . . . providin' you know where to sell him." He paused, gazed from the blood bay to its rider, then rolled up his eyes and said: "All right. Forty dollars. But that's my bottom dollar, and only because you an' me is going to work out a sort of workin' partnership."

Jack stuck out his hand without saying a word. They sealed the sale with a handclasp, then rode along slowly, side-by-side, for anyone who happened to be watching, and Jack was certain there were watchers, to see their casual approach to those distant, screening trees.

Jack kept watching ahead. Roger and Sam were in those trees. By now they had had ample time to complete their scout of the Evansville area, and get back there. As he kept watching, he said: "Mister Craig, we're out away from everyone. Maybe if we just spoke out with each other." He turned to meet the smaller man's crafty, shrewd look. "I trade off about four or five strings each ridin' season."

Craig was not fazed. "I can supply you with that many, and more. Both mules and horses. Nothing rank nor ringy. We got to keep a good reputation."

Jack kept eyeing the older man. "That's a lot of horses and mules."

Craig nodded. "For a fact. You worryin' that maybe I can't come up with 'em?"

"Can you? We're not talking about worn-out critters. I never handle anything like that."

"I can," replied Morton Craig, looking ahead, then turning slowly to Jack. "I got to find two more suppliers to replace those two that got raided a few days back." He winked at Jack. "But around Evansville there are fellers who need the money and the work."

Jack did not look away. "How?" he asked quietly.

Craig evened up his rawhide reins, spat to one side, furrowed his brow, then said: "Just take my word for it. I can supply them."

Jack slowly shook his head. "Mister Craig, I got to do better'n that. Talk is cheap." He waited before adding: "I'm not too interested in where they come from, except that I don't want to go trailing into some territory that's just been raided, with horses in my string that got some cow outfit's brand on them."

Craig relaxed a little. "I'll make damned sure you know where not to go, when you pick up each string."

Jack said: "We're talking about stolen horses."

Craig's smile was strained as he met Jack's gaze. "Well, any time a man handles a lot of horses he's goin' to get some now and then that's been. . . ."

"Mister Craig . . . straight out. I already told you I'm not too particular."

The wiry man nodded his head curtly. "They're stolen horses and mules." He continued to ride alongside Jack, looking directly at him.

The trees were getting close. Jack looked from them to Morton Craig and mirthlessly smiled. "All right. Just be damned sure you can supply me, and be double damned sure you don't let me trail 'em back into the same country where someone stole 'em."

Craig smiled from ear to ear, not amused but enormously relieved that the fencing was over and his new friend had not batted an eye. "I'll keep you from ridin' into trouble every way I can, Mister Pate, and to make it easier for both of us, you write me a letter a few weeks ahead of time and let me know you'll be arrivin' here, so's I can have the animals ready for you. Just address the letter to Mister Cantrell here in Evansville."

Jack showed a flicker of that mirthless smile again as he turned off the road toward the screening trees where the little creek ran. "Need a drink," he explained. Morton Craig turned toward the trees, also.

X

There were two men back in town who would have understood instantly, when those two unshaven men strolled forth from the trees—the stockier of the two men smiling around perpetually squinted eyes—but Morton Craig simply saw two strangers. He stared at them, then dismounted slowly, keeping his horse between the oncoming strollers and himself.

Jack stepped down and shoved a gun into Craig's back. The horse trader turned very slowly, astonishment imbedded in his face.

Sam walked around the horse, still smiling, not uttering a sound as he leaned and lifted Craig's six-gun away. Roger did not even draw his weapon. He simply stood there, considering Craig with interest.

Jack said: "This here is Cantrell, the feller those horse thieves were peddling their stolen animals to."

Craig's jaw sagged. He twisted to gaze steadily at Jack Pate. As full realization soaked in he said: "God damn."

The three partners ignored this. Roger said: "What's he got to do with the stage robbery?"

Jack was leathering his Colt when he replied: "That's what we're going to find out. Let's ride up the pass a couple of miles where folks won't see a little fire."

Roger nodded. "Yeah. But maybe he'd talk without havin' the soles of his feet burned with a red-hot cinch ring."

They all three stood looking at Craig. The surprise had been so complete that Morton Craig was still floundering. But he understood the implication about that cinch ring and the fire. "What the hell are you talkin' about?" he asked, and waved his arms. "I never in my life robbed a stagecoach!"

Sam kept grinning. "Maybe you didn't, mister, but I'm going to bet ten dollars you know who did rob one over near Fort Morgan a few days back."

Craig stared at Jack Pate. "Who are you?" he asked.

Jack offered an indifferent reply. "Those fellers who robbed that coach . . . who are they? Never mind about me."

Craig continued to stare. "You're the three fellers who caught Alf and Will and cleaned them out."

Sam kept smiling. "Next time they steal horses, mister, you better make sure whose horses they are rustling."

Craig looked skeptical. "All them horses belonged to you fellers?"

"No," stated Sam. "Only three of them. But we took back the others as well. And a few other odds and ends. Mister, if you told them to keep on raiding the Fort Morgan country, it's your fault they got caught and cleaned out. Not ours."

Jack waited until this exchange was completed, then got back to his original topic. "Which four men robbed that coach five miles south of Fort Morgan, Mister Craig?"

As before, the horse dealer said he had no idea, that he had never stopped a stagecoach, and knew nothing about that particular robbery.

Roger and Jack exchanged a glance, then Roger turned back where his horse was, speaking over his shoulder. "I guess you're right, Jack. Let's ride up the pass out of sight of the village."

Morton Craig watched Roger for a moment. When he was convinced Roger was not bluffing, he said: "Alf and Will stopped that stage."

Jack slowly shook his head. "There were four men, not two."

"Well, they maybe took a couple of friends along," Craig explained. "All I know is that after they got cleaned out, they swore they'd make it back off the folks over there. They was mad clear through. They quit me, said they wouldn't work for me no more . . . that as soon as they got a decent grubstake, they were going to leave the country."

"So they robbed that coach," murmured Jack. "How much

did they get off it?"

Craig professed not to know. "They wasn't hardly speakin' to me by then. I got no idea what they got. But there was a couple sacks of mail. I heard 'em talking about that."

Sam said: "And a bullion box."

Craig screwed up his face. "There wasn't nothing said about a bullion box." He continued to stare at Sam. "You fellers aren't lawmen. I told Alf you wasn't."

Sam smiled and said nothing. Roger strolled back to listen. He heard that last comment and looked steadily at Morton Craig. "You don't have to be a lawman to get mad when someone steals your horse, mister. Lawmen haul 'em in for the judge to deal with. Us fellers do the judgin' on our own."

Craig was perspiring. He raised his hat to mop off sweat. As he replaced the hat, he faced Jack again. "You fellers don't favor the law, I can see that. We can still work something out."

Jack's answer was frank. "Yeah, we probably could have . . . once. But right now we want those four fellers who raided that stagecoach."

"Why? You had money on it, or something valuable? Listen, I can likely get your stuff back from Alf and Will. There's no sense in makin' a war out of this." Craig swung his glance from Sam and Roger back to Jack. "Fellers like us are entitled to make a living, but we sure as hell can't do it fightin' among ourselves."

Jack remained unmoved. "For the last time, Mister Craig . . . who were the other two stage robbers?"

"I told you the truth. Alf and Will were in on it, but that's all I know for a fact. After they got cleaned out, they wouldn't hardly speak to me. Somehow or other they decided it was my fault."

"Who do they normally run with in Evansville?" asked Jack.

But Craig was adamant. "You can do what you want, I still

can't tell you any more because I don't know any more."

Jack said: "Tom Burlingame?"

Craig fidgeted. "They been hangin' around his shop since they been back, but I don't know that he was with them on that job."

Roger turned his back on Morton Craig and addressed his partners. "We can kill the whole damned day standin' here. Jack, we got to get one of those horse thieves. Get both of 'em if we can."

It sounded logical enough, but of course the problem was how to accomplish it. Jack knew better than his partners did how suspicious and watchful the people in the village were. He also knew that, although by a narrow margin he had escaped detection, he was still regarded with suspicion. "After nightfall," he told Roger Bemis, and related his experience over in front of the blacksmith's shop. Morton Craig had not heard this before and listened with interest. Ordinarily Craig would probably have had some comment to make, but by now his sole concern was his own safety. He said nothing, and his crafty, narrow face showed that he was considering his own dilemma.

Sam jerked a thumb in Craig's direction. "What about this one? If he don't ride back, maybe folks'll wonder."

Jack had already thought about this. "He and I'll ride back in plain sight just like we rode out. His cabin is on the west side of the road. There's a new pole corral out back with four mules in it and a band of horses. You fellers creep around there after dark and come in from out back. I'll leave the back door unlatched. Be damned careful. If anyone sees you, the whole darned town'll come down on us. It's a nest of horse thieves."

Roger looked doubtful, but all he said was: "Where do those two fellers bed down at night?"

Jack faced Morton Craig. "Answer," he said.

Craig answered. "In a cabin south of my place. The feller

who owned that cabin rode south two years ago and no one's seen him since." Craig scowled at Jack Pate. "You'll get caught at this sure as hell. The folks in Evansville got eyes in the backs of their heads."

Jack's response was dry. "Four eyes aren't any better'n two, if you can't see in the dark. . . . Mister Craig, we're going back now and you're going to act normal, and stay right beside me the rest of the day. Give him back his gun, Sam . . . unloaded."

Sam complied. He shucked out the loads and dropped the useless gun back into Craig's hip holster. Then he smiled and addressed Morton Craig. "I sure hope nothin' goes wrong, partner. But if it does, you're going to be the first one to head for the sand hills. I'll see to it myself."

Roger and Jack spoke aside for a moment or two, then Roger and Sam stood aside while Jack and Morton Craig got back astride for the ride back. After they had turned out of the trees in the direction of the village, Roger wagged his head. "What the hell are we going to do with four lousy highwaymen? I don't much feel like takin' 'em back and handin' them over to the folks at Fort Morgan."

Sam's answer was curt. "Take 'em back, hell. All we want is what they took off that coach. And if there wasn't a bullion box, I'll eat my horse."

"Who said there was a box on board?"

"Well, the coach that arrived in Fort Morgan the night before had a box aboard. We all three seen them liftin' it down."

"Sam, damn it, that don't mean there was a box on the stage these fellers robbed. You heard that horse dealer . . . those fellers got a couple mail sacks. Aside from that we know they robbed the passengers." Roger looked irritably at Sam. "There was no bullion box, and I'll lay you odds that what they got out of the mail pouches and off the passengers wasn't as much as that old cowman and those town fathers offered us for finding these highwaymen."

Sam groaned. He had it fixed in his mind that there was a bullion box. At least that there should have been, and on that basis he had been spending his idle time considering what he would do with his share of the loot.

But Roger was a practical man. More practical than Sam was, which Sam fully realized. Both Roger and Jack were practical, shrewd men. Sam wagged his head. "Then what in hell's the sense of going through all this?" he asked.

"Five hundred dollars from over at Fort Morgan," stated Roger. "And maybe whatever we can take off Alf and Will. Altogether, if we're lucky, I'd guess we might pick up a couple thousand."

Sam scowled. "Split three ways? Roger, I hid more'n that under the floorboards of my room back at Fort Morgan."

Roger did not argue, he simply said: "We're over here, and we're up to our hocks in this mess. What do you want to do, saddle up and ride off and leave Jack down there?"

Sam subsided, but the disillusionment would require considerable getting over. But Sam's disposition was not subject to sulkiness or gloom for very long. He was by nature a man of rough humor, native resourcefulness, general indifference to most values other men respected, and he was generous. He was also fearless and deadly in a fight.

If there actually had been no bullion box, he would have to scrap all those earlier plans and concentrate on fresh ones. He began doing exactly this as he and Roger returned to the trees to take their horses out on ropes and let the animals fill up. They had all afternoon to kill. The best way to do it was to make certain the animals that would be under them tonight were rested and fed.

XI

Morton Craig was craftily busy with private thoughts for half the distance back to his corrals. Once, he offered Jack Pate some advice.

"You'll never bring it off. Evansville's a place where folks watch everything and everybody."

Jack did not doubt this, but he and his partners were not gun-heavy lawmen who rode into a place with a challenge on their lips. They had been surviving for some years now by guile, by using all the perfected deviousness of their outlaw trade. They had seldom been in positions where peril was not a constant companion.

Craig also said: "I can't understand you fellers. What the hell are you helpin' the law for?"

Jack could have answered that very easily. He and his partners were not helping the law. Not consciously anyway. They were helping themselves. By Jack's calculations, including the reward offered over at Fort Morgan and whatever they might be able to pick up along the way, it was not impossible that he, Sam, and Roger might not come out of this with about $1,000 each.

He said: "Mister Craig, if things were different, Evansville might be just the town my partners and I would like to live in, when we're not on the road. But this time we got other ideas."

Craig shook his head. "You'll never make it."

Jack turned. "We'd better make it." He did not fill out that threat because he did not have to.

They got back to the outskirts of town. A short, thick man wearing a heavy, checked red and black shirt was leaning on a tie rack and watching their approach. He closed his clasp knife, tossed down the stick he had been whittling on, turned, and casually walked southward down through town.

Jack sighed. This would be a hell of a town to visit a widow in at night.

They got back to the corrals and dismounted. Morton Craig was unnaturally quiet as he pulled his saddle and removed his bridle. He watched Jack, but after a while, conscious that even when Jack did not appear to be keeping an eye on him, he was being watched, Craig leaned on the corral, rolled a smoke, and woefully eyed his corral full of livestock. "We sure could have made us a killin' workin' together on these animals," he said.

They fed the livestock and went inside the cabin. It was a typical single-man's boar's nest. It smelled stale. There were caked cooking pans on the dirty old wood stove, and tin plates plus several cracked and handleless cups in a big, tin dishpan half full of cold, greasy water.

Craig built a fire, draped his hat from a broken set of buck antlers, scratched, and eyed Jack Pate. "You hungry?" he asked.

Jack, looking around, shook his head. He was hungry, but not *that* hungry.

Craig started a meal. Once, when he started out of the kitchen, Jack growled at him and he turned back, saying: "Hell, I was only goin' after a tin of bakin' soda to make biscuits with."

"Sure," Jack agreed dryly. "And a handful of slugs for your gun. Mister Craig, don't take chances and you just might come through this with a whole hide."

Craig worked a moment at the stove, then turned. "You can't take four fellers out of Evansville. It's crazy to even try it."

Jack straddled a chair and watched his reluctant host. "We can do it," he replied quietly. "Right up through that gap and out the far side and down to Fort Morgan."

Craig made a painful face. "I'll explain something to you, Mister Pate. Everyone around here either has the law lookin' for them, or is doin' something they hadn't ought to be doin'."

"Like you . . . dealing in stolen horses?"

"Yeah, like me. Like everyone else in this place. Do you think we haven't long ago worked out systems of protection? I'm not goin' to tell you what they are, but, take my word for it, you're not goin' to ride out of here and through that pass with no prisoners."

The coffee was boiling. Jack said he would take a cup of it, and, as Morton Craig turned to draw off two cups, someone rolled a big fist across the roadside door. Jack swept his coat back in one smooth gesture. Craig turned, saw him do that, and swallowed hard. "Let me get rid of 'em," he muttered. "Whoever it is, let me get 'em away from here."

Jack nodded and arose. "I'll aim at your back from the doorway here. Mister Craig . . . be awful careful."

The horse dealer stumped through his littered, smelly little parlor. Jack cracked the kitchen door and leaned to look and listen. Even before he could make out the caller, he knew who he was by his deep calm voice: Tom Burlingame, the blacksmith.

Craig said: " 'Evening, Tom."

Burlingame answered smoothly. " 'Evening. That feller who bought the big mule off me, Mort, is he around?"

Craig cleared his throat. "Somewhere, I reckon. He also bought a mule off me. He's comin' back in the mornin' to get it, and maybe some of the horses. What about him?"

Burlingame's reply was in that same unhurried, deep voice. "Alf and Will figure he's one of those fellers who raided them on the east side of Turner's Gap. They been all day makin' up their minds. But you know, I got doubts. Those two idiots looked him right in the eye this mornin' and wouldn't make a positive identification."

"Well, what you want me to do about it, Tom?"

"First, I want to know where he is, then I want him kept occupied while I hunt up his outfit and search his saddlebags. If he's one of those raiders, he's not going out of here alive. If he's not one of them, then Alf and Will are goin' to get the sharp edge of my tongue. They're gettin' to be a pain in the rear anyway, losin' that herd, lettin' someone clean them out, and settin' around now, sulkin' and loafin'. I got enough to worry about without gettin' involved in something as silly as this."

Craig was sympathetic. "If he shows up this evenin', I'll take him over to the saloon. Someone over there will see, and let you know."

Burlingame seemed satisfied. "Good enough. Find out where he made a camp. Otherwise, it'll take an extra hour findin' his outfit."

Craig nodded. "I'll do it. As for Alf and Will"—spite crept into the horse dealer's voice now—"the sooner they clear out the better. They must have got enough off that stage to ride on. They're a liability around here now, anyway."

"What they got off the coach," stated Burlingame, "wasn't enough. I know that for a fact. They want to raid another one. I told them not to. Not around Fort Morgan, lawman or no lawman. You can't keep on raidin' the same territory even if they don't have a constable over there. And I don't want them to do anything that'll jeopardize us over here."

"You got the authority to order them out, Tom."

"Yeah. And I figure to do it. But first I want to know about this feller who bought my mule. Once that's cleared up, I'll get rid of Alf and Will." Burlingame started to turn away. "I'll put out the word at the saloon. When you show up with this stranger, if he comes back tonight, they'll let me know."

Craig closed the door gently, turned, and saw Jack's cocked Colt as Pate stepped into the kitchen doorway. Craig ignored the gun to say: "You heard it all. Now what?"

"We stay right where we are until my friends get here," replied Jack.

Craig went back to the stove where greasy bear meat was sizzling, giving off a powerful, gamy aroma. "He won't just put out the word at the saloon, Mister Pate, he'll put out word all over town," stated Morton Craig, as he turned with a plate in his hand, heading for the kitchen table. "Tonight, everyone is goin' to be watchin' for you." Craig sat down, gazing at his curled, cooked black piece of meat, and fished around for his clasp knife. "God-dammit, Mister Pate, someone is goin' to get shot tonight sure as I'm settin' here." He looked up, sly eyes showing frustration—and fear. "I'll give you another piece of advice."

Jack sipped his coffee in silence, watching the older man's face in the fading daylight that came inside through a fly-specked, cracked window.

"Catch Alf and Will, Mister Pate. That had ought to be easy, if you're sly and quiet in the dark. Clean them out, and the three of you get astride and ride hard. You might make it. But if you try and find the other two stage robbers. . . ." Craig sat, shaking his head with slow, hard emphasis. "You'll get yourself killed. And you heard Tom . . . he wants Alf and Will out of here, anyway. Likely he might not even try very hard to catch you fellers, if all you do is go after Alf and Will."

Jack motioned with the tin cup. "Your haunch steak is getting cold."

Craig swore under his breath, opened the clasp knife, and started carving the tough big piece of meat. He looked up once, wagged his head, and went on with his meal.

Jack got a second cup of coffee, took it back to the chair, and sighed as he sat down. He had been in his boots since long before sunrise. He would probably still be in them all night and perhaps for most of tomorrow. He thought about his involvement here in Evansville, and came to the conclusion that, if he could do it all over again, he wouldn't do any of it. But here he was, in Craig's cabin with Roger and Sam to arrive shortly now, as the night settled lower by the moment, so, like it or not, he had no choice but to see it through.

He rolled and lit a smoke. Tobacco fragrance helped dispel the rank smell of that meat Craig had cooked. "How did it happen all you folks in Evansville got into the horse-stealing and outlaw business?" he asked Morton Craig.

"People got to live," Craig answered. "And not everyone is in it, anyway. Some are just content to lie low for whatever reason, because we got a good warning and alarm system here. As you're going to find out tonight." Craig wiped grease from his lips with a stiff, soiled, old blue bandanna. "We can't raise livestock up here . . . the season is too short and there's not enough ground. Turner's Gap has been a route through the mountains for a long while. We just sort of started takin' advantage of opportunities, is all. There's no other way to make it any more. The Army don't need pot hunters nor scouts . . . the Injuns is mostly quiet . . . the cowmen down south don't hire men like they used to. Some fellers work out, but there's not enough work for all of us. So we just get by as best we can." Craig shoved back in his chair. "Where are you wanted?" he boldly asked.

Jack sat gazing across the room without answering.

Craig shrugged. "It's all right with me. I can recognize 'em the minute I see 'em. That friend of yours who's always grinnin' . . . the feller with the ivory handles on his gun . . . I swear I've seen him somewhere, maybe on a Wanted poster, but I've seen that face somewhere before." Jack's long silence did not seem to inhibit Morton Craig. "You fellers are no more on the side of the law than I am . . . than Tom Burlingame or anyone else up here is. Mister Pate, use your brains . . . you can live here safe from the law. Join in with us, and you'll make out just fine."

Jack drained his second cup of coffee and finished his smoke, arose, and stepped to the door in the back wall to lift the latch so the door would swing inward under the slightest pressure, then he sat down again, "You are almost a convincing talker, Mister Craig. Almost."

Craig was encouraged. "You heard Tom. Those two damned idiots didn't get much off that stage. Not enough to risk your neck over."

Jack kept smiling. "But they're not the only ones we got in mind cleaning out, Mister Craig."

For the first time the horse dealer's eyes reflected sudden dread. "I got nothing," he bleated, and gestured. "Look around. You see anything valuable in here?"

Jack did not respond. He lifted out his six-gun, turned the cylinder, wiped dust off the barrel with a sleeve, and eased the gun back into his holster. Craig watched all this and for once was willing to be quiet. Only when Jack raised his eyes and their glances crossed, did he act as though he might speak, but Jack spoke first. "Who were the other two?" he asked quietly.

Craig thought it was an offer. "If I find out and tell you, you fellers will leave me alone?"

"No," Jack said dryly, "but we won't slit your throat. Who were they?"

"I told you and told you . . . I don't know. That's the gospel truth. But I could find out."

"You just set there and digest your supper," Jack told the horse dealer.

Time passed, darkness settled, two men walking down the back alley, talking about dance-hall girls up in Laramie, laughed and kept on walking, their voices growing fainter as they progressed southward.

Ten minutes later a gun barrel pushed the door open a little at a time. Craig and Jack watched. There was part of an arm visible but not until the door was fully open did Sam Starr step forward. He saw Craig, then Jack Pate. "All right?" he asked softly.

Jack nodded, and Roger came in from the opposite side of the door, cocked six-gun in his fist. Roger barely more than glanced at Craig as he stepped in, eased off the dog of his Colt, and holstered the weapon. Then he shoved back his hat and said: "We rigged out the other horses. They're in a shed near this gent's corral. One was that blood bay you was ridin' today, Jack."

Sam wrinkled his nose. "What the hell you fellers been cookin' in here?"

Jack arose, reset his hat, and left Sam to watch Craig while he and Roger went to the next cabin, the place where Craig had said Alf and Will were living.

Darkness helped a lot. The moon might arrive later but right now there were stars and darkness, with the stars mitigating the darkness very little.

Roger said: "Did you know they got fellers around here who just sort of patrol back and forth?"

Jack hadn't seen anything like that, but, after all Morton Craig had said, he was not surprised. "It's an outlaw town," he told Roger, then related what Burlingame had told Craig about that stage robbery. Roger's reaction was almost pleased.

"I told Sam there was no bullion box. If we come out of this with five hundred each, not countin' what they'll pay us over at Fort Morgan, we'll be doing good."

Jack stopped in the darkness, gazing over where a feeble flickering light shone in the cabin where Alf and Will were camping. While he studied the building, he said: "I figure we can come out better than that, Roger. That horse dealer back there's got a cache, or I'm an Indian's uncle."

Roger brightened a little, then he also turned to study the log house dead ahead.

All the houses in Evansville, as well as the few stores, had been made of logs. This near the high mountains there was no better, or cheaper, building material. This particular cabin was square, low, and massive, with two windows, one in the north wall, the other one in the front wall facing the roadway. There were two doors, as well, one in front, one at the back.

Jack said: "They're inside. Which door do you want?"

Roger did not care. "Front or back. Don't make any difference."

"Don't shoot. Whatever happens, don't shoot. This damned town is a powder keg tonight." Jack faced his friend. "Which door?"

"The back one. If they try to get out, I'll brain them."

Jack turned in the opposite direction, darkness lay in layers all around, and over across the road, southward a few doors, there was the muted sound of men gathering in a saloon. Otherwise, the village seemed peaceful enough—except that Jack knew Tom Burlingame was looking for him, was waiting for word about him, and that meant there were others who were also interested in his whereabouts.

Before he stepped over the rotten porch planking in the front, he made a slow and very careful study of the roadway. Several men were leaning at a tie rack down in front of the saloon, relaxed and smoking as they talked, but elsewhere, up near the cabin where Jack was standing, there was no one.

He stepped wide over the punky boards, palmed his Colt, felt gently for pressure on the wooden door latch, felt it yield slightly under his hand which indicated that there was no locking bolt behind it, and pushed the door open. It did not make a sound.

Two men were eating at a rickety table where a guttering lantern was burning. They were hatless and hunched over. Neither of them knew they were under a gun until a gust of colder air came in from the front doorway, then they both looked up. Alf, the horse thief with the beard, showed exactly the same expression of stunned disbelief that he had showed that night Sam, Roger, and Jack had risen up around them out of the grass.

Jack stepped inside, eased the silent door closed, and gestured with his six-gun. "Drop 'em. And do it slow."

The horse thieves obeyed stiffly and clumsily. As before, when they had faced Jack Pate, the light was poor, their astonishment was complete, and recovery was slow for both of them.

Then Alf said: "It *was* him, Will."

The shaven outlaw sat twisted on his bench looking at Jack, saying nothing. It did not matter now that he had hesitated about making a positive identification, and he realized it, but it had been a terrible mistake. He seemed also to realize this.

XII

It was quiet in the log house. So quiet in fact that the sounds from the saloon across the way, southward, did not penetrate once the door was closed.

Jack ordered the horse thieves to stand up, which they did. Then he herded them to the rear wall and watched them as he opened the alleyway door. Roger stepped in looking around. When he saw the horse thieves, he said—" 'Evening, gents. Haven't seen you in quite a spell."—then he went over to the table and helped himself to someone's full cup of black coffee, watching the men against the wall.

Jack holstered his six-gun. "You can make this easy or hard," he told Alf and Will Smith. "Who was with you when you stopped that stagecoach south of Fort Morgan?"

Neither outlaw answered right away. They were confused, upset, and afraid. Roger put aside the cup and went over to look in the stove. It was brightly burning. He turned back. "The way this works," he told the horse thieves, "is right simple. First, we gag you, then we pull off your boots, then we heat a cinch ring and, when it's red hot, we put it against the soles of your bare feet. . . . Who were the other two?"

Alf's dark, turgid gaze show dogged stubbornness. His bearded, coarse features closed down in an expression of unyielding defiance and he would not say a word. But his partner had nerves closer to the surface. He looked once at Alf, then fidgeted when he faced Jack and Roger. "One was a feller folks called Jasper. I never heard his second name, and names don't matter around here anyhow."

Jack nodded. "Good. Where is Jasper tonight?"

Will had no idea. "He was only here in town for a couple weeks. Camped back in the trees a ways, and right after we stopped that coach, he taken his share and lit out. Said he had a date down in Mexico, and never even come back to town with the rest of us."

Jack's disappointment was not very great. In a way he was relieved, because, as Morton Craig had been saying all afternoon and evening, getting out of here with four prisoners would not be an easy thing to do.

Jack took a long shot and said: "Tom Burlingame was the other one."

Will looked at his partner. "They already knew, I didn't tell them." Evidently there was some code among the men of Evansville about revealing names, or perhaps deeds, but in either case Will's comment left his captors believing the punishment for breaking the code might be grisly enough to impress most men.

Alf still darkly glared and kept his bearded mouth closed.

Jack went to the table, took an empty cup to the stove, and filled it from the pot over there. Then he looked at Roger, showing irony in his expression. If Jack had known this morning Tom Burlingame was one of the men they had come over here for, he probably could have brought Burlingame out to the trees, too, and left him with Sam and Roger. This damned life was full of ifs, and except for them a man might live twice as long.

Roger said: "How do we get him?"

Jack sighed. "Somehow," he muttered. "We'll herd these two next door, then figure on it a little."

They kicked the guns under a wall bunk, took their captives out into the back alley, blew out the lamp, and closed the back door. Alf stalked along, still doggedly silent, his dark eyes with their muddy whites darting back and forth as though he would use any opening that arose to get at his captors. But none arose. He was not in the hands of greenhorns.

When the four of them walked into Morton Craig's kitchen, Sam recognized the prisoners. He arose and stepped around them with a wicked wink at dour Alf. Craig and the horse thieves eyed one another. Finally Alf spoke. "You son-of-a-bitch," he said gruffly to the horse dealer.

Craig portrayed surprise and wonder. "For what?"

"You damned well know for what," snarled the bearded man. "For helpin' these fellers."

Craig was prepared to protest but Jack growled him into silence. Looking at Craig, Jack asked where Tom Burlingame would be tonight, and Craig, under those baleful dark eyes, squirmed. Sam stepped to the sink and picked up a large butchering knife. He smiled as he turned toward the horse dealer. Craig blurted it out.

"He lives next to his shop. He stays pretty much to home most nights. Tonight . . . well, you heard him at the door . . . he'll be home waitin' for word of your whereabouts."

Alf's malevolent glare was fastened upon Morton Craig. The horse dealer would not look at Alf, and, as Jack turned with a nod at Sam Starr, the horse dealer sidled close and spoke in almost a whisper. "Get those two out of here. Whatever happens, take care of those two. If you don't, if they get loose, they'll tell Burlingame what I just said. He'll skin me alive."

Jack looked at Roger. "You mind keeping an eye on this bunch?"

Roger did not mind at all. He went to the stove for some coffee, and gazed at the tag end of that strong-smelling bear steak. He was hungry, but, as with Jack, that particular prospect did not arouse any interest in him at all. As he turned, Jack and Sam were leaving. Sam closed the door gently and Roger leaned on the sink, gazing at his prisoners. "Set," he commanded. They all sat down, watching him. "Now mind your manners and you might make it."

Alf glowered. "You ain't goin' to use that gun, mister."

Roger agreed. "No." He held up the big butcher knife. "I'll use this."

Alf was undaunted. "You'd never get that close to me."

Roger gazed steadily at the horse thief. "Keep on talking, and you'll find out."

Alf grudgingly subsided. Caution, and perhaps a little doubt as well, made him decide not to force a fight. Roger looked capable enough, and there was no doubt at all that he would indeed use the knife—maybe even his gun if he had to.

Craig was as nervous as a cat on a hot tin roof. So far, there had been talk, and a little activity, but no real peril. He wanted things to remain that way. But he also wanted Alf and Will silenced. They were the only people in Evansville who could point accusing fingers at him. What had subtly happened was that Morton Craig's daylong association with Jack Pate, and with his partners Starr and Bemis, had got Craig into an unenviable situation. He would be able to talk his way out of it, most probably, up to the point where he had succumbed to fear and had told the three partners where they could find Tom Burlingame. That was pure and simple betrayal. If Tom Burlingame ever found out about it, Morton Craig's life wouldn't be worth a red penny.

He watched Alf and Will even more intently than he watched Roger, but as far as Roger was concerned, he was a nerveless man, fatalistic up to a point, and perfectly willing to kill. Those attributes were indelibly stamped on his face. Alf was about forty years old; any man who had lived as he had, had survived because of a developed ability to read men. Armed, he might have challenged Roger. Unarmed, looking at Roger leaning over there sipping coffee, the tie-down off his belt gun, Alf's defiant hostility remained leashed. He could be patient for an excellent reason. There was no alternative.

Will made a smoke and offered Alf the makings, but Alf refused with a bear-like wag of his head.

Roger had made his assessments, too. Craig and Will Smith were dangerous, but only providing they got an upper hand, whereas the bearded, muddy-eyed man was dangerous just sitting over there. One careless move and Roger would have a battle on his hands. He watched them all, but let his gaze linger most often, and longest, on Alf.

When he finished the coffee, he said: "Horse trader, where's your money belt?"

Morton Craig lost a lot of color. "I don't have one. Mister, all I got is about fifteen, sixteen head of livestock, and what you see here in my house."

Alf turned venomously. "You damned liar! You got a cache. You always had cash to pay us with."

Craig's hands opened and closed while he furiously glared.

Roger watched them, and asked the same question again, but this time he picked up that big butchering knife. He also said: "I don't figure these fellers like you very well. They might not raise a hand if I cut your throat."

Craig's mouth was dry. "What more do you want from me, for Christ's sake! I been helpful and co-operative."

Roger conceded this. "Sure you have. Scairt peeless, but co-operative. Now we want your cache."

Will Smith dropped his smoke on the floor and ground it underfoot. He did not actually smile but there was a gleam of satisfaction in his glance. Clearly he did not have any more use for Morton Craig than Craig had for Will and his partner. This, of course, had been obvious to Roger—had in fact been the basis for his present tactic. They were divided, they were enemies, and he was confident the horse dealer did have money hidden around the cabin.

"You're goin' to bleed like a stuck hog," he told Morton Craig. "One big swipe with this thing across your windpipe and you'll flop like a gut-shot deer. . . . Where is the cache?"

Alf was enjoying this, particularly the pallor on Craig's features and the deep distress in his eyes. "He ain't bluffin'," Alf said.

Craig held out for another couple of minutes, but when Roger straightened up off the sink, Craig caved in. He pointed toward the cook stove. "Behind there, down low at the base of the wall. There's a length of rotten log that comes out."

Roger did not turn and look over. He stepped to one side and motioned with the knife at Will Smith. "Get down there and dig it out," he ordered.

Will shot Craig a look, then arose to comply. Roger kept to one side where he could watch all three of them. He put the knife aside and palmed his six-gun. Looking at Alf, he said: "If you think I'm afraid to use this thing because of the noise, go ahead and try me."

Will grunted. It was hot behind the stove. He scrabbled among the lower wall logs, shoved back his hat to study things, then probed and pulled some more. One short length of log came away in his hands. He looked at the thing. It had been carefully whittled to fit, then it had been stained to blend perfectly with the adjoining logs. Where it had been wedged in, there was an opening about a foot long and about six inches high. Back in there, the log was punky from too many years of being soaked by winter storms and baked by summer suns. He got down low and felt around, then grunted and leaned back with two soiled little flour sacks in his hands. He looked at Roger.

"Get 'em all," Roger ordered.

Will leaned and felt around again. When he hauled back this time, he was shaking his head. "There aren't no more."

Roger pointed with his gun barrel. "Set 'em on the sink and go back to your chair."

After Will had obeyed, Roger grabbed one of the little sacks, hefted it, then, using just one hand and his teeth, pulled loose the drawstring and tilted the sack. Greenbacks spilled out. Each little sack was crammed full of greenbacks. Roger smiled for the first time that night.

"How much is here?" he asked Morton Craig.

For a moment the horse dealer could not answer. His dry mouth was only part of the inhibiting problem. He had always been an acquisitive and miserly man. What was over there on the dirty sink was not just his working capital, it was also his savings.

When he spoke, it was half a croak. "Four thousand, five hunnert dollars."

Alf and Will stared from the little flour sacks to Craig, then over at Roger, whose surprise was just as great. As he holstered his six-gun Roger picked up both little sacks and shoved them inside his shirt. Then he said: "Help yourself to coffee, gents. Just be right careful how you go about it. Horse trader, you got any whiskey around here?"

Craig weakly pointed to a cupboard. Roger found the bottle and tossed it to Craig. "You need this more'n you need coffee," he said in a cheerful voice, then stepped back to watch Alf and

Will fill cups at the stove and return to their chairs.

Roger's smile faded but did not quite die. He and his partners had become convinced they were not going to come out of this situation with much profit. Jack and Sam would be surprised and delighted.

Roger rolled a smoke, enjoying Morton Craig's obvious distress. He lit up and shook his head at the horse dealer. "I had no idea dealin' in them paid better than stealin' them," he said. "Go ahead, take a drink. You sure look like a man who needs one."

Craig drank deeply.

XIII

Sam Starr was one of those blithe individuals who, even in a perilous situation, acted as though he were either immortal or half-witted. He stood in the dripping darkness opposite the blacksmith shop watching the small lighted cabin next door, and said: "I hope they got something to eat over there. I could chew the rump off a bear if someone'd hold its head." He did not appear to be the least bit worried that the town and everyone in it was against them. Even its distance from the closest point of safety for them was against them.

There were several men, armed and casual, who seemed to be patrolling among the houses and stores. Sam saw them and was almost indifferent to the danger they posed. He stood studying the log cabin next to the blacksmith shop, and, when a large, bear-like shadow passed in front of a lighted window, inside the house, Sam said: "If he's a big man, then he's at home."

Jack had worked out their itinerary in his mind, but only up to a point. He studied those patrolling men, guessed when it would be safe to cross the dark roadway, but beyond that point he had no plan except to get the drop on Burlingame.

They had to do that. One gunshot and all Evansville would come boiling out into the roadway, armed and aroused.

Sam eyed the lighted log saloon, but whatever his thoughts he kept them to himself this time because Jack pointed and spoke. "We can get across the road and down alongside the shoeing shed. Then we'd better sidle out back."

Sam hitched at his shell belt, gauged the distance, and, when Jack finally stepped away from the darkness, he moved at his side.

Three men emerged from the saloon unexpectedly when the partners were midway across the road. Jack slackened his stride instead of lengthening it. He looked up, and, when those three townsmen looked back, Jack threw them a casual wave. Two of them waved back. The third man was holding a bottle in his hand and raised it to his lips.

Jack and Sam got in beside the shop where another pall of pitch darkness sheltered them. Neither of them spoke as they waited a few moments, listening to the half-drunk loud discussion going on up in front of the saloon. Then Jack relaxed. They had an ally tonight: John Barleycorn.

Blacksmith shops all smelled the same, even with the doors closed. Sam wrinkled his nose, looked around, and led the way around behind the shop where piles of cast aside horseshoes were mounded into a careless pile and where buggy spring leaves and worn-out wagon tires lay at random. Beyond, southward, was a small lighted window.

Jack had adjudged Tom Burlingame so he had no illusions. What he wanted to do was enter and catch Burlingame the way he had caught Will and Alf, but Burlingame was an altogether different kind of individual. Jack had never seen him armed, but that did not have to mean much, either, especially now that Burlingame was aroused about Jack.

Sam nudged Jack and pointed. A bony-tailed rank-looking

thin dog was nosing in the alley behind Burlingame's cabin. "He'll bark sure as hell," Sam whispered, and picked up several small stones that he began peppering at the dog to turn him back. Initially, the dog paid no attention, then he looked around, and, when one of those pebbles struck him, he jumped, tucked that long tail, and ran southward. Sam smiled in satisfaction.

They had to cut wide out and around behind the shop to avoid stumbling over discarded steel. The rear of Burlingame's cabin was no different from the rear of most other buildings in Evansville. When they got over there and sought another dark place, there was one small rear window and a heavily reinforced bolted slab door, otherwise the wall was long, made of notched-in fir logs, and had an overhanging set of eaves that extended more than a foot from the wall.

This time, Jack could not cover both doors. Anyone standing around front at the blacksmith's front door would be visible to those patrolling watchers.

He shook his head as the doubts began multiplying, then, as he stepped to the door, he said: "Don't use your gun, Sam. Don't shoot."

Starr nodded without looking entirely convinced as he studied the heavy door a few feet away. "How many are likely to be in there?" he asked, and then, before Jack could respond, he said: "Why not just take back the two we already got and not run any more risks?"

They had not said they would return with the stage robbers; they had simply promised to try and find them, and, if they returned with Will and Alf, the people around Fort Morgan would probably be satisfied. But Jack Pate was a thorough man. He was also susceptible to challenges, and Morton Craig had stirred that trait in him by all those predictions of disaster, and how they could not get out of Evansville with prisoners.

Instead of replying, he went closer to the door, palmed his

six-gun, leaned and listened. If there was conversation beyond, he did not hear it. Those log walls and that bolt-reinforced thick door would have deadened any but the loudest sounds.

He raised his left hand and felt the latch, but this time it resisted pressure, which meant it had a bolt through the latch on the far side.

Sam leaned to crane up the alley, then he hissed and turned to fade into darkness as a slow-pacing man in a checked red and black woolen shirt came ambling along. As Jack turned toward the sheltering darkness beside Sam, he recognized that man. He had been at the upper end of town whittling this afternoon when Jack and Craig had ridden back. At the time Jack had thought he was a watcher, and now, as the man came walking along without haste, Jack was sure of it.

That bony-tailed lanky dog was working his way back up the alley. The patrolman saw him and growled at him. This time the dog hesitated long enough for the man to swear at him before turning southward again.

Jack and Sam did not especially fear discovery. They had their guns in hand. They simply wished to avoid it if they could. If they could not avoid it, they would put the patrolman down with a dent in his skull. But the burly man in his checked shirt was watching the raw-boned dog as he strolled past. Just once did he turn to glance in the direction of Burlingame's rear door, then he passed on by.

Sam let his breath out slowly and soundlessly, holstered his gun, and remained a moment longer when Jack moved away, to make certain the patrolman did not return.

This time Jack's hand did not quite touch the door when the sound of someone on the other side withdrawing the bolt came out to him. He swung, motioned for Sam to flatten, and did the same. There was no time to dash for sheltering darkness.

The door swung inward, orange lamplight fell outward, and a

woman came forth, looking neither right nor left as she headed straight across the alley to an outhouse. Jack's quandary was acute. He had never struck a woman over the head, and this one moved too swiftly in any case. She entered the outhouse, closed the door, noisily dropped the bar from inside to lock the door, and Sam stepped up to lean and look inside the house, not the least interested in the woman. What evidently pleased Sam was that, now, they had clear access without having to knock and perhaps arouse Tom Burlingame.

Sam reached, touched Jack, and jutted his jaw to point. Tom Burlingame was on through the kitchen, his back to the rear of the house. Fortune had taken a hand. Jack entered the house, his course clear, and Tom Burlingame did not turn until Jack was less than fifteen feet from him with Sam back there filling a doorway.

Burlingame did not show astonishment. He looked from one face to the other one, then he looked at the guns and lowered a hand in which he had been holding an old newspaper.

If he was armed, there was no outward sign of it. Jack took no chance. "Put the paper down and walk to the door, and, Mister Burlingame, move easy. We're going over across the road to Craig's place . . . without trouble, unless you make it."

Jack was in a hurry. That woman would not remain out back much longer.

Burlingame was by nature a deliberate man. He acted that way now as he stood where he was and said: "Mister Pate, you are a fool if you think this is going to work."

Jack gestured. "The door. Move along."

Burlingame turned, crossed to the front door in three strides, opened it, and looked out, then he started through. Jack hastened to be close when they both emerged. Sam came last. He closed the door and darkness swept in around them. Both Sam and Jack holstered their weapons. Burlingame did not hesitate, nor did he seem to be very desperate as he strolled across the roadway and turned northward.

A small, dark man arose from a bench out front of a store, showed white teeth in a smile at Burlingame, nodded to Jack and Sam, and stepped to the edge of the plank walk on his way across to the saloon. Jack eyed him, wondering if somehow or other Burlingame had passed him a sign. It did not seem so.

Until they were around behind the Craig cabin Tom Burlingame neither spoke nor hesitated, but back there he stopped and turned. Looking first at Sam and Sam's ivory-stocked gun, then at Jack, he said: "You *did* rob Alf and Will."

Jack gestured ahead. "Go inside."

Burlingame did not move or shift his gaze. "I'll give you one chance, Mister Pate. Walk away right this minute, with your friend, and I'll let you go. Ten minutes from now it will be too late."

"Inside," repeated Jack.

Burlingame turned, went to the kitchen door, pushed on inside, saw Will and Alf sitting there, saw Morton Craig's expressions of disbelief first, then fear, and eyed Roger, whose bulging shirt front was very noticeable.

Jack said: "Roger, you and Sam can get the horses. I think we've got to move pretty fast now."

Burlingame had showed almost no emotion to this point. He did not show any now, but he said: "Pate, this is your only chance. Leave now and ride fast."

Sam went with Roger to get the saddled horses from out back. As he and Roger were loosening the tie ropes, Sam said: "This town gives me the creeps. They all talk like they know somethin' we don't know."

"They got watchers out and patrolmen. I guess you got a right to be nervous," stated Roger. "But if we can make it through the next few minutes, I think we'll have a fair chance."

A pair of men appeared out in the back alley, where they halted to watch Sam and Roger lead out those saddled horses. One of them started across in the direction of the shed as he said: "Hey, Morton, you know the rule." The second man started forward, also, but he passed around the side of the corral and was more distant when his companion got up close enough to see he was not addressing Morton Craig. He stopped. Sam and Roger were strangers to him. He looked over where his friend was, then lowered thick brows as he swung back to say: "Who are you fellers? Is Craig around?"

Roger answered calmly. "Yeah. Craig's over in the house. We're sort of friends of his."

The second patrolman arrived and stood gazing at the saddled, bridled horses. "You fellers just ride in, did you?" he asked.

Sam spoke up from slightly to one side of Roger. "Yeah, just come in. What's this about a rule? What rule you talkin' about, mister?"

The first patrolman turned slightly apologetic. "I seen some saddled horses over here and just figured it was someone ridin' out. We got a rule around Evansville no one rides out after nightfall unless they got Burlingame's permission. Tonight, he didn't give no permission, so when I seen these saddled horses. . . . I didn't know you boys had just entered town."

Sam smiled affably, white teeth showing in the darkness as he moved ahead. Roger masked his partner's move by talking, and, when Sam was close enough, he drew. It was an infinitesimal blur in the night, then he cocked the Colt. Both townsmen stared. Roger went ahead, disarmed the patrolmen, stepped behind them, and struck hard, twice. Both patrolmen collapsed at Sam's feet.

Roger looked from the unconscious men to Sam. "So that was it. Anyone a-horseback after sundown without permission is a target." He reached for the lead ropes and turned toward the cabin.

Sam held all the shanks while Roger went into Craig's kitchen. He was in there long enough to have explained to Jack what had happened near Craig's corral, then he and the others came out. Sam distributed reins. Only one man did not have a mount and yet by rights he should have had the best mount because most of the horses belonged to him. Jack settled over leather, gazing at Morton Craig. "You been pretty free with advice today," he told the horse dealer. "Now I'll give you some. Get on a horse and get out of here as fast as you can." Jack turned. Sam had tied Alf's and Will's hands. He and Roger had the reins to their horses. Tom Burlingame was staring straight at Morton Craig. When Jack waved for Sam to lead off, Burlingame was directly in front of Jack. He shook out a little loop and dropped it lightly over the large man's head, yanked slack until the lariat noose was snug around the big man's throat, then Jack urged his horse away. Burlingame said nothing about being roped like that. None of them had anything to say until they were northward through the darkness beyond view from Craig's cabin, then Jack called for Sam to turn in the opposite direction, to head southward rather than northward. Neither Sam nor Roger hesitated but Tom Burlingame frowned at Jack as though he might speak, but he maintained silence.

Jack had made a particular point of seeing to it that Morton Craig knew he would take his friends and the prisoners through Turner's Gap. If there was pursuit, it would go up through the pass, and shortly now there would indeed be pursuit. Jack knew that to be a fact, too, but not until they were south of town, heading in the general direction of Cedar Brake, did the triggering mechanism detonate.

Jack had carefully placed five six-gun bullets from his shell belt in a tin can from Morton Craig's kitchen, and as he had herded everyone out to mount up, including Craig, he had stepped aside, opened the stove, and eased the tin down upon the dying embers of Morton Craig's supper fire.

He had realized it would be some time before there was enough heat to cause the bullets to explode. In fact, when the abrupt rattle of fierce gunfire erupted back there in Craig's house blowing apart the cook stove and blasting the night with gun thunder, Jack had not expected it to happen for at least another ten or perhaps even fifteen minutes. Alf, Will, and Tom Burlingame twisted to look back. Jack gestured for Sam to pick up the gait. He was satisfied Craig would tell everyone the kidnappers had fled out through Turner's Gap. Even so, the best thing for Sam, Jack, and Roger to do right now was to cover a lot of ground—fast!

XIV

They reached Cedar Brake with cold coming through the night to trouble them until they donned jackets. They passed around the settlement at a quiet lope, and a mile onward, when Burlingame stood in his stirrups to look back, Jack called for a halt.

They all sat motionlessly for a few moments, listening. There was no sound of pursuit back there. Burlingame eased down in his saddle and eyed Jack Pate. "Maybe you'll pull it off," he said, without any particular show of animosity. He was the most sphinx-like individual Jack had ever run across. As they started onward, Burlingame reached into a shirt pocket, brought forth a plug, offered it to Roger, who declined, then Burlingame bit off a chew, tongued it into his cheek, and called over to Alf and Will.

"Now are you satisfied about who robbed you?" he asked sarcastically.

Alf's answer was blunt. "Yeah. But that's only half the trouble. Craig helped these fellers pull this off. He told them a lot of stuff to help them." Alf sent a glowering glare in Roger's direction. "And that feller showed his gratitude by cleanin' out Craig's cache behind the stove. Got four thousand dollars in them little sacks inside his shirt."

Burlingame may have been surprised, but Sam and Jack turned to stare while Roger patted his puffed-out shirt and smiled at his partners. "Four thousand *five hundred,*" he said, correcting Alf.

Sam laughed, then they boosted the horses over into a lope again, and passed steadily downcountry. Where they veered westward to find the stage road leading to Cedar Brake, the country was flat enough to enable their animals to cover a lot of miles without effort.

Sam's nose for direction encouraged him to take the lead and finally swing slightly southeastward. No one said a word as the riders followed after.

The cold increased as the night advanced. Once, Roger held up a hand. They all halted to listen. Horses were below them, moving east in a loose trot. To experienced horsemen it became evident that they were loose animals, not ridden ones. Sam blew out a big sigh of relief and led off again.

There was a moon but no one had heeded it. Nor did it make any difference now, but if it had shown back at Evansville while the three partners were trying to capture their hostages, it would no doubt have increased their risk and their peril.

They halted at a warm-water creek miles out from anywhere, got down to rest their legs, and give the horses a chance to drink and briefly crop grass. So far, the animals were holding up well.

Burlingame ignored his captors and asked Alf for a fuller explanation of Morton Craig's treachery. Alf was only too glad to answer. He related everything that had been said in Craig's kitchen, including the horse dealer's information about how the manhunters might be able to capture Tom Burlingame. When Alf had finished, Burlingame turned to Will Smith. "That's the truth?" he asked. Will nodded his head.

Sam had been listening to all this. He was smoking, standing easy with a lively gaze passing among the prisoners. Then he smiled at Burlingame. "Mister, everybody loses some of the time. You can't surround yourself with fellers like Craig and these two and not get sold out sooner or later."

Burlingame looked stonily at Sam and his ivory-handled six-gun. "You should have been a preacher," he said dourly, and faced Jack and Roger. "You got four thousand. I'll add a thousand to it. We're more'n midway between Fort Morgan and Evansville. You turn me loose so I can get back to Evansville about the time you reach Fort Morgan, and we'll be quits." Burlingame reached inside his shirt, low, and pulled forth a thin doeskin article resembling a belly band. It was much narrower and softer than an ordinary money belt. He tossed it to Roger, who was closest, but he kept looking directly at Jack Pate. "That's your thousand."

Roger dug out the warm, folded greenbacks, counted them by moonlight, shoved them into a shirt pocket, and flung the little money belt to the ground. "We're doin' a little better all the time," he said, and turned toward Jack. "We'd better be getting' along."

Pate and Burlingame were still looking at one another. Jack said: "Sam? Roger?"

As far as Sam was concerned, it did not matter whether they arrived in Fort Morgan with any of their prisoners. He said: "It's all right with me. He can't get back up there in time to do us any harm. Not even if he rounds up a posse and tries to get back down here. Sure, turn him loose if you want to, Jack."

Roger was less casual. "And suppose he dogs us and back-shoots someone in the dark?"

Jack did not believe Tom Burlingame was armed, but he deferred to Roger by saying: "If you figure we'd ought to take him on with us, give him back his thousand dollars."

Roger stared. "Give it back?"

"Yeah. He made a fair offer."

Roger looked pained. "What in the hell? Jack, he don't mean no more to us than that horse dealer we cleaned out."

Jack did not argue, but simply said: "They aren't much alike. Craig was a snake to begin with."

Roger thought a moment while everyone watched, then he threw up his hands. Foremost in his mind was the fact that he was not going to hand back the $1,000. "Turn him loose!" he exclaimed, and stepped over to lift off the noose that left Burlingame standing free.

Will protested. "Hey, you fellers got more'n that off us when you caught us with them horses in the pass. That ought to entitle us to go free, too."

Jack ignored the horse thieves as he addressed Tom Burlingame. "Head out," he said. Burlingame nodded, twisted to catch his reins, and swing up. "Obliged," he said to Jack, and got a warning back. "Don't shag us. Don't try to keep up with us."

Burlingame turned back at a walk, his big upper body erect as he rode off into the darkness. Roger kept wagging his head about this as they all got astride again, and Will Smith complained bitterly as they struck out again, angling more easterly now because Sam's sense of direction told him they were roughly parallel to Fort Morgan.

The country was open. They left some breaks behind to the east and had miles of starlit grassland on ahead as well as on both sides. Roger kept watching their back trail, but, if Burlingame was back there, he had to be a long way back because there was no sign of him.

They spooked some bedded cattle and Sam's horse snorted

as he shied. Sam did not curse the animal, but he complainingly reasoned with him about the foolishness of being frightened by red-backed cattle.

Jack's tiredness increased along with the cold, until, shortly before first light, he was slouching along, dozing for a few seconds at a time.

Roger was behind the horse thieves. They watched Jack's tired slump, but, when they looked back, Roger was there, erect and alert. They probably would not have tried anything anyway, even though they were bitter. More so after being ignored after Burlingame had been set free, than before.

They were close enough to the south road leading from Fort Morgan by predawn to hear, then also to see, a stagecoach heading south with its four-horse hitch in a sloppy lope. It was the first coach out of Fort Morgan for this particular day.

Sam blew on stiff fingers and watched, then turned toward Will with a question. "How much did you gents get off that stage you robbed?"

Will regarded Sam from sullen eyes, but he answered. Like Alf, he had long ago decided that Sam would be the most likely of the three partners to use his gun. "Four gold watches, a diamond stickpin from a peddler's necktie, and seventy-one dollars."

"And the mail pouches," Sam added, blowing on his fingers again.

"There was nothing in the letters. Not a lousy dollar," stated Will, his sullenness deepening. "We took them because they was there, but what we figured on was a box . . . and there wasn't none." Will kept looking at Sam. "You fellers got a hell of a lot more off of us than you got off Burlingame. You dassn't turn us in at Fort Morgan, anyway. We seen you rob Craig and we seen you let Burlingame, who was with us when we robbed that stage, give you his money to ride off."

Sam stopped blowing and flexed his stiff fingers. He turned straight in the saddle and, without saying another word, booted his horse over into a lope again. There was a thin line of new light against the uneven far horizon. Daylight was close by.

Jack slackened to a steady walk when they reached the Fort Morgan road. He was in the lead as they turned northward toward town. So far, all they could make out up ahead was a dark, low blur where Fort Morgan was, but a half hour later they could see roof tops. That was when Jack halted in the center of the road and said: "We can't get up there before sunrise." Then he added: "Those two will bleat their silly heads off. If we could have got them into town and locked up in the dark, it would have worked."

Sam had an answer for this problem. "Knock 'em over the head."

Jack did not see this as the solution. "We won't go into town with 'em, we'll take 'em out to that old cowman's ranch." He left the road up another mile riding west on an angle that would take them out around Fort Morgan. Neither Sam nor Roger questioned his decision. Probably because they agreed with it. But an hour later with the sun showing and the whole world brightening, Roger had a question. "Griffith'll have his hundred, but how do we get the four hundred from the townsmen?"

Jack's answer indicated that he had arrived at a conclusion about this some time back. "We leave Alf and Will tied to a tree, and tell Griffith where they are. By the time he finds them we ought to have found that storekeeper, collected the rest of the money, and be on our way"

Sam broadly smiled. It was a simple scheme, and perhaps that was why it appealed to him. He winked wickedly at Alf. He had been baiting the disagreeable, bearded horse thief off and on since they had ridden south from Evansville. Now, he did it again.

"Trouble with fellers like you is that you don't have enough sense to be good at this business. Now me and my partners . . . we're professionals. We got brains."

Alf seemed poised to rip out a savage retort, but Sam's wide grin and cold, bold stare stopped him. He looked away, would not look at Sam again, at all.

They did not know the exact location of Griffith's outfit, and in fact they would have settled for any cow outfit, but good fortune brought them to a big dead tree that had been shorn of its top and all its limbs. There was a large letter *G* burned into the trunk a third of the way up, about the height of a tall man standing in a wagon bed. It still did not have to be the Griffith outfit, but they dismounted, tied Alf and Will to the boundary tree, and, when Will made one last, very impassioned, plea, Sam rolled and lit a smoke and shoved it between Will's lips, grinned wickedly at Alf, who refused to look at Sam, then they swung up, leading two horses, and rode along the old wagon ruts.

It was a long ride. Better than two miles by Roger's satisfied estimate. He had been worrying for fear the ranch might be too close to that old tree with the letter *G* branded into it.

They saw riders heading out of a dusty yard with thin new-day warmth beginning to freshen the day. The buildings were old, made of logs, and several of the smaller ones still had their original sod roofs, but the barn, cook shack, and main house were roofed over with sugar-pine shakes, something that had obviously been done much later.

There were four riders heading out. Jack, Sam, and Roger halted back a goodly distance to allow the range men to get well away before they continued on to the yard. Alec Griffith was emerging from the cook shack sucking his teeth. When he looked up at the sound of a steel shoe striking stone, he stopped dead in his tracks, staring.

The three men coming toward him abreast were unshaven,

rumpled, gray-faced with fatigue, and red-eyed. He spat aside, walked down to the nearest tie rack, and leaned there, watching.

When Roger was closer, he said: "Good morning."

Old Griffith nodded, straightened up, and returned the greeting. " 'Morning, gents. You look like you could stand a decent meal. There's plenty of leavings inside. Tie up and come on in."

They dismounted stiffly, looped their reins, and followed the cowman back into his cook shack, where a glaring *cosinero* stiffly stood by a large black iron range. Griffith ignored the cook's indignation. "These here are friends of mine, Muley. They been out a long while. Feed 'em."

The cook complied but he banged the plates down before filling them, and, when he brought over the coffee pot, he put it down, hard, and made no move to fill the cups. Then he went back to his stove, his back stiff with indignation. A hallowed ranch rule had just been violated. If men missed breakfast—or any other meal—regardless of the circumstances, it was just too damned bad; they had to wait until the next mealtime rolled around.

But Griffith ignored his cook's attitude as he sank down opposite the three partners, shoved back his hat, and said: "Did you boys do any good?"

Jack spoke around a mouthful of food. His partners did not even glance up. They were starved, and the warm, wonderful smells inside the cook shack brought out all their hunger.

"We got two of the fellers who robbed the stage, and one kept on going south into Mexico." Jack paused to drain his coffee cup. Griffith reached for the pot to refill it.

"There's another one. His name is Tom Burlingame. He's head Indian at a place called Evansville, northwest of here."

Griffith nodded. "Evansville. That's a damned renegade town and always has been. You couldn't fetch this one back?"

Sam and Roger stopped chewing to hear their partner's answer. Jack dug into his plate and ate for a moment before replying. "Yeah, we could have, Mister Griffith. But we didn't. You fellers can go after that one if you're a mind to." Jack looked steadily at the cowman. "You got that hundred dollars on you?"

Griffith reached slowly into a pocket. "What about the loot from the stage?" he asked, counting out greenbacks.

"Those two we brought back got it on them. Or they cached it up in Evansville. We were sort of in a hurry to get out of there alive, so we didn't hang around hunting for it."

Roger picked up the greenbacks, rolled them, and shoved them into the same pocket of his soiled shirt where he had cached the $1,000 from Tom Burlingame.

"Seventy-one dollars, some watches, and other stuff," stated Sam scornfully. "I thought there was a bullion box on that stagecoach."

Griffith thinly smiled. "That went out before dawn this morning. We been getting a little spooky about shipping bullion out lately."

Sam sat there, gazing at the cowman, fork poised but motionless. "This morning?" he said. "Before daybreak, this morning?"

Griffith nodded and turned toward Jack again. "You lock those two you brought back in the jail house?"

Jack reached for his cup as he answered. "Are you goin' into town this morning?"

Griffith nodded. "Yeah, as soon as I do a little work, I figure to ride in. A feller applied for the marshal's job yesterday. The town council is goin' to meet and look him over. They invited me to be there."

Jack smiled. "You'll see those two fellers we brought back, then," he said, and pushed away the empty plate to arise. "Let's go, Sam, Roger."

Griffith went out to the tie rack with them. They left two

tired horses tethered at his hitch rail, swung around, and rode back out of the yard in the direction of Fort Morgan.

Sam laughed when they were miles away. "You can sure tell a decent lie, Jack."

Pate frowned. "I didn't lie to him. I just didn't say we'd locked those fellers up. He'll ride right past them when he comes to town, and we need the time."

XV

They stabled their horses with the day man who had just arrived down at the livery barn, with instructions for each animal to be grained, fed, watered, and curried, then they sauntered over in the direction of the general store where a clerk with black cotton sleeve guards from wrist to elbow was sweeping off the plank walk. Jack entered alone. Roger and Sam took up positions on each side of the door where they had an excellent view of the roadway and the other buildings north and south.

A number of townsmen came and went up at the café, single men, mostly, or husbands whose wives could not be routed out this early to prepare a meal. Paul Benson, the fat stage driver, was talking to a man out in front of the corral yard office, northward and upon the opposite side of the roadway. The man he was standing with was wearing a green eyeshade. He was thin and grizzled. He was probably the company's local manager but neither Roger nor Sam knew him. Nor were they particularly interested in him. Or the fat stage driver.

Carl Hanson approached his store from the south with some large, leather-backed ledgers under his arm. He walked right past Roger, who had turned to avoid a meeting, entered the store, and, when he saw Jack Pate idly conversing with his clerk, he stopped stonestill for a moment, then walked on up, smiled as he placed the ledgers on a counter, and gestured for Jack to follow him.

They entered a dingy little cluttered cubbyhole of an office near the rear of the building. The storekeeper motioned to a chair and asked if Jack would care for some coffee. Jack sat, but declined the coffee. By his estimate he and his partners had perhaps two hours to do what they were here to do, which would be adequate, he felt, providing circumstances did not require them to dawdle too long.

He related the crucial aspects of what he, Sam, and Roger had accomplished, asked for the money, and said Alec Griffith would arrive in town this morning with Alf and Will Smith. He also explained about Tom Burlingame, saying the same thing he had told Griffith, and letting it remain that way. The fourth highwayman was by now down in Mexico.

Hanson listened, asked about the loot, and, after Jack explained to him that it consisted of a diamond stickpin, four gold watches, and $71, the storekeeper wagged his head. "Why would men risk prison or maybe even getting shot for that?"

The answer was easy. Because they had not known what was aboard the stage, had thought it would be a lot more, and it hadn't been. That was all there was to it.

Hanson did not ask why they hadn't lodged Alf and Will in the jail house but he was interested in other aspects of what had occurred, and he seemed especially interested in Evansville, which he said had been notorious throughout the area as an outlaw town for many years.

Jack knew this. He had also had it confirmed by Alec Griffith, so he said: "My partners and I'd like to settle up."

Hanson had a small, massive steel safe in a corner of the office, but he did not go there for the money; he withdrew a fat leather purse, meticulously counted out a number of greenbacks, and without a word handed them over. Then he went to stir the fire in his wood stove. There was a small graniteware coffee pot atop the stove. While he was occupied at the stove, he said: "We got a feller who used to be a sheriff down in Texas applying for the constable's job, Mister Pate. But we been discussing this the last day or so, and, while he's qualified enough, we decided to offer the job to you, again." Hanson turned, smiling a little. "We'd even let you put your friends on as deputies."

Jack stood up. The coffee smelled good but for once he was not in the mood for it. "Thanks all the same," he replied, stuffing the greenbacks into a trouser pocket. "It'd cost Fort Morgan too much to have three lawmen when you can hire this Texan as just one man. Besides, you don't have enough work for three lawmen hereabouts."

Hanson was not confident about this. "The way things been going lately, Mister Pate, we might need three lawmen. Horses stole right out of the livery barn, stages gettin' robbed no more than five miles from town. . . ." Hanson shook his head and filled a cup from the pot on the stove. "I tell you, things sure aren't like they used to be when folks had respect for the law."

Jack went to the door and turned back to smile. "We got to get some rest, Mister Hanson. See you again."

The storekeeper stood, nodding and sipping coffee, as Jack walked away. Maybe Pate was right. Maybe Fort Morgan did not need three lawmen, and for a fact it would be a lot of expense having three of them. He drained the cup and went back out front to get the ledgers and return to the office with them. It would be an hour or so before customers began trickling in. He had that much time to complete the bookwork he had not completed at home last night.

Sam Starr had a question as soon as Jack appeared. "When do we get our stuff from the boarding house?"

Jack said—"Right now."—and led the way. Up in front of the harness works they passed a brawny man with pale eyes and droopy moustache who was having his first smoke of the day. He said—" 'Mawnin', gents."—and turned slowly to study their backs after they had passed along.

Jack said: "That's the Texas sheriff they're figuring to hire as town marshal."

Not until they were on the boarding-house porch did Roger look back, then he dryly said: "We better get our gatherings and roll our hoop. I know that son-of-a-bitch. He was a deputy over around Tucson one time."

Jack and Sam looked back, too, but the Texan was no longer out front of the harness works; he had strolled southward and across the road in the direction of the general store.

The boarding house smelled of greasy fried meat and spuds. The partners went along the dingy corridor to their rooms, worked busily for a few minutes, then met out in the hallway. They left the structure by the rear door, picked their way through a decade of discarded débris in the weed patch on their way to the alley, and walked briskly southward. Jack thought they might still have an hour, but there was no reason to put this to a test. He turned toward Sam. "You got your cache?" Sam had indeed got it. He would have abandoned all his other possessions at the boarding house, but not his cache. Roger, too, had stuffed saddlebags. He had also removed the money from his shirt, both inside it and outside it, and had shoved that into his saddlebags, too.

They were approaching the rear doorway of the livery barn when Roger said: "By rough figures, I think we each got to come out of this with about maybe as much as two thousand and two hundred dollars."

A hostler wheeled forth a barrow of stall cleanings, dumped it against a mound of similar compost, then leaned on the upended barrow handles while watching the three partners approach. He had only finished caring for their horses ten minutes earlier.

Out in the front roadway someone sang out in a loud call.

"Hey, Alec, what you got there? They don't look too good."

That was all the partners needed. Jack's additional hour had telescoped into several minutes. Sam went after his horse with aggressive singleness of purpose. Roger and Jack fanned out the same way and the hostler, leaning on the barrow handles, looked on in mild surprise. Then he reluctantly turned back to help, but no one needed him. In fact the three unshaven men rigging out their horses worked faster and more efficiently than the hostler had ever worked. When they were ready to ride, Sam flipped a silver dollar to the hostler, and as slow as the man was in other ways, his hand moved with half the speed of light to snatch the cartwheel out of the air. Then the three unshaven men mounted inside the barn, which was strictly against livery barn rules, and reined out the back way.

In front, a man sang out to Alec Griffith from up the roadway a short distance. "You the new lawman, Alec?" It was called out in high humor but Griffith did not smile when he called back: "Get Carl Hanson over here to the jail house. He's got the keys I think. And, Frank . . . you seen those three fellers who brought back the horses when they was stole a week or so back?"

Frank answered easily. "Not hide nor hair of them. But I heard tell they'd went after them stage robbers. I'll go get Carl."

Jack looked back. Only the hostler was visible in the rear barn doorway, craning his neck after them. Sam saw this and said: "He'll tell 'em we rode south."

Jack had already surmised as much, so they rode south for two miles, then crossed the stage road down where someone had recently driven a band of cattle, and mingled their tracks with other tracks of shod horses, heading east.

Roger sighed. "That was a right nice vacation back yonder . . . until those bastards stole our horses and commenced being obnoxious."

Sam disagreed. "I was damned tired of just eatin' and playin' cards. A man gets all plugged up with fat livin' like that." He looked back, saw nothing to bother him, looked forward, and said: "Where we goin', Jack?"

"Some damned place where we can sleep for a week," answered Pate, "and shave, and buy some clean clothes, and let these horses have a few days of standin' in tree shade."

Roger laughed. "You know where that place is?"

Neither Jack nor Sam knew so Roger told them. "Heaven. There's no place on earth us three can find all that, and not run into the law as well."

It may have been true, but riding eastward, safe from pursuit, with dozens of miles of open, sun-bright country around them, it seemed that surely there would at least be a hidden cañon with water and tree shade in it. To most people that would have been asking very little. To the men in Carl Hanson's store back in Fort Morgan, it seemed to be a certainty. Even Alec Griffith, who knew the Fort Morgan countryside as well as any man alive, scotched the prospective town marshal's urgings that a big posse be made up to ride hell-for-leather in pursuit, simply by saying: "All you'll do is ride your butts off." Griffith grinned a little. "If those are the same fellers you been talkin' about, Marshal, they wouldn't go anywhere except where you'd least expect to find them. And in this territory . . . take it from me, I was a lawman once, too, many years back . . . there are a hundred places for men like that to drop out of sight."

The prospective town marshal spoke with exasperation and urgency. "I told you gents . . . Pate, Bemis, and Starr are wanted from here to hell and back for just about every crime except murder. There's rewards on each one of them. We could swoop down on them and end three careers of lawlessness, providin' we quit standin' around here like a bunch of crows on a fence, and get a-horseback."

Griffith gazed at the storekeeper, whose expression was also calm. "Carl?" he said.

Hanson fingered the top of his store apron and looked at the other members of the town council who were leaning on his counter alongside Alec Griffith. They gazed back. "Well, it's up to you gents. For my part, I never rode with a posse in my life, and I'm about the worst marksman in the country. . . . And it seems to me those fellers brought back our stolen horses, got the stage robbers, did everything we asked of them, so if. . . ."

"But, by God," exclaimed the Texan, "they're *outlaws!* Not just penny-ante outlaws but rustlers, horse thieves, bank robbers, and highwaymen!"

Griffith said: "I guess we got to take your word for it, partner. You'd ought to know. You're a professional lawman. But when we was listenin' to those two worthless bastards I untied off my boundary tree and fetched here to the jail house, I got to confess, I wanted to laugh. For thirty years no one's ever been able to do what those fellers did over at Evansville. And a lot of men have tried. Personally I can't ride with no posse and I can't spare any range men to ride, either." Griffith straightened, still showing ironic amusement in his gaze. He stood a moment looking at the quiet, thoughtful councilmen, then walked out.

The Texan gazed after him, then turned and said—"Most cowmen are on the side of the law."—in a disgruntled tone of voice. "But not that one."

Carl Hanson faintly frowned. It seemed useless to try and get this man to understand that, outlaws or not, those three partners had broken the back of the reign of lawlessness that had existed in the Fort Morgan country for months.

One of the other councilmen straightened up off the counter, slowly. He was chewing a little pipe and paused long enough to say: "I got to agree with Mister Griffith." He looked steadily at the Texan. "But if you want to take over as town marshal from today on, it'll be all right with me. Just let what's happened around here before today slide right on past." Then this man also departed.

One by one they all left, until only the Texan and the storekeeper were there. Hanson agreed with that councilman who had said he was willing to hire the Texan as town marshal from today on.

"Just let this other thing die. Keep order here from now on."

The Texan stood a moment in thought, then he nodded. "All right, Mister Hanson. Maybe I can understand how you folks feel. But from now on . . . no wanted men in Fort Morgan no matter how helpful they are."

Hanson nodded. If Fort Morgan had an official lawman, there would be no need for unofficial ones to serve the community. After the Texan had strolled out into the bright roadway, Carl Hanson grinned, then laughed. When his clerk came along looking at him oddly, Hanson regained his customary composure and got to work around the store. But it stuck in his head that wherever those three outlaws were, it probably was better than being inside a store, and whatever they got involved in months and years from now, it would probably be much more exciting than weighing out five pounds of dried beans, or peddling kegs of horseshoe blanks.

* * * * *

Man Behind the Gun

* * * * *

I

"Jase, he's dead."

"I know."

"He looked like he was trying to talk. . . ."

"Go get the wagon."

The youth stood up slowly. "No," he said. "There's something else got to be done . . . you fetch the wagon."

The older man looked down. He was taller, thicker. There was something quietly oaken about him. A little of the gray day's bleakness in his face. Some of its wintriness in his eyes. "Do like I said. Get the wagon." As though it mattered, he added: "It'll be dusk before long . . . there's a storm coming."

"Jase. . . ."

"First things first. You don't want him left lying here, do you? Then get the wagon."

The youth started away, and for a long time his brother stood there without moving. Finally he twisted at the hips and looked back. The youth was a stripling, all suppleness and grace, with a mighty store of quickness in him as his mother had had.

He looked down. The white hair stirred a little under the fingers of a low breeze. The blue eyes were as steady in death as they'd been in life. The thrust of jaw was the same. Everything was the same—just the life was gone. And off a way the big black horse stood, head down, drowsing.

And farther out the land rolled and dipped like water, tan water pigmented by bunchgrass and sage. And the tang of autumn lay briskly in the air. The smell of it was overhead where tattered old clouds, all gray and gritty, went hurrying.

The big man went down on one knee and smoothed back the white hair, picked up a hand that was thick, solid, and held it.

He was still like that when his brother returned with the wagon, got down, and stood still.

"Jase. . . ."

The big man got up heavily. "Let down the tailgate."

A gust of sharp wind came, roiled their coats, and fled southward.

"Jase. . . ."

The big man stooped in silence, lifted his father, put him on the wagon bed, arranged his arms and legs, and gripped the sides of the wagon. His big red hands were white around the knuckles. He turned toward the younger man. "Sometimes you talk too much, Arty. Get up on the seat and take him home."

When the wagon was in motion, Jason went to the black horse, swung up, and reined after it. The sun was engulfed by a great, swollen dark cloud. The wind came stronger, lifting off the ground, swirling, pushing the horses' manes upward along their necks.

The younger man drove without looking back, shoulders bowed as though crushed with pain, back bent. Behind, Jason plodded along. Just once did he raise a fist and smash it down upon the saddle horn.

When they got to the cabin, a gust of squall rain hit, pounded, and passed. Unheeding, they took the dead man inside, lit lamps, and laid him out upon his bed. The cabin was damp smelling, rank, and close with range smells—saddles, sweat-stiff saddle blankets, gun oil, horse sweat.

"Arty, I'm going to town. Sheriff's got to be told."

"Sheriff," Arty said thickly. "What good'll that do?"

"You get a fire built and sit with him. I'll have a box sent back."

It didn't occur to Arty to wonder why Jase didn't take the wagon and bring the box back. It didn't occur to him that Jason was deliberately deluding him, because Jason wasn't deceptive. Even now, with their father dead in his lean-to bedroom—bullet hole high in the chest—Jase was quiet, steady-eyed, oaken appearing. Imperturbable Jason Swift, taciturn, big, strong as an ox, unhurried, and unhurrying.

Outside, the storm was prematurely darkening the world. There was the constant choking sound of wind, the intermittent patter of rain, the smell and feel of tumult. Jason swung aboard the black horse and rode eastward.

Later, atop a gritty knoll, a crooked flare of white lightning came. Then there was thunder and torrents of water, not raindrops but sheets of water that struck the ground, hissed and boiled around the black horse's feet.

And below, warm orange lamplight shown from buildings, gray with a sheen that sparkled when the lightning arced, white and sputtering. He held the sodden reins chokingly tight, then went on past, and drew up behind Chiloquin at a back alley littered with refuse. There wasn't a soul in sight anywhere. Horses tied to rails on either side of the roadway were hunched up, tails splayed against shivering flanks by the wind, saddles glass shiny with water.

There were sounds. He heard them in the interludes between blasts of wind, distant and soggy sounding. Northward along the walkway, buildings looked unreal, stilted and ugly. He went as far as an overhang and there he stopped, facing eastward across the sea of mud. Around the spindle-hung doors of the Ute Valley Saloon there was light of a yellower kind; more brilliant and hot-looking. He stood, still and cold, hushed except for the flicker of his father's eyes, steady, wintry now, older by far than their years.

He crossed through the mud, and stomped on the far side plank walk, hesitated briefly, then shouldered into the saloon. Brilliance dazzled him, warmth swept up and left a musky perfume in his nostrils. Someone nearby exclaimed in a startled way. Jason looked around. The face was unfamiliar but the man's apparel was that of a rider. He was holding a mug of mulled ale in his fist, staring over it at Jason. He blinked. "Ought to get next to the stove, mister," the rider said. "You're wetter'n a newborn calf."

Jason's gaze swept past the stranger's face, lifted and fell, then stopped. He said: "Mister, I'm in a hurry. See that red-headed feller yonder at the bend of the bar? Feller next to that man in the white hat?"

"Yeah."

"Wonder if you'd do me a favor and ask him to come outside for a minute . . . got something important to tell him."

The rider nodded. "Sure," he said, and started to move away.

Jason went outside and stood in the darkness with the galloping rhythm of rain overhead on the plank awning. He shivered, used a limp handkerchief to wipe his palms and the butt of his pistol. The storm was worsening. Rain, under the overhang, stung. The wind screamed and swirled, buildings creaked, loose boards slapped—a riot of sound and turmoil riding the night.

Yellow light shone off a bare red head. The doors were flung outward and a man stood twenty feet away, swinging his head, a slow, careless smile dimming when he saw no one.

"Balester."

The redhead turned, twisting his body. "Yeah?" he said. Then he froze, lips parted.

"Surprised, Balester?"

"Didn't expect you, Swift. What d'you want?"

Jason's elbow crooked, drew back, and stiffened. The wet gun muzzle tilted steadily upward.

"Swift!"

"Didn't you expect us to fight back, Balester?"

"What're you talking about?"

The hammer clicked back, and in all that bedlam the sharp little sound carried. Balester was like stone.

"Who-all was with you?"

"I don't know what you're talking about, Swift. I. . . ."

"About a murder you committed today. Who else was there?"

"You're crazy. I don't. . . ."

"Who else?"

Balester swallowed hard.

"Take it with you then," Jason said. "I think I know who the others were anyway."

Balester was flinging away when Jason fired. He drew upward, looked incredulous while the screaming wind sucked away the gunshot sound. His half-drawn gun fell in the mud beside the plank walk, when he collapsed.

Jason walked northward through the storm as far as an alleyway before he crossed the road and went back to his horse.

With the wind subsiding, the rain becoming more monotonous than terrible, he rode northwest as far as a sprawl of buildings in a sodden meadow, and there he left the black horse again, walked through the mud as far as a log bunkhouse, and tossed several rocks against its door. When the opening yawned wide and gusty light spilled outward, he was looking into a man's sleep-coarsened features on which a scowl lay.

"What you want, mister? Why didn't you knock 'stead of throwin' rocks?"

"This is important. I want to talk to Ted Sloan."

"Well, come in out of the wet."

"I got no time. Tell him to hurry up."

The scowl faded, was replaced with curiosity. The rider

strained to see the dark shadow's face, couldn't, and turned away.

Jason wiped his hands again, drew out the pistol, and wiped it, too.

"Yeah? Come up here close . . . I can't see. . . ."

"You could see well enough to murder an old man a few hours back."

The tousled head went up; the body stiffened. "Is that you, Swift?"

"Who else were you expecting . . . who else did you murder today, Sloan?"

"I didn't murder nobody."

"You're a liar. Balester. . . ."

"If he told you that, he's the liar . . . not me."

"You were just along for the ride."

"I didn't have no hand in the. . . ."

"Let's hear your version of the killing."

"I had no hand in it. I was ridin' with Balester an' Cook an' Pete Cuneo. We seen your old man and headed over his way. . . ."

"To talk," the quiet, dry voice said. "Just to talk."

"Balester sang out, an', when the old man turned, he was holdin' a gun. Pete hollered he was goin' t' shoot. I was goin' for my gun when one of them shot first. I don't know which it was. That's how it happened."

"You know which it was, Sloan. You know as sure as day follows night. Which one?"

"I don't know. That's the gospel truth, Swift."

"Sloan, Balester is dead. I killed him in Chiloquin. I'm going over to Cuneo's now. I'll kill him, too. Then I'm going to visit Cook. If I ever see you again in Ute Valley, I'll kill you. No matter where I see you, I'll kill you. I won't sing out, and, if your back's turned, I won't hesitate. Now come down here where I am."

He herded the bare-footed man through the mud where the black horse stood, mounted, and leaned down. "Turn around, Sloan."

"No. Listen, Swift. . . ."

"I'm not going to shoot you. Turn around!" He swung the pistol as Sloan turned. The black horse splashed mud over the prostrate form.

The rain had stopped. It was deathly still. A winter moon rose over the hushed, naked land. And Jason Swift cut due west, lifted the horse into a long lope, and held him to it for miles, reined down to a walk, and finished the last lap to the Cuneo Ranch with predawn bitter cold thickening his marrow, making his fingers stiff and awkward.

"Cuneo!"

A dog came out of somewhere and barked in stiff-legged excitement. The cabin was dark and silent.

"Cuneo!"

Within, a muffled voice garbled an oath. "Yeah? Who is it? What ya want?"

"Hurry up, Cuneo . . . this is important."

"What's important? What's so cussed important it won't wait till sunup? Who is it . . . what the devil ya want at this hour?"

"Get up!" Jase called back, thumping the door with one big fist. "Hurry up. It's got t' do with old man Swift."

The garrulous voice faded out. A hand wrenched at the door bar, threw it off, and swung the panel inward. There was a gun in the man's waistband. Aside from britches he was unclothed, and his hair was awry. Pete Cuneo was a small man, whipcord lean, tawny, with a narrow chest, and a stubble of black beard. He had a big ugly nose, vigilant brown eyes with sharp gleams of yellow in their depths, and at the sight of Jason Swift his breath went out in a rush.

It was an even break. They went for their guns at a distance of not more than ten feet. The explosions came almost together. Cuneo went sideways and backward as though struck by a powerful blow. He slid down the door with both hands over his middle and made gulping sounds. Jason left him like that.

Riding southward, while the sharp cold made his teeth chatter, Jason rubbed at a raw red welt above his hip where powder burn had rent the cloth and stung his flesh.

At James Cook's place there was an air of prosperity, a scent of hay, a look of cleanliness. He left the black horse behind the log and sod barn and crossed the rear yard as the sun rose over far away hills. He struck the rear door with his fist and planted his legs wide. A woman came, stared at him, and blinked.

"Where's Cook?"

"Eating breakfast."

"Tell him a man wants to see him."

"Won't you come in?"

"No, I'm in a hurry. Tell him it's about what happened yesterday afternoon . . . and hurry."

She moved away. Beyond the door Jase could see a scarred maple dresser, a blurry big mirror above it. Voices came—a man's in quick inquiry, a woman's in rapid, fear-tinged gustiness. He moved clear of the opening.

"Who's out there?"

Jason stepped back still farther, drew his gun, and waited.

"Who is it?"

Silence.

"Blast you, Swift . . . I know who it is."

"Then come out and take your medicine."

"Come in and get me."

"You'd like that better. Easier to shoot men when they aren't set, isn't it?"

"Darned right . . . him and you both. Him and any others butt in here and steal range." Cook swore.

Jason went to the edge of the cabin, stepped down off the porch into the mud, and went along the rough side, turned again, and guessed which shutterless window would be the one. He approached it, bent a little, rose slowly, and saw movement among the corner shadows beyond.

"Turn around, Cook."

Cook did, whirling and lashing out with a shot that sang through the opening. Jason fired. Cook let off a shrill scream. He thumbed off another shot, and another. Jason fired again and Cook broke in the middle, bent far over and kept right on going, face down. The woman screamed, and Jason's teeth went on edge from the sound. He went back to the black horse and rode in a westerly way, slowly, with a taste of ashes in his mouth, a sense of emptiness inside his head, and a soddenness in his stomach.

Back at the cabin where his brother was, Jase put up the black horse, grained him, went into the cabin from the rear, and began to discard his dark, wet clothing. Arty was there, watching him. Neither of them spoke. Arty went to the table, drew out Jase's .45, sniffed it, opened the trap, and revolved the cylinder slowly, slowly closed the trap, and put the gun back in its holster.

In fresh, dry clothing Jase turned his back upon Arty, made a breakfast of thick bacon and mush, ate it standing up, and, after he laid aside the bowl, lit a cigarette. Then Arty spoke.

"Where's the box?" There was bitterness in the youth's voice, in his clear blue gaze, in the drawn-down expression of his mouth.

"You'll have to get it, Arty," Jason said in his unruffled way. "I won't have time."

"Who did you kill?"

"All but Ted Sloan." He looked sardonic. "Cuneo, Cook, Balester." He tolled off the names in a lingering way.

"Oh, Jase. . . ."

Jason spoke again, unheeding. "There's room enough here for all of us, Arty. They knew it. Paw knew it. He wouldn't fight them except that they made him. When they came, he didn't have a chance. You saw that."

"You outlawed yourself, Jase. Why didn't you let me . . . ?"

"I don't have a lot of time, Arty." Jason looked through the partly opened door. Gray shadows lay beyond. He dropped his eyes to the lean youth's face. "Now you bury him, Arty."

Arty laughed, a brutal sound. "Then what? They'll be after me, too. They'll burn this cabin, maybe haul me off to prison."

Jason shook his head. "No. It was just one man with a gun. Folks saw me like that . . . alone. There'll be posses out. I've got to go, Arty. Just one thing for you to remember. We're going to do what he wanted. We're going to keep this piece of ground. We're going to keep our cattle on this range. That was his dream. We're his sons."

"We?"

"I'll be around, Arty."

"Jase, I can't."

"Bury him, Arty. Buy a box in town and plant him right here near the house. Put up a railing to keep critters out. They won't bother you too much, I don't think. If they do . . . well, they brought this on and that's the way it's got to be. You see that as well as I do."

"But not like this, not with you hiding. I don't think he'd have wanted us all killed over this ranch, Jase. I really don't."

Jason left his brother in the cabin, saddled the black horse, and rode westward toward the broken land where timbered arroyos and great slopes swept upward, where the forest's peace lay, and the sun burned with a soft, clear warmth, until he was lost in far places. He rode far beyond sight of the whirling press of riders who swept up to the low, squatty cabin and dismounted with slamming boot steps, and faces of twisted steel.

Arty rubbed his palms along his trousers, listening to their clamor. He eyed the clumsy shotgun and decided against it. They were too many.

"Come out, Swift, unarmed and with your hands over your head. Hurry up now, or you'll go back to town tied crossways."

He opened the door and saw them, their wild, hot eyes and merciless mouths, their guns and coiled ropes upon the saddles.

"Come down here. That's good . . . hold it. Jeff, feel him for a gun or a knife . . . these Texicans usually carry both."

"He's unarmed."

The sheriff lowered his carbine, let its snout point downward. "Where's your brother?"

"I don't know."

"He's lying."

"I'll handle this, Curt. Was he here?"

"Yes, he was here. After breakfast."

"Which way did he go?"

A voice from behind the cabin called out: "Tracks back here! Fresh tracks goin' toward the badlands."

The sheriff's mouth quirked. "I figured," he said, then nodded at Arty in cold triumph. "Them others I sent'll probably run into him."

Someone said: "Where's your old man, kid?"

"In the house."

"Fetch him out."

"He's dead."

The sheriff's brows drew down slowly. "Dead? How?"

"They shot him yesterday a couple miles from here."

A tall man with an angular face, deep-set gray eyes, and a carbine to lean upon asked: "Who shot him?"

"The ones Jase shot."

There was a stir of movement in the posse. The sheriff waved one hand toward the cabin. "Go see, Mike, will you?"

The tall man went past Arty into the cabin. While he was gone, there was a strange silence. When he returned, they all looked up at him.

"Dead, Sheriff. Shot through the chest."

The lawman's carbine slanted still lower. "Yesterday afternoon, you say? Why didn't you 'n' your brother let me know?"

Arty's arms ached from being held high. "We let you know when they shot our horses, ran off our cattle. What good did it do?"

A posse man went over by the porch and sank down upon a box there. "Let him put his arms down, Sheriff," he said.

"He never gave them a chance, Arty."

"They didn't give our paw a chance."

The man by the porch said: "Put 'em down, kid."

Arty lowered his arms, flexed his fingers to get feeling back. There was a hot, dry burning in his throat.

"Say," a man said grumpily, "we going to stand around here all day, or go after him? If he's got a two, three hour start, we'll need all the time we can get."

Others echoed him. The tall man leaning upon the carbine was studying Arty with sardonic eyes. The older, stubbier man dawdling by the porch heaved himself upright with a sigh. They began to mount their horses. The sheriff made no move to turn away.

"Someone's got to take this guy back to town an' lock him up."

Men moved away impatiently. A shockle-headed man with a pair of moving, watery eyes volunteered. He had a shotgun on his lap. They put Arty in his care and trotted stiffly around the cabin, westward.

"Where's your horse, Swift?"

"In the corral back of the barn."

The restless eyes smiled deceptively. "Naw, let's not bother going near no buildings. Let's you just start walking." He emphasized the direction with the shotgun muzzle. "Move!"

Arty walked with the soft, measured sound of the rider behind him.

People saw, knew him. They watched as he went by toward the jail house. Shame, hatred of what was unjust, burned in his mind, in his heart. He looked up only when the man with the watery eyes pushed him inside a strap-steel cage, slammed the door, and closed a big hasp and lock.

It was the door's clanging finality that echoed in his mind. "What're you locking me up for?"

"You're his brother, ain't you?"

"But I didn't shoot anyone."

The man shrugged, tossed the key upon a table, drew up a chair, and sank down upon it, tilted it far back. "All 'coons don't kill chickens," he said, "but when you see 'em you kill 'em, don't you?"

It was late, after midnight, when the posse returned, worn and short-tempered. They were townsmen for the most part, though, and more weary of the chase than antagonistic toward a killer's brother. The sheriff dismissed them, told the watery-eyed man to get some supper and return later. Then he pulled the chair closer to Arty's cell and sank down upon it in a slouching way.

"Tell me the whole story, Swift."

"I didn't see any of the killings."

"I don't mean them . . . I mean how this come about."

"When we took up land here a year ago, the other cowmen said the country was getting cluttered up . . . too many cattle for the range. They said we couldn't turn out."

"So you turned out anyway."

"It was our right. We got as much right as they have."

"What other trouble was there . . . besides them horses that got shot and the cattle you said were run off?"

Arty looked into the smooth, ruddy face. "Besides that? That's all, except the threats. They put warning notes on the trees. Even nailed some to our cabin one night."

"Who were they?"

"The ones my brother shot. One he said he didn't shoot . . . Ted Sloan."

"Did he say why he let Sloan go?"

"No."

"All right, these fellers threatened you, you say, and then what?"

"Paw told us he was going to look for some cattle we couldn't find. When he didn't come in, we went tracking him. There he was, dying."

"Dying? Wasn't he dead when you found him?"

"No. He died while we were standing there."

The sheriff leaned forward on his chair. "What did he say before he died?"

"Nothing. When we rode up, he smiled at us both. Just smiled and lay there. Then he died. He was trying to say something. Never got it said."

"And so your brother rode out and killed three men on nothing more'n your pa's smile and some ideas who his killers were?"

"I don't know what he went on. Only Jase . . . he isn't easily roiled. He doesn't make mistakes."

The sheriff stood up, yawning, made a cigarette, lit it, and exhaled. His eyes were thoughtful and merciless. "Don't he?" he said. "He made the dog-gonedest mistake of his life when he went after them men, mark me, boy. The dog-gonedest mistake of his life."

"Let me out of here."

The sheriff smoked in a heavy, tired silence. After a time he said: "How old are you, boy?"

"Twenty."

"That so? Y'look younger."

"When will you let me out of here?"

A shrug. "Maybe tomorrow. You're in here for your own sake. There's the devil to pay in your neck of the woods. Those men had brothers an' friends an' relations. They're going over the whole cussed country looking for a Swift. Let 'em have tonight to get some of it burned out of 'em. Then I'll turn you out. But listen, kid . . . quit the country. Get out. If you don't, you'll get a shot between the shoulders one of these days. Your brother's made things like that."

"I didn't shoot anyone."

"I know," the sheriff said. "Neither did John Wilkes Booth's landlady . . . but they hung her just the same. You can thank your brother for making things like that, kid. You're marked . . . they'll kill you inside of a year for what he done. So take my advice . . . saddle up and keep going. Go a long way off . . . back to Texas. That's where all you Texicans belong, anyway. Troublemakers. . . ."

The sheriff walked away, lit a lamp at the far end of the cell-block, and closed the door after himself.

Beyond the high barred window Chiloquin was sleepless despite the lateness, the sharp, bitter night, the sob of a growing wind.

Arty sank down in the gloom with his head in his hands. Men of twenty don't cry. Whimpers of grief come awkwardly, but there is a dry, hollow hurt, as though the world had collapsed, shattered around their feet, and turned to something hateful.

Finally he lay back, but sleep wouldn't come. Instead a choking sense of overwhelming loss stifled him so that he turned to the wall and pushed a fist hard against his mouth. What would *she* think? What land was worth four dead men? Remembering how he'd wanted to kill them himself, horror filled him.

Cold came through the little window, damp cold riding the wings of a steady blow that would sweep the last leaves of autumn from the ridges. A howling wind sucked up under the jail house's pole-end rafters with a mocking, husky sound of laughter.

On the crossing from Texas, at a dismal place called Tiburon, his mother was buried. They'd camped four days making a carved paling for her grave site. . . . Then, on to New Mexico, across its burning sands to Colorado, to Ute Valley where great hunkering mountains squatted lean flanks upon the valley's edges. Where this disaster had struck.

Sarah . . . corn-silk hair and snapping black eyes. Full, willful mouth, rich and red and tantalizing. He turned from the wall, struggled upright on the edge of the cot.

Jase, who had showed him things with a patient gravity, never lost patience with a younger brother who wanted short cuts to all ends. Big Jason, his soft, rumbling chuckle, so rare of late, his slow-kindling humor with its attendant crinkling lines around the wide blue eyes.

Their father, with a strange power in his hands that could winnow the wildness from a mustang's heart, bring a calf back from the verge in the cold, terrible winters, or rest with a strange, haunting gentleness upon a gangling boy's shoulder, restraining without prohibiting.

And those others—Balester, Cook, Cuneo, Sloan. He lifted clenched fists and held them so that the white glow of moonlight fell across their gnarled bones. In a quiet whisper he spoke to no one in the night.

"It's all right, Jase. I want them dead. I want them all dead."

He dropped the fists, and a strange, intent brightness was in his gaze. Ted Sloan wasn't dead. Ted Sloan was there, as he'd always been—loud-mouthed, irritating, patronizing. Jase had left him one. Thinking back, he remembered the peculiar way Jase's eyes had clung to his face when he had said Sloan was still alive. *Jase wanted it that way . . . wanted one for his brother to get.*

He stood up and moved toward the high window, drew up a little nail keg, and stood upon it, looking out into the silver night. He smiled.

Dawn found him still peering out. When the sheriff returned, he rattled the door and flung it wide with a sour smile. "All right, kid, I'm turning you out early for a reason. Go back, plant your old man, and keep on going. They'll be looking for you by late sunup, so you got to make tracks. Get it done and get on your way to Texas, and when you see your brother, tell him it's just a matter of time. Every day he stays alive and free means it's just getting that much closer to the time he'll be caught. Tell him that for me. They never escape . . . none of 'em."

Arty went out into the chilled stillness. His horse was there, saddled, fresh. He stepped up and went due west from Chiloquin. He rode all the way home without seeing a soul, not even any cattle or horses.

He buried his father on the prairie by the cabin while the wind lashed and hooted. The wind was a fury; it made their spindly cottonwoods, planted the year before, creak in a gaunt, hurting way as though above the shallow grave.

After a while the great white shroud would sift down upon it all. Soon a whiteness would cover the unmarked, narrow mound in the wintry, booming silence of Ute Valley.

He stood there like a carving, with the lead-slate sky above, the troubled short grass below. He made a prayer with his lips, against the blackness in his heart, and never heard them coming until he turned toward the cabin, intending to get his pistol, carbine, and the old scatter-gun. And his heart, beating faintly, turned to ice.

Eleven of them sat there, perfectly motionless, watching him. Three were Cuneos. He knew them by their swartness, by their slightness. Some of the others were familiar in an obscure way—relations probably, friends of the men Jase had killed.

Back among them a man dismounted. It was a slow blur of movement, deliberate, unhurried. The man twisted and turned until he emerged from the group of silent men. Ted Sloan.

"Art, come here."

He made no move to obey. The wind ruffled his thick hair; the hat in his hand hung limply. Sloan turned, said something the wind caught up and threw skyward. Others dismounted; several started forward. When they were close, they seemed huge, their faces smoothed by the dark beauty of violence. They lunged, and he flung away. They fell upon him. He fought. Voices rose in grunting symphony, in panting profanity, for Arthur Swift was supple, as lean and tough and vicious as any of them.

They bore him down, pinioned his arms. Someone yelled in thick exultation: "Hang him . . . lynch him!"

"Give me that whip!"

"Here, Sloan! Hey! Stand him up and tear his shirt off. Get the bend out of his legs."

"Aw, lynch him. Wish Cook's widow could see this!"

Struggling did no good, but he twisted, wrenched, and someone swore when he was kneed. A raw red fist came out of the mêlée and crunched against his temple. Lights exploded behind his eyes, and loud whooshing sounds rang in his ears.

"Stand back."

He heard it dimly, and his eyes were filling with water when the lash made its singing sound, broke against his chest with staggering force. Pain came—a red eruption of it that flooded his body, drowned his dimmed senses.

"He's out . . . he's hangin' limp. Get some water, somebody."

"Water nothin' . . . just hold him up."

He felt no more.

There was a soughing wind whipping under the rafters when he opened his eyes, a dull pain burning like fever in him, but it was strangely warm in the darkness.

"Drink this."

The man was angles and shadows, indistinct. They were in the cabin. There was a snapping fire in the iron stove. He was on Jase's bunk. The dark shape bent over.

"Drink it. Come on . . . while it's hot."

He drank, seeking features that weren't recognizable in the gloom. He held out the cup and felt it taken away. For a time there was nothing but tiny rustling sounds, then the flare of a match, the glowing end of a cigarette that dulled while he watched it.

"You got a pretty good hiding, didn't you?"

The voice was so calm, so slow and steady, he thought for a moment it was Jase's. But it wasn't; the tone was different. Still, there was something familiar. . . .

"Shouldn't have wasted so much time, kid."

"Who are you?"

The dark head bent lower. There was a faint glimmer of strong white teeth. "Plenty of time to talk of that. Right now I'm interested in your brother. Where is he?"

"I don't know. Who are you? Why don't you light the lamp?"

"We don't need any light," the deep, soft voice said. "Besides, it might draw them back."

Memory stirred. Ted Sloan and the plaited, rawhide drover's whip. He moved a hand, an arm, felt his chest, and pain broke out anew. He ground his teeth against it. His chest was like jelly. The arm dropped down.

"Did you see them do it?"

The angular shadow bobbed its head twice, said nothing.

"Did you see Sloan? He's the one Jase let go."

"Forget it, kid."

Arty made a wild sound deep in his throat. "Sloan. . . ."

"I said to forget it. That's how people get outlawed . . . remembering things like that . . . like the killing of your pa."

He rolled his head toward the ghostly blur of a face. "I'll never forget that . . . whoever you are. Never. An' when I'm able. . . ."

"Listen, Swift, it was wrong, sure, but legal wrong . . . not frontier wrong."

"What?"

"Like this, kid. Where there's law and plenty to back it up, men'd go to prison for this. Here, the law's got no great backing, so men've used their own laws to settle things. It's simple, kid, the oldest law on earth . . . an eye for an eye and a tooth for a tooth. But that's Injun law, not white man law. You go kill this Sloan . . . you'll be hunted, probably killed . . . sure as the devil you'll get caught and sent away. You'll ruin your life."

"They marked me," Arty said, feeling the ridges and welts and places where a sort of flesh jelly was. "I'll carry these marks forever. Forget it?" He gave a hoarse laugh.

"It isn't the marks on your hide, kid . . . it's the ones they put inside your head. You've got to get them out or you'll be like your brother . . . hunted, outlaw, never still, never able to sit down of an evenin'. No family, no wife, no girl. It isn't worth it, kid, believe me. I've seen too many who wouldn't shake it off. Most of 'em I saw stretched out."

The big shadow rose, stood towering in the blackness, and a cold, silvery moon touched the curling hat brim, the angular, even features below it.

"Who are you? Were you with them?"

"I wasn't with them. I rode up later, just as they were finishing you up. They left when I shot in the air."

"Who . . . ?"

"Remember the feller with the posse yesterday who went in and looked at your pa?"

Arty remembered. A tall, thin man leaning upon a carbine, detached, watchful, silent. "Yes," he answered.

"Well, that's who I am. Deputy U.S. marshal. I was passing through Chiloquin, dropped in on the sheriff for a visit, and he got me to ride along. Name's Mike Meaghan."

Arty let his head fall back. "Lawman. We lived here a year and no lawmen come around. Now. . . ."

"Now they're all over the place, aren't they?"

"Yeah."

"Listen, kid, you got any friends around here who'll look after you until you're able to travel?"

He thought of Sarah, shook his head bitterly. "No, not now."

"Who was there . . . before?"

"A family . . . like us, like we were . . . starting up out here."

"Who are they?"

"The Lances, Sarah and her paw. Her mother died in the crossing, too."

"Where do they live?"

"Five miles due north where the river makes a break around a headland. They call it Big Bend."

"I'll get your wagon."

"No. . . ."

The deputy marshal stood looking down without speaking.

"They won't want me, especially her father. He's against violence. He's a Bible reader. By now he'll know about Jase."

"Who else, then? You've got to have care for a few days, until you can sit a saddle."

Arty rocked his head shallowly. "I'm not sitting a saddle,

mister. I'm not leaving. I was going to . . . but not now. I didn't think Jase was right killing all of 'em. Now I do. And Sloan. . . ."

"Swift, I'll tell you again. Shake that off."

He closed his mouth under the marshal's stare. Somewhere westward was Jase. Westward, too, was forgetfulness, peace, until he could get around again. From that lost country all tangled, and broken, he would emerge later, for, as Jase had said, they'd come to Colorado to run cattle. No bushwhacking murderers would keep them from it—not with their blood and flesh a part of Colorado.

"I'll get your wagon."

He turned his head enough to see the tall, lean frame pass beyond the cabin door. His mouth was locked tight.

II

The night was cold, the hour late. Mike Meaghan said nothing, watched the horse's rumps swing rhythmically ahead of the wagon. Behind him Arty lay swathed, breath steaming, eyes steadily upon the mighty curve of eternity overhead. The moonlight made his features sharper, his flesh pale.

It was getting gray when they swung into the Lance ranch yard. A rooster crowed and a dog crow-hopped toward them, hackles up, barking. There was a glow of light past a small window, and after a moment the door opened a crack and a man's shaggy head peered out.

"Mister Lance?"

"Yes."

The deputy marshal kicked the foot brake, looped the lines, and got down stiffly. Arty heard him talking to Lance and drew his mouth down, picturing Lance's face, the way it would close, lock out the knowledge that Arty was there in the wagon. The voices went on fitfully. There were awkward lapses of silence. Then he heard footsteps hurrying over the frosty ground, and a head appeared over the wagon's side.

"Arty!"

"Hello, Sarah."

She scrambled up, swung down beside him. Her eyes were immense. He returned her stare and they were both silent. Then other footfalls, and Meaghan loomed up, John Lance beside him. The shorter man's face was shadowed. He let out a soft breath. Meaghan went to the tailgate and fumbled with it, let it down, and glanced over at Lance with raised eyebrows, waiting.

"Hello, Mister Lance."

"Hello, Arty. Guess you need a mite of rest, boy."

"Naw, I'll be all right. This was his idea, not mine."

"Can you walk, Arty?"

"Sure." But he wasn't sure. He hadn't tried.

"I'll help you. Sarah, go fix the cot."

She climbed out of the wagon. Meaghan's thin face followed her through the weak light. He bent, slid his arms under Arty's pallet, and lifted. Arty was embarrassed and indignant.

"Put me down, darn it."

Meaghan's mouth quirked. He stooped, set Arty on his feet, and held his arm. There was a galling pain that felt like slow fire eating away his chest. He looked stoically at the ground, took a step, another step, and found it hurt no more when he moved.

Inside the cabin the atmosphere was heavy with the aroma of greasy food. Arty felt an unexpected, ravenous hunger. Sarah watched, rooted to the floor, when Mike Meaghan removed the blankets, helped Arty lie back on the little cot. John Lance stood transfixed by the jellied ruin of Arty's chest. His face got very white.

"Sarah, get some warm water and clean rags."

Dressing the wounds made them hurt like fury. Arty's eyes smarted, but he fought monumentally to keep his face blank. It fooled none of them, but it did make their work easier. When it was over, Mike Meaghan straightened up from wiping his hands and looked with unmistakable longing at the burdened stove.

After he ate, made a cigarette, he sat down beside Arty. Sarah was busy in the kitchen cleaning up; her father was out doing the chores. They were alone in the low-roofed parlor.

"See, kid, he was glad to have you. Now listen a minute. . . ."

"You going to preach some more?" The blue eyes were scorning, defiant.

Meaghan drew on his cigarette. A ripple of muscle moved along his jaw. "Y'might call it that, only it's for your own cussed good. These folks are kind . . . they're going to take care of you, patch you up. Most folks are like that."

"The Sloans like that . . . the Cuneos?"

Meaghan regarded his cigarette and nodded. "I think so. If your brother hadn't gone kill crazy, I reckon even those folks'd have come around in time." Meaghan turned, looked directly at Arty. "I'm a little older'n you. I've seen a whale of a lot more of life'n you have. In my business you meet more bad ones than good ones. And you know, kid, I haven't lost faith in humankind, so why should you?"

"You ever see your paw dying with a bullet in him?"

"No, but look at it this way. The man who killed your pa got his. He got killed, too, see? Only it wasn't done legally, so now his killer, your brother, is a hunted man. The point is, if you keep on bein' bitter like you are now, kid you'll wind up being hunted, too. And all it'll get you is killed."

"I'll do mine fair and square."

Meaghan's gaze grew ironic. "Will you? A kid like you . . . go up against grown men who were teethed on guns? Heck, they'll kill you so quick no one'll know what hit you . . . you least of all."

"Quit your dog-goned preaching. Just because I can't get out of this chair. . . ."

"That's why I'm doin' it, Arty. I don't want to get you after I get your brother. Don't make me."

Arty smiled without humor. "You? Get Jase? You'll never see the day you can hold a candle to my brother, mister, never."

Meaghan went on: "If you kill this Sloan or some of those others, it'll start the chain reaction for you like it has for your brother."

"What do you mean?"

"You kill Sloan, more Sloans go after you. You maybe kill another Sloan. They'll still be after you. Sooner or later one of them'll get you. If your brother's still around, he'll go after the one killed you. See what I mean? It's endless. One gunfight always starts more gunfights. No one ever wins them. I know what I'm talking about."

"Save it for church," Arty said sharply.

Mike Meaghan stood up. He looked thoughtful. "All right, kid. I didn't think you had the brains to understand anyway, but I tried."

"Listen, Deputy, when I'm able, I'm going back to our ranch. Our cattle'll be scattered all over the country. I'll have to round them up."

"I know. What about it?"

"Do you think those men're going to let me ride the range after the very cattle they killed my father over . . . and my brother killed them over?"

Meaghan's thoughtfulness drew out in silence. He moved his feet, stood hip-shot. Finally he said: "Well, I'd sort of hoped to get home for Thanksgiving. Reckon I won't make it. All right, Arty, I'll take care of that end of things."

"How?"

"Easy. Restraining order against every man who says he's an enemy of the Swifts."

Arty laughed. "Against their guns, too? I guess where you

come from things're different, Deputy. Ute Valley law's sort of a loose-rope kind. I know. We went to Sheriff Whitney a lot of times. It not only didn't stop them from running off our critters and shooting our horses . . . it didn't even slow them down when they caught my paw out alone."

"Maybe, maybe not. U.S. marshals are a little different, though." Meaghan turned toward the door, scooped up his hat, and held it. "You'll see what I mean the first time someone raises a hand against you, if what you're doin' is legally right." With one hand on the panel, he smiled. "Kid, do us both a favor. Be a man about this trouble, not a trigger-happy kid."

Arty heard him whistling as he drove the wagon away. It sounded strange, out of place, but, oddly, there was something about the tunelessness that was effective. He wondered about Meaghan.

Sarah cared for him. Her father said little those first days, but his eyes were eloquent. There was a vast depth of understanding in John Lance that neither Arthur Swift nor his daughter comprehended. Sarah was the first to discover this. It happened after Arty had been at the Lance place two weeks. He was beginning to ride again, would be gone from daylight till dusk. He rode with his shell belt laden with slugs, his pistol riding loosely by his side, and a stumpy carbine butt jutting upward from his saddle. Rode the Ute Valley range with a restlessness that led him to every cranny, every lift of land, and through the sprawl of trees that fringed the cattle country. Slowly he found scattered bands of his father's cattle, and one chilly November day when there was an inch of snow on the ground he sat motionlessly in his big sheepskin coat watching a Swift calf sucking a Sloan cow.

When he got back to Lance's that evening, there was a hard, glowing light in his glance, a wealth of silence, deep and forbidding, in the way he moved, ate his supper, helped John Lance with the outside chores, and then retired.

Sarah was listless. She sat in the warm lamplight watching her father stoke up the stove. "Pa, he keeps getting worse."

John turned, gazed at his daughter a moment, then adjusted the damper while speaking. "None of them were easy men, Sarah," he said. "Where they come from life is hard . . . the people come to be just as hard. It's in them, honey."

"But tonight. . . ."

"I noticed. He saw something today, I expect." John let his arm drop down, stood back looking at the stove. Almost casually he said: "The old man was like iron, but different from Arty or Jason. He believed. Yes, Amos Swift believed."

"Arty doesn't."

John sank down upon a bench and looked at his daughter. At eighteen she was robust, strong, and very pretty. He looked down, rubbed his palms together. "No, Arty doesn't. Neither does Jase. Amos told them the Word, I know, but, honey, never forget that a Texican's Lord is a lord of war. Not like our Lord."

"It isn't right, but that isn't what scares me, Pa. What I'm scairt of. . . ."

"I know. That someone'll kill him. Well, let me tell you something, Sarah. Couple days back I was out checking the cows for springers. Bad for them to calf this late. Anyway, I came across pine cones set atop rocks. Back a ways was a lot of pistol casings."

Sarah looked interested but uncomprehending.

"The boy's practicing with his guns, Sarah. He's practicing every day, I'd say. Maybe for an hour at a time."

As the significance of this sank in, Sarah slumped lower. John looked at the stove, heard its merry, busy sounds without heeding them. Warmth increased around them.

"He's going to fight them, Pa."

John nodded.

"You've got to stop him."

John looked up at her. "I can't. Maybe you can, Sarah, but I can't." He was quiet a moment. "It's bad, honey. Not just for him, for them, but for us. If he kills Sloan or one of the Cuneo boys, or any of those others who were in on his whipping, they'll come here. By now everyone knows he's staying with us. In town, men I've known since we came here look away when I pass. I knew that would happen when we took him in, Sarah. That didn't worry me a whole lot, but this does. This can mean we'll be burned out at the very least. At the most, we might be shot."

Sarah's fingers were interlocked, the knuckles white and rigid. "There must be a. . . ."

"Sarah, the one thing I've been sitting here for the last hour waiting to hear you say, you haven't said."

"You mean . . . have him go away?"

John nodded.

"Oh, we can't, Pa. We can't turn him out. It'd drive him to Jase, and that'd be the worst thing in the world. You know that."

"No," John Lance said gently, "I don't know that at all. If he's going bad, Jase at least could show him how to be bad and stay alive." John stood up, went to the stove with a heavy tread, set the damper for the night, and looked down at his daughter. "Sarah, he's not a saint by any measure. Tell me something . . . why is it that women always love the bad ones, the wild ones, the ones who trail trouble behind them like a flag? Tell me why that is, will you?"

She answered without meeting her father's eyes. Her voice was almost a whisper. "I don't love him."

"Yes, you do, honey."

She didn't argue, and after a long interval of silence John crossed the room. "Good night, Sarah."

"Good night, Pa."

She thought of it until the bitter cold etched white lacing upon the windows and tree limbs popped with sub-zero brittleness. Then she, too, retired.

But the worry followed her, stayed warm and restless in her mind. It was still there in the morning when she stoked up the stove and prepared breakfast.

When Arty came in from milking and pitching feed to the horses, she turned and looked squarely at him. His blue eyes were clear and bright. His cheeks were flushed red below the shiny sweep of his reddish hair. He was handsome, so handsome her breath caught in her throat.

He set the pail upon a table and looked at her. "What was that for, Sarah?"

"What?"

"That stare."

For a moment she didn't reply. "I want you to hook up the sleigh and take me for a ride this morning, Arty."

"This morning?" he said, surprised.

"Yes."

"Well, I sort of planned to ride over by Blank Rocks today, Sarah. I haven't covered that country any too. . . ."

"You can do that tomorrow."

"Oh. . . . Say, do you want to get something in town, is that it?"

"No, I just want to go for a sleigh ride in the snow."

"Don't want to visit or anything?"

"No." She turned away when the blood beat into her cheeks.

"Well, all right, Sarah."

They went after breakfast. Arty tucked the lap robe around her and didn't smile, didn't meet her eyes until they were well out in the white world with the steam of their breath lying feather soft in the incredible stillness.

When they came to the corrugated bank of Willow Creek,

Sarah asked him to stop. He drew up, let the lines slide through his fingers.

"Sarah?"

She lifted her face to his, moving very close to him under the robe so that he could smell the pine scent of her hair, the scrubbed freshness of her.

"Kiss me, Arty."

His blue eyes grew oddly pale in the ruddiness of his face. He let the lines go and very gently reached over, took her by the shoulders, and turned her a little. She quivered; her eyes fled from his face, grew wide with fear, with something that made his heart grow still.

"You're scairt, Sarah."

"I know. I'm ashamed of it, too." She still didn't look up into his face. "Kiss me, Arty."

He did. He bent his face and kissed her very softly, very gently. She dropped her head upon his shoulder.

"I reckon he was right."

"Who was right?"

"Pa. He said I loved you."

He found no words. In that moment he understood that the language of love, like the language of the snow-bound countryside, was silence.

He was so lost in the quicksands of his discovery, Sarah called his name twice before he answered. "Yes?"

"What will you do with the ranch?"

He twisted his head to look down at her. Only long lashes above the pertness of her nose showed, dark lashes with a soft curve that made him think of music.

"Do with it? Why, keep it. Run it like Paw and Jase wanted. That's the whole thing, Sarah. They want to run us out. They killed Paw and made Jase an outlaw, but we aren't the running kind. I'll keep it, get it back going again come spring." Dark memory stirred in him. "Not many cows left . . . I expect they shot them . . . and no calves, but what's left'll do to start with."

"It would be a home, wouldn't it?" she said slowly, softly.

"It'll be more'n that. It'll be a good ranch again, you'll see."

The muffled fierceness in his voice didn't escape her. She stirred, close to him under the robe. "Arty. . . ." He moved, drew away a little. She looked up. There was a bitter look in his face.

"Sarah, back there at the creek, you were going to preach to me. Don't spoil this . . . don't make kissing you a price I got to pay for something."

She was motionless. Gradually her gaze fell away from him, went out over the dead-white world. With instinctive bitterness she said: "I'm not asking you to pay for a kiss, Arty. I'm trying to make you see that . . ."

"I know," he said shortly, retrieving the lines, flicking them, turning the team, and starting back. "I know what you're trying to make me see, Sarah. I got something else I can see a whole lot clearer . . . Paw's grave."

When they were back, he helped her down. She stood inside the barn while he unharnessed, put the horses up, forked feed to them, and came up beside her, brushing chaff off his sheepskin coat, head down, eyes averted.

"Makes a person sort of hungry, doesn't it?" He looked up hopefully.

"I'll fix supper," she said, and started for the cabin.

He trailed after her, brows down, mouth bleak and stubborn.

John looked at them when they came in. His eyes lingered longest on Arty. "Got below zero last night," he said cheerfully.

Arty shrugged out of his coat, tossed his black hat upon it in a corner, backed up to the stove, and stood there like stone.

John cleared his throat. "Got enough hay over at your place for the critters you've pushed down that way?"

"Yes."

"Sometimes I wonder if it's worth it, feeding six months, grazing six months. Working like a slave putting up summer hay and feeding it out all winter long." John ended on a high note, as though inviting discussion.

"It's worth it."

John nodded, gazing past Arty at the busy stove. "I reckon," he said. "I reckon. Well, expect I'll go out and look around a bit. Gets tiresome sitting here all the time."

He left, and Sarah leaned upon the edge of the kitchen doorway. "Supper's ready. Where's Pa?"

"Went out for a spell."

"Well, you come eat, anyway."

He went, washed, made bear-like sounds behind the roller towel, tossed the water out into the snow, ran crooked fingers through his hair, and started to sit down. Sarah moved close to him. Without speaking, she put her arm up, leaned against him. He felt the remoteness within him crumble.

"No price, Arty," she whispered. "Kiss me again."

He did, and was startled at the quick, eager response he got. He held her close and put his face down beside hers. They stood like that without moving, silent, until she squirmed, then he let her go and felt for the chair, sank down upon it.

She spoke while working at the stove, without looking at him. "Indians read things in the cloud shapes. Did you ever see them do that?"

"Yes."

"I don't believe it but I think it's beautiful, the way they interpret things."

"Sort of sad, seems to me," Arty said, snugging up his chair.

She stopped moving. He knew she was staring at him, was standing close to the table looking down.

"It's sad." There was an unaccustomed harshness in her voice.

"We're sad, too. I don't need their cloud shapes. I know what's going to happen."

He looked up finally. "Cut it out, Sarah," he said.

"No. In the sleigh I let you do the talking . . . now you let me do it. I know you've been practicing with your guns. I know you've found something on the range that makes you all the madder. But, Arty, can't you understand that one man won't stand a chance if you start a fight?"

"I'm not starting anything. I told you that before. They started it. I'm going to finish it."

"I don't care how good you get with your guns . . . they'll ambush you. You just don't stand a chance . . . not one man alone."

"I stand a chance all right. Besides, I'm not alone. There's Jase."

"Jase! Where is he? How can he help you? He's hiding for his life. Maybe he's a thousand miles away. Maybe back in Texas. Wherever he is, he won't be around when you need him."

He got up with a lithe, abrupt movement, went through the kitchen door, crossed the little parlor, scooped up his hat, crunched it upon his head, flung into the sheepskin coat, and left the cabin. He skirted the opposite side of the cabin from which John Lance usually entered, crossed to the corral, saddled up, mounted, and rode into the quiet white world to the forlorn cabin he had helped his father build.

There he put up the horse, fed him, and stood in the gloomy sod and log barn.

A cow bawled.

Aroused by the sound, he went out into the snow and cupped his hands, called, repeated the mournful sound until he saw frosty red backs, gaunt, tucked-up ribs, moving toward the barn. Then he worked until the early shadows came, forking hay to the humped-up cattle, hearing their rattling horns, their grinding jaws. Finally, in the fast fading light, he sank down upon a sawbuck and gazed moodily at the eating animals.

He went into the house, built a fire in the stove, and rummaged, made a pot of mush, and ate it hot but without sugar or cream.

He went to his bunk, lay upon it fully clothed, reached down, shifted his gun, and stared at the thickening shadows.

He didn't know when he fell asleep but he knew why he awakened. The stove had gone out and freezing cold had settled within the cabin. He got up, built another fire, lit it, and ate more mush, now cold and unpalatable, and waited until the heat made the sluggishness leave his marrow. Then he went to the door and looked out. It was false dawn; the sky was like sheet lead, its swollen belly low and nigh to bursting. Snow weather. He stomped his feet, thinking a diet of mush for three, four days wouldn't be good.

When he stepped out past the door, snow crunched underfoot with a shattering echo. Immediately several cows bawled. He went around to the barn, fed the cattle again, rubbed his horse down, and scraped the bottom of the bin for a bait of grain.

The cold was intense, reaching inside his clothes and touching his flesh with a stinging dryness. He saddled up and rode easterly toward Chiloquin.

It was when he was topping a hillock with jack pines like rough beard stubble around him that he saw the first horseman. The animal was down a slack rope, his rider kneeling in the snow with one arm making quick whirling motions. From that distance it was impossible to see what the blur of dark wet body below the kneeling man was, but he knew. The man had roped a calf, was hog-tying it. His purpose was either to cut a bull calf or to brand whatever he had caught. No rider would ever mistake that up and down motion of the tying hand, the way the saddle horse stood back on the rope. He drew farther back among the pines and watched. That was when he noticed the second man.

Perhaps a thousand yards away, moving stealthily, keeping a rise of land between himself and the kneeling man, the second rider was edging up closer. A pale sheen from one fist would be a pistol. Arty sat motionlessly for a moment, absorbing what he saw, and then he dismounted, drew out his carbine, and waited. In the back of his mind was a determination to get a closer look at the calf the kneeling man was working over.

When the calf was tied, the kneeling man stood up, struck at his pants legs with a gloved fist to knock away the snow. He stood a second, gazing downward, then threw his head up and looked around. The sweep of hat brim hid his face. He started to move away, beating his hands together. Puffs of steam preceded him.

The stalking rider had dismounted. Only his head was visible over a snowy ridge. Arty knew he was there or he wouldn't have attached any significance to the small dark blur far out. When the first man was busy gathering twigs, scuffing snow aside to find them, the second man belly-crawled still closer. He was behind a chaparral bush when the first man knelt near the calf, whittled kindling, lit it, and fanned it with his hat. He was so engrossed he didn't hear the second man until he spoke.

"Freeze, mister!"

The words carried clearly to where Arty was. The kneeling man stiffened, made no movement, and didn't turn his head.

"Stand up. Now put your hands above your head. That's good." The first man walked up behind the cowman, plucked out his pistol, and tossed it backward into the snow. Then he went around in front of his prisoner. "All right, put 'em down. Now then, what were you fixin' to do?"

"Brand this calf. What you mean . . . ?"

"Rope it. Where's this calf's mother?"

The cowman rolled his head sideways. "Over in the trees somewhere. She took off when I roped the calf."

"What's your name?"

"Jack Cuneo."

"What's your brand?"

"My brand's C Bar, but this was one of my cousin's critters. The feller Jase Swift killed. His brand was C-in-a-Box."

"So this calf's mammy was a C-in-a-Box cow . . . right?"

"Yes. Who the devil are you?"

"Deputy United States marshal. Name's Meaghan."

Arty waited to hear no more. He led his horse back away, mounted, and rode back the way he had come until he was out of sight and sound, and then he began a zigzagging ride until he found fresh cow tracks. Following them wasn't hard in the crusty snow, and, when he found a cow, she bawled at sight of him, moved with dismay and excitement. He sat a moment staring at her, then swore coldly and got in behind her, herding her toward the place where Mike Meaghan and Jack Cuneo were.

When the cow smelled the little fire, she bawled again, threw up her head, and lumbered through the snow. Bursting out of the trees, she gave another call, and this time her tied calf sent back a pitiful bleat. It triggered the old cow's anguish. She bawled repeatedly, went crashing through the snow toward the astonished men near the fire.

When Arty came out of the jack pines, he had his carbine across his lap. He flicked Mike Meaghan a glance, then stared hard at Jack Cuneo. When he was close, he drew up, dropped the reins, and looked down at the tied calf. Back a way the cow was fidgeting, bawling, wanting fearfully to come closer, unable to overcome her inherent mistrust of humankind enough to do so.

"Deputy . . . cut her loose, will you?"

Meaghan acted as though he hadn't heard. His pistol, cocked, as steady as stone, swerved to include Arty in its orbit. "Put up that carbine, kid."

Arty complied, then rested his hands upon the saddle horn. "Cut the calf loose."

Meaghan motioned toward Cuneo. "Take the ropes off it."

Without speaking, Cuneo bent, threw off the lasso rope, unwound the pigging string, slapped the calf smartly over the kidneys. With a wild leap it regained its feet, let out a tremulous bawl, and fled. The old cow was moving frantically from foot to foot. When the calf swept up beside her, she lowered her head, rattled her horns at the men, and backed away. The calf bunted hard and began to suck.

Arty turned back toward Cuneo, his face sardonic-looking, his eyes unblinkingly hard and cold. "That a C-in-a-Box calf?" he asked quietly.

Cuneo stared at the cow and calf without answering. Mike Meaghan holstered his gun, rolled one fist inside the other one to take away the sting and stiffness. "What do you have to say about that, Cuneo?"

"Mistake," the man answered shortly.

"Yeah, mistake all right. Been a darned sight more'n that if I'd waited until you put your mark on the calf. Been rustling then." Mike looked up at Arty. "Where'd you come from?"

"I was watching both of you from that jack pine hill back there. When I heard what he told you, I went and hunted up the old cow, saw she was one of mine, and drove her down here for you to see that, too."

Cuneo's dark, hard glance was fixed at Arty. There was an utterly unrelenting hatred showing. Arty returned the stare.

Meaghan cleared his throat, spat, shrugged his sheepskin coat closer, and began stomping his feet. "Arty, how many calves would you say you're out?"

"I don't know. We never finished tallying wet cows before

Paw got killed. Quite a bunch, though."

"You got some bagged-up cows among your herd right now?"

"Yes, couple dozen as near as I can say."

"Well," Meaghan said, "this is a bad time to be driving cattle, but, if you want to make a case out of this, I'll fix the legal end of things."

"What do you mean?"

"Round up your cows and drive them to this feller's place. Let your mammy cows wander among his calves. If they pair up . . . and if some of his branded calves suck your cows . . . you've got a perfect case against a rustler."

Mike stood there, tall, thick-looking because of his extra clothing, watching Swift. Cuneo was looking straight ahead, out to where the cow and calf were standing.

Arty sniffed. The air, razor-sharp, was getting colder. He shook his head slightly. "It's going to snow, Deputy. If it's a blizzard, I'd lose more'n I'd gain trying to drive 'em through a snowstorm."

Meaghan glanced upward, frowned a little. "Might hold off long enough. How far from your place is this man's ranch?"

"About six miles."

"If we started right now, the three of us . . . we'd probably make it."

"You got guts," Cuneo said, "thinkin' you can make me help you do this."

Mike smiled frostily. "I *can* make you . . . don't kid yourself on that score." He looked at Arty. "What say?"

Arty nodded without speaking, and Meaghan gestured toward Cuneo. "Watch him until I fetch my horse."

Left alone, Arty felt warm inside. After all this time the law was finally taking a hand.

"Swift, you're making a mistake," Cuneo said with menace in his voice.

"It was you made the mistake."

They rode back through the gray day with Jack Cuneo between them. No one spoke until they were within sight of the cattle eating near Swift's barn. Mike Meaghan looked thoughtfully at the animals, then turned a quizzical expression upon Arty. "I thought you were staying with the Lances."

"Did you?" Arty said shortly, and urged his horse ahead a little.

Meaghan watched him in silence, then shrugged and looked at the dark man beside him. "Cuneo, remember you're under arrest. If you make a break for it, you won't get far. I've never yet seen a horse could outrun a bullet. All right . . . get on the wing across from Swift."

They drove the cattle away from the ranch with no effort. Having full bellies, the animals went readily enough. It wasn't until the first big flakes came swirling down, slow, powdery, that Arty felt an urge to hurry. He knew Colorado's winters; he also knew the way blizzards could come, so deceptively mild at the outset. Dozens had perished because of that lazy gentleness. He edged closer to Mike Meaghan.

"Still a couple miles to go. Maybe one or the other of us ought to go up and point for them . . . break a trail they'll follow in case this gets worse."

"Go ahead," Meaghan said casually. "I'd rather stay back here where I can see between Cuneo's shoulder blades." He threw the younger man a thin smile. "Good thing I rode out this way today, huh? Doesn't seem much doubt about this one at least."

"The others are as bad," Arty said cryptically. He lifted his reins a little. "What made you pick a day like this to ride out?"

Meaghan was making a cigarette. He had his reins looped, his gloves tucked under one arm. "A hunch," he said. "Just a hunch."

Arty looked disbelieving. "You mean you thought this might happen?"

Meaghan lit, exhaled, and wagged his head. "No, not this. I thought your brother might pick a day like this, when folks weren't out, to come down and hunt you up." Meaghan turned, looked steadily at Arty. "I'm not sure I wasn't right, either. How come you were at your home place instead of over at Lance's?"

"I come over here to feed the cattle now and then, that's how come."

"Aw," Meaghan said softly, "we both know better'n that, kid."

"Do we?"

"Sure. I rode by Lance's this morning, early."

"What of it?"

Meaghan removed the cigarette, held it between his fingers. "You and Sarah had an argument."

"Blast you!" Arty said wrathfully, and kneed his horse out.

Meaghan watched him crunch ahead, pass Cuneo without looking at him, curve in ahead of the leaders and ride southeast, erect and stiff in the saddle. He squinted his eyes a little, pondering.

When the snow was coming down heavily enough to obscure vision, Arty plodded to the top of a barren knoll, windswept clean of snow, turned in his saddle, and flagged with one arm. Meaghan watched Cuneo. The dark rider was leaning forward in his saddle. Maybe he was cold. Meaghan reached forward, slid his carbine from the boot, and laid it across his lap. Maybe Cuneo was getting ready to flee.

They went over the ridge, and, through the thickening blanket of white, Meaghan saw buildings, gray, squatty, and cold-looking. Somewhere up ahead a cow bawled. Out of the gloom came a muffled answer. Other cows bellowed.

When Meaghan pushed the cattle up, bunching them, he was

closer to Cuneo. With a soft call he drew the man back beside him. Arty had opened a corral gate. It took a little maneuvering to get the cattle inside because the snow hid the opening, but when it was accomplished, and the three of them were standing outside beside their horses, Arty handed his reins to Mike. He crawled through the poles, opened a gate where Cuneo's cattle were milling, and let the animals mix.

Gaunt and motionless, the men stood back watching. Inside his sheepskin coat, Arty had his gun in his fist. Cuneo was transfixed. Meaghan's cigarette was damp and dead between his lips. A soft sound passed his teeth in a hissing way. Arty swung his head a little. There was a shaggy calf sucking one of his cows. On the calf's ribs was a livid red brand, fresh enough still to show singed hair. It was a C Bar.

"See that, Deputy?"

"I see it."

Arty's gun came out, low and glistening with wetness. "What you got to say, Cuneo?" he asked coldly.

Without looking at either of them, Cuneo said: "A slick's a slick. When you find one on the range, Swift, you mark it."

"No I don't. Never have. Neither did my Paw or my brother."

"Even the ones you can't mammy up?"

"Even them," Arty said. "You're a thief, Cuneo."

"That's enough of that," Meaghan cut in sharply, turned, and saw Arty's gun for the first time. "Put that thing up, kid."

Arty grew silent but made no move to holster his gun.

Meaghan's eyes lifted to his face. Without speaking, he walked behind Cuneo, and swung in between Cuneo and Arty. "Put that gun up, Swift. Any guns used around here, I'll use 'em."

Arty's hand moved, and the gun disappeared within his coat. He looked back toward the cattle.

There were other calves sucking his cows.

"How many did you get all told, Cuneo?" Meaghan asked.

"I got nothing to say."

Meaghan looked surprised. For a moment he just stared. "All right, cowman," he said finally. "Get on your horse and let's head for town."

"Let me tell my wife where I'm going."

Meaghan gave a hard, humorless smile. "Get on your horse."

Arty gathered up his reins, swung up, and waited. Cuneo was turning toward Meaghan when he spoke again. "She's got a right to. . . ."

"Yeah, I know," Meaghan said shortly. "She's got a right to know you been arrested, like she's got a right to ride ahead and warn any friends you got. Get on that horse!"

III

Chiloquin was indoors when they rode down the muddy roadway. What people were abroad moved through the late cold hastily. A few wagons were tied before stores. Down by the sheriff's office the hitch rail was empty. There, Mike Meaghan tied up, off-saddled. Arty waited until Jack Cuneo was on the ground being herded toward Whitney's doorway before he, also, got down.

Inside, Sheriff Whitney was drinking coffee with his back to the little iron stove. He held the cup thrust out, motionless, when the three men entered. His eyes flicked from one to the other, came to rest upon the deputy marshal. "What you got, Mike?"

"A rustler. This feller, Jack Cuneo, rustled some of Swift's calves."

"You sure?" Whitney said.

Arty stood by the doorway, silent. Meaghan looked ironically amused. "Sure? Yeah, I'm sure. I didn't ride through this blamed storm for exercise."

"But didn't you see any sign of the one you went after?"

"Jase? No, not a sign." Meaghan sank down upon a bench. "This'll do for a starter, though," he said, tugging off wet gloves. "Lock him up, Gordon. I'll sign the complaint myself."

The sheriff took Cuneo away. When he returned, he ignored Arty. "Listen, Mike, that guy's got more relations than you can shake a stick at. They'll be madder'n wet hens over this."

"Tough," Meaghan said shortly. He got up, crossed to the stove, and backed up to it, looking at Arty. "I got an idea, kid. Suppose you 'n' me sort of make the rounds with those cows of yours."

Arty unbuttoned his coat against the room's heat. "In this snow?" he asked sarcastically.

"We can wait it out."

Arty snorted. "You may be a good lawman, I don't know, but you sure aren't any cowman."

"Why?"

"Because if this keeps up for a couple more days, the snow'll be too deep to drive through, to start with. To finish with, the longer those bagged-up cows are away from their calves, the less chance there is that they'll ever claim them."

"Oh. Then I expect we can't wait, can we?"

Arty looked disgusted. "We got no choice. Snow's too deep, mister." He turned toward Sheriff Whitney. "I expect now you'll believe what's been going on, won't you?"

Whitney didn't answer. He went to his desk and sat down. Arty waited a moment, pulled open the door, and went out.

Down the road the Ute Valley Hotel, a rickety frame building, thrust its oversize false front skyward. Along the slanted ridge a long rope of snow lay, muff-like and powdery. He started toward it.

Passing one of the narrow gaps between buildings, he heard his name spoken: "Come in here, Arty. Don't just stand there."

He went. It was dark and damp; buildings on both sides

touched his shoulders.

"Jase!"

"Yeah. Trailed you from Cuneo's place."

"Cuneo's?"

"Yeah, I was waiting for him to come back. Saw him ride out about dawn, but he was too far away."

"What'd you want with him?"

Jase's steady eyes were sunken, brighter, his face leaner. There was a hard white ridge above his mouth. The lips were flat-looking; the jaw molded to flinty squareness.

"I heard about the beating they gave you, kid."

"And?"

"I had an ambush laid for him."

Arty leaned sideways against the building. "He's in jail, Jase." For a moment he struggled with his thoughts. "Listen, Jase, the law's finally acting. There's this deputy United States marshal named Meaghan. . . ."

"I know who he is, Arty. He's been couple a days behind me for a month now."

"He's helping. Leastways it was his idea, pairing up our cows with Cuneo's calves, that got Cuneo arrested."

"That's fine," Jason said without conviction, "only I want Cuneo dead. No one whips a Swift like they did you, kid. No one. . . ."

"Jase. . . ."

"How's Sarah?"

"She's fine."

"What's old man Lance say about all this?"

Arty shrugged. He was looking down in a troubled way. "He doesn't say much. You know how he is, Bible reader and all. No violence, turn the other cheek. . . ."

"Yeah. I'll tell you where there are some more of our critters, Arty, only you can't prove anything. Sloan's place. There's eleven dead cows quarter mile from his corrals. Shot."

Arty's eyes smoldered. "Did you see him shoot them?"

For the first time Jason smiled. "Yes, I saw him do it, only I can't testify."

"No. . . ." Arty was thoughtful. "How about calves?"

"He's got some. Why do you think he shot the cows? So's you can't pair 'em up, kid."

"Oh."

"I made a mistake, Arty, not shooting Sloan. I'll get him, though."

Arty fisted his hands and dug them deep into his pockets. "Jase, leave things be for a while, will you? This deputy marshal. . . ."

"Arty, that deputy marshal's after just one thing in this country . . . me. Maybe he caught Cuneo, but he did it accidentally. What he really wants is me. I'll lay you odds he was after me today when he came across you and Cuneo."

Arty shifted his stance, looked at Jase, saw how he'd thinned out, grown more alert. Heard how his drawling voice had changed, too, become whiplash sharp, quick. He reached out and touched his brother's sleeve.

"Jase, take a long ride. Go back to Texas, up to Montana. Don't stay around here."

"He won't get me."

"I'm not thinking of that. I know he won't. I'm thinking of the risks you got to run every cussed day and night. Besides, hanging around here'll only make things worse. And you can't do a lot, Jase, not with every man's hand against you. Go some place, start new."

Jason straightened up. A forbidding look came fleetingly over his face. "Aren't you forgetting something, Arty? Paw?"

"No, I'm not forgetting Paw . . . not forgetting anything, only. . . ."

"That rawhiding they gave you?"

"Nor that."

"Then just hang and rattle, kid. We'll be back in the saddle, you'll see. Say, you got any money, Arty?"

Arty had. He gave all but a few dollars of it to his brother. Jason tucked it away and lay a thick hand upon Arty's shoulder. "Don't soften up. Come spring things'll get mighty warm for our enemies, Arty." Then he left, a big, a wide shadow fading down the little gap between two buildings into the frozen darkness at the far end.

Arty went to the hotel, got a room, and paid an extra dollar to have a roustabout haul buckets of hot water for a bath. When he was in bed listening to the soggy drip of snow water outside a window, he thought about Jason. He'd changed, and Arty knew the outlaw life had done that. The steady eyes were sharper, restless. There was a cold, calculating ruthlessness in them. The big body had thinned out, toned down to pantherlike quickness. Arty turned under the quilts, squirmed, and finally fell asleep.

By dawn he was dressed and had eaten. When he crossed to the livery barn, the deputy marshal was sitting there, long legs shoved out in front of him, smoking a cigarette. He looked up with a smile.

"Figured you'd be along."

Arty went past without speaking, got his horse, cuffed him with a rice brush, saddled and bridled him. When he turned the animal once, after the manner of experienced horsemen, before mounting, he saw that Mike Meaghan was already sitting his saddle, watching him, obviously waiting. He stood stockstill, looking upward.

"Just thought I'd ride with you."

"I don't need company."

"No, I don't expect you do, but you got it."

Arty clenched his fist around the reins. "Where I'm going won't interest you."

"Back to your home place? Oh, I'm interested in the ranch myself."

"That's not where I'm going."

"Up into the mountains, maybe?" Meaghan said in a soft-sharp way.

"No, not into the mountains." Arty swung up, lifted his reins.

"Out to Lance's? Only I don't believe you're going there."

Grasping that, Arty urged his horse away. "That's exactly where I'm going," he said thickly, thinking he'd shake the unwanted companionship that way.

But Meaghan reined out, too, and smiled. "That's good, kid, because I sort of want to talk to John Lance a little."

There was nothing to do. Arty rode in profound silence, acutely aware of the thin man's gangling form beside him. He didn't speak for the entire trip, and by the time he hauled up in the Lance yard anger was choking him. He hadn't wanted to see the Lances. He hadn't wanted to see Sarah.

A horse nickered from the barn. Arty looked over that way. John Lance appeared in the doorway with raised eyebrows. He had a short-handled manure fork in his hand. He set it aside and came toward them, dry-washing his hands.

" 'Morning, Arty . . . Marshal. Sarah's got coffee on."

They got down. Arty shot the lawman a dark look, passed him on the way to the house, opened the door, and saw Sarah look up quickly. She straightened slowly without speaking, staring at him. He ducked his head as though breaking through brush, went deeper into the room, and let voices fill the silence. Sarah went into the kitchen; her father set out crockery cups, a sugar pot, some heavy spoons. Meaghan dropped down into a chair, ignoring Arty.

"This is a powerful big country, Mister Lance, and I been

thinking maybe you could shorten up a lot of ridin' I've got to do."

Sarah brushed past Arty, mumbling: "Sit down. Don't stand there looking like a storm going to break."

Arty shucked his hat and took a chair, gripped the hot cup of coffee with both hands, and stared into its dark liquid depths.

"I'd be glad to do what I can," Lance said. "But Arty here knows the country better'n anyone around."

"I know," Meaghan said dryly, "but for what I got to do I don't think he'd fit so well."

Sarah looked across at Meaghan swiftly. Her father's mouth dropped open, closed swiftly, tightly. Gradually Arty's eyes left the coffee cup, went to the marshal's face, and clung there.

"Like what?" Arty asked.

"Hunting down a killer."

"I'm sorry," was all Lance said.

"That means you won't help me?"

"Yes."

Meaghan sipped coffee, set the cup down slowly, revolved it with one long-fingered hand. "I didn't have to say this in front of you, kid, only I thought it'd be best, both of us knowing where we stood. . . ."

"Why don't you ask me to help you?" Arty said bleakly.

"First place . . . you wouldn't," Meaghan said. "Second place, after last night, I'm not sure I'd want you to."

"Last night?"

"Yeah, after you met your brother."

Arty's throat tightened, threatened to cut off his wind. He gripped the cup tightly, lifted it, and drank. When he set it down, he was calmer. "Know a lot, don't you?"

"No, not in time anyway. I didn't hear he was around until this morning. Feller saw him riding out, westerly." Meaghan turned back toward John Lance, told him about arresting Cuneo with Arty's help. Instead of looking pleased, Lance looked almost ill. He dropped his gaze to the table, remained silent.

Sarah moved behind Arty's chair. "Come gather eggs with me, Arty."

He arose stiffly without looking at either man, picked up his hat and coat, and followed her into the kitchen. When she was bundled up, they went out into the pale light. Inside the hen coop she turned and closed the door behind him.

"Was it really Jase?"

He studied her. "Seems like I'd better just keep quiet, Sarah," he said. "That feller's got ears like a deer."

"He was foolish to go into town, Arty."

"Maybe. Sarah, I'm sorry. . . ."

"Are you? Me, too."

She went closer, raised her arms; the sweater she'd thrown across her shoulders fell away. Dropping his head a little, he found her mouth.

They stood a foot apart looking at one another. He reached up with his fingers and pushed a tumbled strand of taffy hair away from her cheek.

"Guess I love you, Sarah." She started to move past him. He reached out, caught one bare arm. "That deputy in there, Sarah . . . I've got to shake him. He's danged near living in my clothes with me."

She half turned to face him. "Why do you have to shake him? Are you going to meet Jase?"

He shook his head. "It isn't that. I've got something else to do."

"What?"

"Say," he said a little coldly, "in Texas women don't question their menfolk."

"This isn't Texas, and I don't want to be a widow before I'm a bride."

He let go of her arm. She went to the nests, rummaged, began to fill the pockets of her apron with brown eggs. Speaking to him without looking around, she said: "I know what you want to do, and I've thought about it, too. If that lawman can't stop you, I can."

"What? What are you talking about?"

"About shooting the Cuneos, Ted Sloan, any others you've got in mind to shoot."

"How can you stop me?"

"Two ways. I've thought them out. One way would be to warn the men you're after."

"Warn them against me? Put them on their guard so's they'd be . . . ?"

"That's not the best way, though. The best way would be to have you arrested, locked up until this deputy marshal is finished with what he's trying to do."

"Sarah!"

She flung around. He'd never seen her so white, so hot-eyed, before. "Don't you realize he's going to get Jase? Everyone else knows it by now, Arty."

Arty made a twisted grimace. "He isn't man enough," he said.

She picked up her sweater, threw it around her shoulders. "You fool, Arty. There's only one way Jase can escape that man. That's by going far away and changing his name, dropping out of sight, becoming. . . ."

"He won't go away. He told me that last night."

"Then," Sarah said, "you aren't going to be killed, too. I won't let it happen."

Instead of the mistiness he'd seen in her glance once, now he saw a grim and whole-hearted determination. It shocked him in a way. Women weren't made to talk this way, act so purposeful—or were they? He looked past her at the fly-specked wall.

He was out of his element; this was a strange world to him, this sphere of skirts and blouses, taffy hair and direct black eyes. He remembered his mother, but now he couldn't recall anything of her that would help.

"I'm not going to stand by and see this lawman worry Jase, Sarah, not nohow."

"You can't stop him."

He looked squarely at her. "Would you really warn Sloan against me? That'd fix it so's he could bushwhack me. You know that, don't you?"

She made a motion with one hand. "I was talking. If I knew they wouldn't go after you, I'd warn them."

He smiled bitterly, said nothing.

"But I know they will, Arty. I know something else, too. They've heard about Jack Cuneo."

"How do you know that? We just jugged him last night."

"Because Pa talked to Sloan and some other men this morning about chore time. They were riding for the high country. They told Pa about it."

"The high country?" Arty said, his stomach tightening into a ball. "Why? After Jase?"

"Pa didn't tell me. Maybe they didn't tell him."

"What else would they be doing up there this time of the year? The cattle come down into the valley after the first big snow." He reached around her, caught the door latch, and lifted it. She went out first.

When they were back inside, Arty didn't bother to take off his coat. He held his hat in both hands and said in a low voice: "Sarah, fix me a bundle of meat or something, will you?"

"Why? Are you going to trail them?"

He nodded without speaking. Voices from the parlor came mutedly to him.

She touched his face. Her fingers were ice cold. The fire was out of her voice. "Arty, for me, just one favor."

"What?"

"Take the lawman with you."

Seeing a quick splash of dark color come into his cheeks, she hurried on in a low, insistent way: "He's the law. He could stop them from killing Jase, from hanging him, maybe. Listen to me. There'd be two of you then, not just one, and you'd have the law along."

"After Jase!"

She shook her head. "No! To stop them from murdering him, hiding his body in a snowbank. Arty, please. Those men know the mountains as well as you do. They've got half a day's start on you. The lawman by himself wouldn't get to the first ridge before they'd see him. He could flounder around in those hills for a year and never find Sloan or Jase. We both know that."

"And after we found Jase, he'd arrest him for murder."

"At least he'd have a fair trial, Arty. The other way he'll get hung to a tree . . . no trial at all. Maybe a bullet in the back."

"I can do it by myself," Arty said. He turned away from her, got as far as the back door before she caught him. He shook her off and went outside.

She was rigid in the opening, made as though to follow, but a quiet voice behind her said: "Never mind, miss."

She turned. The big marshal was looking intently at her. Her father was behind him, half shadowed by the larger man's shape. "He's going."

"Yeah, I know. Your pa told me about those men riding through this morning." The intent eyes crinkled in calm humor. "You told him about them out in the chicken house, didn't you?"

"Yes."

"That's what I figured. Well, he's not going anywhere, ma'am."

Arty appeared abruptly in the barn door with his hat riding far back on his head, his coat open, and his face dark with anger. "Darn you, lawman, take the chain off this horse!"

Meaghan edged past Sarah. Her father walked closer to her. Together they watched the lean man cross through the packed snow to the barn door. His voice was as clear as a bell when he spoke.

"Figured you'd want to skip away, Arty. Borrowed Lance's log chain and a couple of locks. Didn't want you riding off on your horse or mine."

"Take that chain off!"

"Sure." The deputy went into the shadowy barn. Arty shot Sarah and her father a short glance and followed. The marshal removed the heavy chain from his own horse's neck first, let it drop, fingered the latigo, snugged it up a little, and leaned across the leather, gazing at Arty.

"Well?"

"Well, what? Take that chain off my horse."

"Glad to, kid. All I ask is one thing . . . your word you'll lead me after those men who're out to drygulch or lynch your brother."

Arty's breath came in spurts. Its steam almost jetted past his distended nostrils. He crooked the fingers of his right hand.

"I wouldn't make that mistake if I were you," Meaghan said, without smiling. "I got one pointed right at you, kid, from this side of my horse." He drew in a big breath, let it out slowly. "Why," he said plaintively, "don't you grow up, get some sense? Every cussed minute we stand here, this Ted Sloan and his pardners are getting that much closer to your brother. I don't need to tell you what they'll do to him if we aren't there to stop it."

"I'm going alone."

"No you're not. We're going together, and you're going to

give me your word you won't run off . . . that you'll lead me where the trouble is . . . or neither one of us goes."

Arty swore thinly. "Trying to make me a treacherous snake an' lead the law to Jase. That's all you want."

"No it isn't. I want your brother, sure, but more'n that I want to keep a lot of fools from getting into the same boat he's already in by takin' the law into their own hands. Remember what I told you one time about gunfights. Well, it applies in this case, too. Those cowmen'll be outlawed for all time if they do what they're out to do. I'll have six men to hunt down, instead of one." Meaghan came out from behind his horse. He had no gun in his hand. He went to a sawhorse and leaned against it, looking at Arty. "Come on, kid . . . you got no choice. The longer you stall, the less chance we've got together. Your word. . . ."

"Arty. . . ."

He turned, saw Sarah framed in the opening. Beyond her stood John Lance.

"If we mean anything to you . . . give him your word."

Arty drew himself up. He wanted to swear, to stamp his feet, to use his gun. He let his breath out slowly, instead. Meaghan was right about one thing: the longer they stood in the barn arguing. . . .

"All right, Deputy, you got it."

"You'll stay with me, not try any monkey business like getting the drop on me, and you'll lead me where those men are going?"

"I said all right."

Meaghan handed John Lance the other key. Without a sound Sarah's father unsnapped the lock, removed the chain from around the neck of Arty's horse. He didn't meet the youth's wrathful gaze, but moved back with Sarah and remained silent as the two men mounted, moved out into the yard.

Sarah walked a little way after them. "Arty?"

He drew up, half turned.

She held up a heavy bundle wrapped in a large gingham cloth. "The food . . . for both of you." Closer, she put a hand on his leg, looked into his face. "Would you, Arty? It's all right. Would you?"

He stared at her. Meaghan cleared his throat. John Lance had his back to them over by the barn. Her fingers closed a little upon his flesh. He bent low, brushed his lips over hers, and straightened up in the saddle.

They rode in a northerly way until the Lance cabin was lost behind, then Arty swung west, and ahead was the purple, snow-crowned lift of mountains.

He had no idea where Jason's hide-out was but it didn't worry him. He and Jase had camped at a dozen spots when gathering cattle early. He knew his brother wouldn't be far from one of them.

Mike Meaghan rode in silence, his eyes fixed upon the great forested slopes ahead that seemed to rise in tiers, each furred with trees. Finally, when dusk was lowering, early and cold, he twisted a cigarette, lit it, and watched the way the smoke hung suspended in the deathly still air.

"Any line cabins or anything like that up in here, Arty . . . trappers' shacks or the like?"

"First off," Arty said curtly, "you can quit calling me Arty. I been called that since I was a baby. It doesn't fit any more."

"All right," Meaghan agreed pleasantly.

"And second, yes . . . there's a few lean-tos my paw and brother and me built up in here against nighting out."

"You expect he'll be by one of those?"

"I don't know where he'll be."

"You didn't ask him last night?"

"Not last night or any other time."

"I expect you wouldn't tell me what he said last night. . . ."

"That's right, I wouldn't."

"We better look for a place to camp," Meaghan said. "Any south-slope meadows in this country?"

"Don't worry. We're heading for a place with horse feed in it."

They rode into the forest and found the footing much better. Pine needles were thick, spongy, but the trees themselves kept most of the snow from reaching the ground. Arty led the way. Meaghan noted the general direction, and when they came to a thin ledge, broke over it and began a steep ascent into a small park. He sought for, and found, enough landmarks to aid him later, should the need arise to relocate the hidden valley.

Arty reined into the fringe of trees, drew up, and bobbed his head forward. "There, that's one of our lean-tos."

The thing was made of pine limbs, pieces of deadfall. It had been cleverly thatched with needles. Inside, to Meaghan's surprise, the ground was perfectly dry. The lean-to faced southward, away from the direction of the wind. He watched Arty drag his blanket and saddle inside, hobble his horse, and begin gathering faggots. He half smiled as he, too, made preparations for the night. The horses grazed away from the trees, and by the time Arty had a little fire going squarely in front of the lean-to, Meaghan was laying out Sarah's food. He whistled.

"Man, if I was a hundred years younger, I'd run you a foot race for that girl, Art. Look here . . . roast beef, a cooked chicken, even a packet she went and made up of coffee. Bless her pretty soul."

"How old are you, anyway?" Arty asked quite suddenly.

Meaghan looked over at him. "Thirty-five. Why do you ask?"

"Oh, I thought you were younger. Maybe twenty-five or thereabouts."

"What's the difference?" Meaghan said. "I get around pretty actively for an old man."

"Well, you're always calling me kid. I thought if you were only a little. . . ."

"Shucks, Art, I didn't mean anything by it. Most folks call you young fellers kid." Meaghan sliced a big piece of meat off the roast with his boot knife, held it out, and Arty took it. "I won't do that any more."

They ate in almost total silence. Once, when wolves howled and their horses snorted, rattled the chains of their hobbles, Arty swore. There was more feeling in the profanity than Meaghan thought the occasion demanded. He studied the younger man's face across the fire.

"What's wrong?"

"Nothing."

"Want me to guess, Art?"

"Can if you want to. I can't stop you."

"Well, then I'd guess you were thinking, if those wolves howl this close, we're alone. Neither your brother nor Sloan's crowd are anywhere around. Right?"

"Right."

"Finished eating?"

"Yeah."

Meaghan got up with the bundle. "Best cache this back of the lean-to then, or some marauder'll clean it out for us tonight."

Arty looked up. "Put it on top the lean-to," he said. "There's more than a few porcupines up here. They'll root out any cache on the ground and climb right over sleeping men to get to them."

Meaghan put the bundle overhead, dropped down, and made a smoke. "Art, you expect we'll ever be friends?"

The suddenness of it startled the younger man. He was slow in answering. "What's the difference whether we are or not?"

"I reckon the most important reason right now is that, if we run into trouble, I'd rather have you as a friend than not. In other words, an outlaw's brother behind me in a showdown gunfight isn't exactly what I look forward to, especially if the outlaw's out in front of me."

"If that happened," Arty said bitterly, "you'd have a little time to pray, but not much."

Meaghan nodded his head fatalistically. "Still stickin' to that old saying about blood being thicker'n water, aren't you?"

"That's the way I was raised."

"Yeah, most of us were, ki- . . . Art. In most cases it's right, too, but not where the law's concerned."

"Rope it, will you? You're the preachingest feller I ever run across."

"Don't mean to be, exactly, only I sure don't want to see you wind up behind the gun."

"Now tell me my brother had no right to kill my paw's murderers."

"Sure, I'll tell you that. I'll tell you something else. When any man, even the President, takes the law into his own hands, he's walkin' smack dab into a pot load of trouble. What's the sense of having laws if everyone operates according to their own lights? Now there's something else . . . if your brother can prove he didn't kill those men in cold blood, he's got a chance. Not much of one, but still a chance. But, and it's a big but, Art, if he goes up against me when I go to take him, that's resistin' arrest . . . a felony."

Arty got up without speaking, went to his saddle blanket, kicked his saddle into position to serve as a pillow, put his feet toward the fire, and settled down. The shadows danced eerily across the lean-to's thatched roof. He wriggled to get comfortable, pushed his belt gun away from his body, and stared upward.

The wolves howled again, closer. He saw Meaghan's shadow

unwind off the ground, grow taller and taller against the fire. He refused to look until the deputy marshal bent, pulled loose his carbine, and walked out into the night. Then he raised his head and watched him, unaware that the fire made his face look indescribably evil with shadows below his cheek bones, in the deep-set sockets where his eyes were, and down around his mouth.

He was still awake when Meaghan came back, glanced down at him, saw his eyes fixed upon the ceiling, and heard him grunt as he sat down again.

"Sure bold wolves you got up here. Came right out into the open near the horses."

"Why didn't you shoot one?"

"And tell the world we're here?"

"If the world's interested," Arty said, "it can smell our fire for a mile off."

"Not if it's sitting by a fire of its own, it can't." Meaghan leaned the carbine near his blanket and saddle, stretched out, and cushioned his head on the leather of his saddle. "Ever have any Indians back in these hills?"

"There are some. It's been years since they were trouble-some, though. Just run off a few cattle now and then, maybe some horses. They've got to eat, too."

"What kind?"

"Utes, now and then a Sioux, some 'Rapahoes, maybe a Cheyenne or two. Lot of mixed bloods."

"Like in Texas," Meaghan said drowsily, and Arty's mind jerked awake.

"You from Texas?"

"Sort of. Been away from there a long time, about fifteen years."

"We were from there originally."

"That so. What part?"

"Port Arthur country."

"I've been there," the deputy marshal said, turning up on his side. "Well, I expect that settles my biggest worry then."

"What do you mean?"

"No Texican ever shot another Texican in the back."

Arty listened to the steady breathing. For a long time sleep eluded him. His chest itched. He scratched it, felt the ugly ridges of scar flesh there, the few remaining scabs. Maybe one Texan never shot another in the back, but there wasn't any assurance it couldn't happen.

Dawn came with its heavy grayness, but, by the time they had the little fire going again, the sun burst through. Meaghan brought in the horses while Arty broke camp, laid out some food, and got ready to leave. The deputy was whistling. The sound was fluted up through the towering trees; it had a wistful sweetness to it. The song was one sung by both sides in the recent Civil War, "Lorena."

Without speaking, Arty saddled, up, waited until Mike had eaten, stowed his carbine in the boot, and swung up. They rode across the little meadow and along a game trail that appeared suddenly among the foremost sentinels of the forest. Somewhere up ahead a blue jay went into paroxysms of sound, warning that men were approaching.

After an hour's riding, Meaghan said: "No sign of riders in here, Art."

"Wouldn't be any, anyway. We're short-cutting. When we get past Blank Rock, we might cut some sign."

They went northerly for what seemed an interminable length of time to the marshal, then Arty swung abruptly westward. They angled along the side of a towering eminence, finally topped it, and Arty reined up. The wind was blowing gustily. It stung like glass splinters.

"This Blank Rock?"

Arty pointed downward. "See that big boulder down there, been split by lightning?"

Meaghan followed Arty's hand with his eyes, and nodded.

"That's Blank Rock. This side of it's sheered off clean . . . there's nothing on it. The other half's down in the cañon there about half a mile off. It's got Indian carving on it."

Meaghan swept the wild country for sign of movement. There wasn't any. He squirmed in his saddle, made a cigarette, and frowned. "You sure you know where they might be, Art?"

Arty didn't answer. He reined off the hilltop and went westerly as far as a steep slide where animals had passed for thousands of years, wearing a trail six inches deep into the living stone, packing the earth so hard it echoed harshly when ridden across. From the sheer edge of the hillside they could see hundreds of miles.

Meaghan, following, grunted. "I prefer flat country," he said. "Man's clothes'd be out of style before he hit bottom, here."

They wound around the sheer slope until the topsy-turvy world settled into a gentle roll of land, reached a twisting, tortured cañon where magnificent trees reached upward. There was a rushing creek down there, each wavelet foaming white and shiny.

Arty zigzagged until he found what he sought: another game trail winding through the sunshine among giant pines. He hadn't spoken in hours. Meaghan let his horse follow, admitting to himself he was hopelessly lost.

When the land began to rise under them, there was another trail bisecting the one they came up on. Arty didn't hesitate. He swung northward, kept traveling in that direction until the sun was slanting off the meridian, then he took another trail going due south. By then they had achieved considerable altitude again. The frozen upthrusts of mountains lay wave after wave until the horizon intervened. When Arty stopped, Meaghan sat there gazing around at the tremendous scope of a lost world. Silently he acknowledged that his wisest move so far had been to press Arthur Swift into being his guide. Without him, and against his brother Jason who also knew this country well, it would have taken him years to find the wanted man in this vast and trackless upland.

"Much farther, Art? I mean, until we cut sign?"

"Not much," Arty said cryptically. His manner had changed. He was wary, watchful, more silent, more taciturn than ever. From this Mike Meaghan drew comfort. They were closer than Arty would admit. He leaned far forward in his saddle, rested both arms upon the horn.

"Art, something I want to say before we get all involved up ahead."

"Shoot."

"No matter what happens, I'll do everything I can to help your brother."

Arty twisted his head, stared. "Why?"

Meaghan's gaze dropped away. "Oh, just call it gratitude if you've a mind to."

"All right, I'll call it that . . . now tell me the truth."

"You. I been battling like a preacher wrestling the devil to keep you from gettin' behind the gun, too. About the only way I see to make sure you don't turn wild is to make cussed sure your brother gets a fair shake."

Arty remained motionless for a moment, then, without speaking, he urged his horse out. Mike followed him. Arty hauled up, and Mike's horse almost bumped into him.

"There," Arty said, pointing to a well-worn cow trail.

Meaghan looked. Fresh shod-horse tracks lay in the cold earth. He followed their direction, raised his eyes, and looked ahead. The trail was an old and well marked one, perhaps twelve feet wide, free of pine needles and brush. "What is this, an old emigrant road?"

"No, cattle trail from the back country. I guess packers used to use it, too. I've heard they did, anyway."

"Pretty good trail, all right. They were going north. What's up there?"

"More of the same."

"I mean meadows, ranches, things like that. We don't want to ride into an ambush."

Arty quirked his bitter mouth into a smile. "Don't worry. I know this country better'n Sloan ever will."

"How about the men with him?" Meaghan asked dryly. "They all greenhorns, too? Look, Art, whenever we're nearing an opening you cut into the trees, understand?"

For an answer Arty reined out without speaking. Meaghan noticed, however, that for all his confidence, he loosened his pistol in its holster.

IV

The shadows were long on the east side of the big trees by the time Arty reined up at the edge of an oval clearing. Stumps showed through tall, tangled grass.

"Go around it," Meaghan said.

"Can't." Arty reined out into the open. Meaghan hesitated, then followed. It annoyed him the way Arty was acting, had acted before crossing the clearing. When they were on the far side, back once more in the shifting gloom of tree shadows, Meaghan stopped and called softly: "Art, why couldn't we go around that clearing?"

"Because there's buckbrush west and south. East is the big cliff."

"Well," Meaghan said, "any more big holes full of daylight, let's go through the brush."

"What you scairt of?"

"Not scairt of anything, but if those men're up ahead a short way, they might have scouts out. Folks do that, y'know."

Arty pushed on. The trail narrowed a little after several miles, and shod-horse tracks were closer, more lumped, and fresher-looking. Riding past a skirted park, Arty lifted his arm and pointed without speaking. Meaghan saw it, another little lean-to shelter such as they'd spent the night in.

"Another of your huts?"

"Yes."

After that Arty rode more often with his eyes on the tracks than upon the country about. Finally he stopped altogether and swung down.

Meaghan dismounted behind him, strode forward. "What do you see?"

"Here . . . their tracks. One split off, went up into the trees." Arty's gaze probed the dark forest. "Someone among them's been in here before, knows the country pretty well."

"Why? How do you know?"

The blue eyes came fully around. "The cabin my paw and brother built lies about half a mile ahead. It's not a lean-to. We always kept it stocked with flour and the like, in case we got caught out in the fall, late."

"I see. So you think someone knew about it, and now they're along with Sloan, maybe guiding him."

"Yes. But more'n that. With that kind of savvy they might creep up on Jase, if he's at the cabin."

"You think he is?"

Arty nodded without speaking, straightened up, and gazed steadily at the lawman.

"Then let's go."

"It's too quiet," Arty said.

Meaghan cocked his head a little. "Yeah, it is sort of quiet."

"We'd better split up here, too. You keep going north on the trail. I'm going up into the trees, circle around, and come down behind the cabin."

Arty was mounting when Meaghan said: "Art?"

"Yes."

"Among us Texicans a man's word's his bond."

Arty swung up, settled into the saddle. "Don't worry," he said, and rode off the trail, disappearing among the trees.

Meaghan mounted and rode slowly ahead. There was an eerie hush over everything, no blue jays, no scurrying squirrels—no movement. He sniffed the air, kept his eyes moving, and from time to time counted the tracks. Quite suddenly, rounding a bend, he saw where another man had left the original party of six. This time the rider had gone down an angling game trail southward. Four horsemen had kept on going toward whatever lay up ahead. Meaghan had a feeling that they were too late.

Looking upward, he saw where the treetops thinned out, revealing the turquoise sky. That meant another opening up ahead. He leaned, tugged out his carbine, and lay it across his lap.

When the clearing showed through the trees, he stopped, still deep in mottled shadows, and studied it. The cabin was weathered, disguised by the growth around it. It faced the clearing but its rear was in the forest. He shook his head at that tactical mistake and dismounted, led his horse behind him, and went forward with caution.

Where the horse tracks stopped, he paused. Droppings indicated how long the men had stayed back in the trees. Evidently they had waited for something. It wasn't hard to figure out what, for the grass out in the little park was well trampled. They had sat back waiting for the owner of the horse that had been grazing there to emerge from the cabin.

He tied his horse back out of sight and went forward afoot. While he was standing beside an immense pine, motionless, listening, studying the park, cabin, surrounding area, a gunshot burst into the silence, shattering it. He drew erect, brought the carbine up, and held it in both hands.

A muffled shout came next, then several calls that echoed faintly among the trees, and another gunshot, Arty must have come across something back behind the cabin somewhere. He started to move forward, caught a glimpse of flashing movement, and froze.

A horseman burst out of the trees with his pistol held high, head twisted over his shoulder. He was spurring directly toward the trail Mike Meaghan was standing beside.

A second rider came out of the trees, but more to the north. He rode only halfway across the little park, then reined up, drew his hand gun, and shouted angrily at the first rider. The fleeing man slid his horse to a dirt-spewing halt.

"It's that kid," the second man said sharply. "Maybe there's more . . . let's get out of here. We done what we come for anyway."

"Wait," the second rider said. "We got a chance to end the tribe of 'em right here."

"No. . . ."

"Got to, you fool. The kid can identify some of us."

The first rider was obviously struck with the logic of that reasoning. He turned his horse, walked it back toward the second rider, handgun trained upon the forest. "Where're the others?" he asked in a quick, nervous way.

"They scattered when he fired. Come on, let's get over toward the trees. We're sittin' ducks out here."

They approached the place where Mike Meaghan stood. He faded deeper into the shadows, held his carbine low and pointed. His right thumb curled around the hammer, snugged it back.

When the men were close to the fringe of trees, two more

riders came jogging out of the trees across the park, saw their friends, and called out softly. The four of them clustered together not fifty feet from Meaghan. The second man who burst out of the forest was obviously the leader. He explained why they should kill Arthur Swift. The others agreed, but there was considerable nervousness among them.

"Couple of us got to stay here by the trail. He'll more'n likely go back this way. We'll pick him off soon as he rides out into the open." The leader jutted a gloved hand at two of the men. "You two go out around him, see, and close in where Jase is. That's where he'll be by now. As soon as you see him . . . shoot."

Two riders broke away. They rode slowly, and Mike watched the nearest one with his heart in his throat, but the stranger was peering intently into the forest ahead.

Mike's mind conjured fact from what he'd heard. His earlier feeling, that he and Arty had arrived too late, was confirmed. Jason Swift had been caught off guard, was back there behind the cabin somewhere. By now Arty had probably found him. At any rate Arty had seen at least one of his brother's assassins and had fired at the man. He was still back there somewhere. Two others of Sloan's crew were stalking him.

Mike stepped out into a little opening where sunshine lay and shouldered the cocked carbine. His voice carried only as far as he wanted it to, and there was a world of menace in it. "Freeze, you two. Watch it! That's better. Now turn toward the east and put your hands on top of your heads. Good. Now lock your fingers." He moved down toward them.

Their horses threw him startled glances, pointed their ears forward, and moved a little, uneasily. He disarmed both men, removed carbines from their saddle boots, cast the hardware far out into the brush that lay down the east slope, and was turning to facc them when two simultaneous gunshots shivered the stillness with echoes. A third shot came moments later. Each of them understood its meaning, stood poised with expectancy, and Meaghan decided he didn't have time to tie his prisoners, when an unfamiliar voice called out in a muted, excited way.

He was moving around behind the men, had uncocked the carbine, and was hefting his pistol, swinging it high, when the shot came, close and thunderous. Its breath upon his cheek was cold. He swung away and dropped, snapped a shot in the direction of the unseen gunman, and rolled.

His captives had disappeared over the slope where Meaghan had thrown their guns. The killer's second shot blew pine-scented mud into his face. He rolled again, frantically trying to reach a gray deadfall. There was no sign of his assailant back among the trees.

When he was almost to the deadfall, a third shot came. That one spun him half around upon the near-frozen ground, and he felt blood gushing under his clothing somewhere, but, strangely, there was no sense of pain, only numbness.

Two voices yelled encouragement off to his right. He knew the unarmed men were down there hunting frenziedly for their guns. They had seen their man score a hit.

From behind the punky old deadfall Meaghan blocked in squares of forest, striving to find his enemy. When he saw a diaphanous gray sift of gunsmoke hanging close to a lightning-split, dying pine, he rested his gun upon the deadfall and fired. Bark flew, a wisp of startled movement snagged his eye. He cocked his gun and waited.

The searchers off to one side and below him were making a racket interspersed with sizzling, excited profanity, seeking their firearms.

The stalemate lasted two full minutes. Mike saw the faint movement then, only because the sunlight reflected off metal. The gunman was lying prone now, pushing his gun hand out from behind the tree by inches. Mike waited, bit his lip straining to see more than the hand. When an inch of shoulder showed, he fired. The man let out a wild yell, rolled completely over, and lay fully exposed. Throwing up his gun, he fired twice at the deadfall. Mike ignored the stinging particles of dead wood, aimed carefully, and fired. The stranger didn't move; his head sank down and rested upon the ground. His fingers opened and closed, opened and closed; the warm pistol lay upon its side in the dirt and pine needles.

Silence descended again, deeper than ever. The men down the east slope ceased their racket. Mike rolled on his side looking for them, afraid they had found at least one of their guns. He understood that they hadn't when he called to them, ordered them to come out into the open and surrender. The sounds of men crashing through brush, past snagging limbs in a hurrying way, going southward, reassured him.

When he propped himself up against the dead tree, put his gun handily close, and looked down where the stickiness was, he heard boot steps coming. Feeling a little faint, he picked up the pistol and waited.

Arty came out of the forest without his horse. He was dangling a cocked pistol from one hand. His face was deathly white, his mouth ajar, his blue eyes darker by shades than they had ever been before. Without speaking, he went around behind the deadfall and looked down at Meaghan.

"Bad?"

Meaghan didn't answer. He unbuttoned his shirt and felt for the injury through his woolen underwear. Probing, he was struck by the unique absence of pain.

Arty knelt, holstered his gun. "Here, let me see." After a moment he wiped Meaghan's blood upon his trousers, spoke without looking away from the exposed wound. "You got to be taken back."

Meaghan quirked a smile. "Sooner or later," he said. "There's one lying over by that split tree. He shot me and I shot him."

"Yeah, I came by him. You got the best of the trade. He's dead."

"Know him, Art?"

An abrupt nod. "Yes, I know him . . . Jack Balester's cousin from over by Cheyenne."

"Was he one of those that hided you?"

Another nod. "Yes."

Meaghan peered at his wound. The bleeding was diminishing; at last he could see the ragged gap in his flesh. It was below his ribs and to the left. As he looked, the numbness began to wear off and pain came in its place.

"You've got to be bandaged," Arty said in the same dull way.

They made the bandage together, and by the time Meaghan had his soggy shirt on again, pain was pulsating with each beat of his heart. Arty got up, dusted mud and pine needles off his pants. "You want to see my brother?" he asked.

Meaghan craned his neck. The look on Swift's face was enough. He'd known anyway. "I reckon not. Not right now anyway."

But Arty wouldn't let it go at that. "You rode a long way to see him, Deputy. Remember, you're goin' to miss Thanksgiving because of him. I'll help you."

Arty's leanness concealed a formidable, unsuspected physical strength. He hooked Meaghan under the arms and lifted. "It isn't far," he said, and kept a tight hold on the wounded man.

They crossed the little park, got to the cabin, and there Mike began to shake his head. "Got a mind full of cobwebs," he said.

Arty let him rest and went after their horses. He returned with their own animals and two others, both saddled, bridled, and with broken reins. He stood in front of the deputy marshal with the same impersonal, brooding expression.

"Come on, it's not far from here."

Meaghan sagged as he struggled to keep up with Arty's heavy tread. The outlaw's brother kept one arm around his waist, and with the other hand he held strongly to Meaghan's arm which was across his shoulders. It was like that when they came to the tiny glade and Mike Meaghan saw the man he'd been after.

Jason Swift was hanging from a straining tree limb. His booted feet didn't miss touching the ground by more than half a foot. He was motionless, his head hung far forward, his hat was gone, and his hair hung in shocks down across his forehead. He was dead, had been dead for some time, from appearances.

"There," Arty said, propping Meaghan against a tree. "Get a good look, Deputy . . . you went to a lot of trouble to see him. Get a good long look."

Meaghan studied the dead man for a moment, then switched his attention to the remaining Swift. "Cut it out, kid," he said. "This isn't helping anyone."

"You wanted him."

"Yeah. Sure I wanted him. Do you think I'd have allowed this to happen if we'd have gotten here first? You know better, Art. Cut him down."

Arty remained standing like stone, gazing with an ill look upon his brother.

"Cut him down, Art."

Without looking away from the lynched man, Arty said: "You've seen enough, have you?"

Meaghan didn't answer, and Arty cut the rope, eased his brother down upon the ground, straightened his arms and legs, and knelt with one clenched fist resting upon the dead man's chest. He spoke without looking away from Jason's set, gray face.

"Did you see the bullet holes, Deputy?"

"I saw them."

"Notice where they were?"

"Yes, in the back. Now go get the horses and let's get him moved down by the cabin."

Arty turned, gazed at the lawman. "Sure," he said, stood up, and stalked through the trees, leaving Meaghan gazing at Jason Swift.

Arty came back, leading two horses. He had fashioned a rude carrier between the horses. They didn't fight it at all, which was unusual. He stopped close to Meaghan. "I'll help you into this thing," he said, lifting Meaghan by the armpits.

"Naw. Just lend me a hand, I can walk it. Put your brother in there."

Arty stood still, gazing at the deputy marshal, then he turned abruptly, stooped, hefted Jase, and put him upon the carrier. He led the horses with one hand and supported Meaghan with the other arm.

They got to the cabin as night was descending. Mike used both arms to get inside. He dropped down at a rough table, lit the lamp, and listened to the younger man working with the horses outside. There was food on a sideboard, but he couldn't have walked that far, and remained standing, if his life had depended upon it.

When Arty finally came in, the gloom was gathering swiftly beyond the lantern's warm glow. He shucked his hat and coat, built a fire in the stone fireplace, arranged some rocks to support a black coffee pot, and went to the bench opposite Mike.

"You hungry, Deputy?"

"No, and quit calling me Deputy. My name's Mike."

Arty appeared not to have heard.

"Where's the one you got, Art?"

The blue eyes lifted. There was a long pause. "Beyond where Jase was. Back in the trees. I saw him moving when I came down toward the cabin. He made a run for a carbine leaning against a tree. I shot him."

"After that one shot . . . a little while after . . . there were some more shots."

"Yeah, another one came pelting out of the trees. We saw each other about the same time. He missed me and I missed him." Arty stirred on the bench. "That other one . . . he was still moving. I finished him."

"Before or after you saw your brother?"

"After."

Meaghan felt for his tobacco sack and papers, began to twist up a cigarette. The room warmed. A scent of coffee rose and Arty went over to the sideboard, picked up two tin cups, filled them, and returned to the table. Mike sipped his, felt warmth and strength flow through his body. He set it down and inhaled the cigarette.

"Where'd you put him, Art?"

"On the porch."

Meaghan drank more coffee. "Did you see this Ted Sloan?"

"No."

"Maybe I did. Is he a sort of sandy-headed feller with a hooked nose, long neck, talks like he's got rust in his throat, rides a ewe-necked Grulla horse?"

"Yes. Taller'n you or me, and thin."

"That's the one did the talking when I jumped them."

"He get away?"

"Yeah. I had 'em disarmed when this other one . . . I think it was the one Sloan'd sent into the woods after you . . . came back. This Sloan and another feller jumped down the slope when the fight started. They were unarmed. Later, I tried to bait them back to surrender . . . they took off afoot southward."

"Four to go," Arty said.

Meaghan watched his face, said nothing, smoked, and drank coffee until the cigarette was used up, the coffee gone, then used both arms to push himself upright. "Help me to that bunk, Art."

When he fell asleep, Arty was still sitting at the table with an empty tin cup in front of him, looking at the fire.

The pain Meaghan hadn't felt the evening before was unrelenting the following morning. He tried several times to get out of the bunk and couldn't. Arty came to the bunk several times, stood there looking down in silence; each time Meaghan apologized for delaying their departure. Inwardly he swore fiercely.

Arty spent the day gathering firewood, studying the sky, making little forays through the forest on horseback just in case, and by evening had inventoried the food, and found that Jase had been amply provided. Mike was fairly hungry that first night, but the next morning he was ravenous. He ate all Arty prepared and asked for more. He got it and ate that, too. Then he made a cigarette and tried to stand up. He was wobbly, weak, and shaking, but he made it, grinning triumphantly at Arty.

"Saddle 'em up, boy . . . I can make it."

But Arty shook his head, guided Mike back to the bunk with a firm hand, and said: "We can't catch them now anyway. Might as well rest another day or so."

Mike rested. There was nothing else for him to do. After five days, though, he was fairly strong again. He was, in fact, cooking supper when Arty came in with a big armload of firewood.

"We can cut and run tomorrow, Art."

Arty dumped the wood, straightened up, and shook his head. "Too late," he said.

Meaghan frowned. "Shake that, will you? We'll get 'em."

"I didn't mean them . . . I meant it's going to storm."

Mike went to the door, looked out, walked beyond the cabin, and sniffed the air. On his way back he saw the still, swathed bundle in the dark shadows of the porch. Arty had sewed his brother into his bedroll. Mike entered the cabin, still frowning.

"Maybe it will . . . smells like it all right. Just the same let's chance it, come morning, if it isn't snowing. What say?"

"All right," Arty replied, sitting down to eat.

The morning came and it hadn't snowed. Mike helped Arty put Jase across a horse, tie him securely. He handed the lead rope up when Arty was mounted and experienced a spell of dizziness when he got astride, and poked his mount out behind the younger man. To dispel it, he smoked. It didn't help the dizziness, but it kept his mind and hands occupied.

They bedded down at the same lean-to where they'd spent their first night out, and the following day were back down in open country. When Mike swung north toward the Lances, Arty let their paths separate in silence. Mike went after him.

"Where you going?"

"To bury Jase."

Mike rode with him. He couldn't help him dig, but he fed the gaunt cattle, built a little fire in the Swift cabin, cared for the horses, and made it a point to be out of earshot when Arty said a clumsy prayer over the second grave behind the paling fence.

Mike was resaddling the horses when Arty appeared in the barn's doorway. "Ready to go?" he asked. Arty leaned on the sill, looking squarely at the deputy marshal.

"Go where?"

"First, to the Lances. Tell them what happened."

"Why? It's none of their business."

Mike's face hardened. "Isn't it? That girl eating her heart out, wondering whether you're alive or dead. The old man's probably wearin' the hide off his knees praying for you. Don't act so tough, Art . . . get some sense."

"All right. I didn't think of those things. Then what?"

"Then we're goin' to Chiloquin. I've got a wire to send . . . then Sheriff Whitney's got a posse to round up."

Arty nodded, accepted the reins of his horse from Meaghan, led the animal out into the yard, and mounted. Waiting for the marshal, looking at the eating cattle, his gaze clouded, and his brows drew down in perplexity. "Wonder how those critters came back here? They're the ones we left at Cuneos."

Mike swung his animal in among the cattle, saw several calves with the Cuneo brands upon them, shrugged, and started past the cabin. "Maybe they got turned out and drifted back. They would, wouldn't they?"

"Yeah, I guess so."

They rode to the Lance place with dusk around them. There was a long path of orange lamplight lying in the snow before the cabin. Arty held out his hand for Mike's reins. "I'll put 'em up," he said.

Mike knocked stoutly, entered with a shallow grin, and saw Sarah's erectness. John Lance stood still, waiting. Upon both their faces was a stillness, a dread. Mike pocketed his gloves, took off his hat and coat, dropped them in a corner, and went slowly toward the stove, turned his back to it.

"Arty's out putting the horses up."

Sarah turned swiftly, disappeared into the kitchen. She neglected to take the heavy sweater. She went out through the rear door and left it ajar, fled across the crunching snow with Arty's name coming from deep inside her.

He appeared in the murky gloom of the barn's opening, and she struck him so unexpectedly he staggered.

"Arty . . . Arty!" She clung to him, said his name, and repeated it incessantly, and kissed him.

"They killed Jase, Sarah."

"Jason . . . ?"

"Shot him, and, while he was dying, they hung him. Shot

him in the back, then. . . ." He dropped his arms, stood before her tall and slightly bent, bigger in the sheepskin coat. "The lawman killed Balester's cousin from Cheyenne . . . that blond-headed feller used to visit Jack. I got another one."

She said nothing. There was nothing to say. The cold went into her, deep. There was no warmth to offset it.

"We brought Jase back and buried him with Paw."

"Come inside, Arty. I'll make supper . . . some coffee."

He didn't move until she touched his arm, tugged at it a little, insistently, then he went with her, moving heavily.

He ate very little, drank some coffee, and wouldn't be drawn into stilted conversation. Finally he left them, went out to the barn, took his saddle blanket up into the hay, burrowed deeply, and slept.

But Mike Meaghan told them everything, and their lamp burned late. He let Sarah examine his wound, redress it with a salt poultice made into a bandage, smoked and drank coffee while answering questions.

Finally John Lance said: "It's hit the boy hard, Mike. He's like a stranger."

Mike looked in a troubled way at the wall. "You know," he said softly, "I thought it would work out with me taking his brother. Since it didn't, I'll never know what the kid would have done. If I knew how he'd have reacted to that, I could tell you how he's going to turn out now." He lowered his glance. "Know what I mean?"

John Lance nodded.

Sarah said: "But it's still so fresh and raw, Mister Meaghan. He'll need time. There's so much confusion, so much hatred in him."

"I don't know about the confusion," Mike said dryly, "but I know about the hatred, and that's what bothers me. Y'see, if he runs across this Sloan, he won't wait for Sloan to go for a gun.

His brother didn't wait . . . the kid won't wait. I know the breed, miss. I know why Texicans turn bad so easy. It's in them. They're a fierce breed."

"They need the Lord," John Lance said.

Mike stopped speaking, looked straight at Lance with his lips still parted, then closed them and shrugged. "Maybe. I'm not going to argue religion with you or anyone else, Mister Lance. All I got to say is that all I know about history . . . it's always been that way. Where the law's not strong, men use the older law of survival, an eye for an eye an' a tooth for a tooth. That's the way it is in Colorado right now. It'll change. Texas changed . . . all the rest of the frontier is changing. So the problem we got right now is to keep that Texican kid from committing murder. A few years from now there won't be a chance for things to happen here like happened to his father and brother. We've got to keep him from the gun just a little longer . . . then time'll take care of the rest. You see what I mean?"

"I see," John Lance said.

Sarah said: "How? He won't stay here. If he goes with you. . . ."

"I aim to take him with me, miss. Keep him right beside me. That way I'll know where he is. That way he can't run off half-cocked, hunt up these lynchers, and murder them." Mike drained his last cup of coffee, and grinned over the edge of it at Sarah. "I'm working harder to keep this kid from becoming an outlaw than I am at catching real outlaws."

"It's more important, isn't it," Sarah said, "to keep one from turning bad?"

Mike nodded. "I think so. I've always thought so. Enough folks keeping enough kids from going behind the gun'd sure make life a whole lot simpler for men like me."

John Lance stood up. "I'll ride over to the Swift place in the morning and read a prayer over Jason."

Mike thanked Lance and let Sarah lead him to the spare lean-to bedroom. After he'd closed the door, he stood a long while in silence, smoked a cigarette until the house was quiet, then slipped out a window, crept to the barn, and peered in. Both horses were there. He went back to the house and to bed.

Sarah rang the breakfast triangle earlier than she was accustomed to ringing it. She had worked hard, by lamplight, to make a hearty breakfast. Her face was red from the stove's heat when Arty came through the rear door. He had washed in snow water. His lips were bluish, his cheeks apple-red, his eyes sparkling. She went to the door and stood on tiptoe, kissed him, and settled back down, threw out an arm as though dismissing him.

"Pa's already at the table."

Arty checked his advance toward the doorway. "Where's the lawman?"

"He hasn't come in yet."

Arty stared hard at her for a moment, then rushed through the room, caught the lean-to door, and flung it open. Mike Meaghan looked around at him.

"What's got into you now, Art?"

Arty flushed darkly. "Nothing. Excuse me."

"You thought I'd slipped away without you, didn't you?"

"Never mind. Breakfast's ready."

Meaghan turned his back upon the door and went on washing.

After they had eaten, they left the Lance place, rode out of the yard with the smell of snow in their faces. Once Mike twisted, saw Sarah waving a shawl, and spoke to Arty.

"Wave to her. She'll catch her death of croup standing out there in the cold."

Arty turned, waved, dropped his arm, and swerved closer to

the deputy marshal. "You tell them all about it?"

"Yes."

"The old man disgusted?"

"Why should he be disgusted?" Mike said with asperity. "He was saddened . . . said he'd ride over and give your brother a prayerful send-off this morning. That doesn't sound like disgust to me. What's wrong with you . . . I mean, more wrong than usual? You've been acting like a bear with a sore since the last time we were at the Lances."

Arty let his horse drop back a little. He didn't look sullen but rather secretively cold, withdrawn, deadly. His silence seemed to aggravate Meaghan. The deputy marshal turned in his saddle.

"You don't want me to call you kid or Arty . . . kid's names. Then act like a man."

The cold blue eyes came up with an icy glow in them. "I'm a man all right. You'll see."

Meaghan jerked his horse to a stop. "Get down," he said. Arty stopped but made no move to dismount. Meaghan slid out of his saddle and spread his legs. "I said get down, Art."

This time the younger man swung off. They weren't more than twelve feet apart.

"Let me see your gun."

Arty looked puzzled. "What for? You goin' to keep it?"

"No, you'll get it back. Hand it to me."

Arty handed the gun over reluctantly. Mike punched every slug out of it, reversed it, and handed it back. Under Arty's perplexed scowl he then unloaded his own weapon, holstered it, and smiled without humor.

"You think you're hell on wheels, Art. Well, I'm going to show you you're not. Go on . . . draw on me."

Arty lowered his head, peered beneath his eyebrows at the lawman. "You got a fever, Deputy?"

"I got no fever and I told you I got a name. Now go ahead

and draw, kid."

Arty studied the taller man. He finally shrugged and moved. He dropped his shoulders a fraction, his right arm making the blurring streak. With his fingers talon-like around the pistol butt, he froze. Meaghan's pistol was leveled at his belt buckle.

Arty licked chapped lips, relaxed, looked in an unbelieving way at the dark snout in front of him. Meaghan holstered his gun with a harsh smile. "Go ahead, kid . . . try it again."

Arty did, moving faster, dropping into a crouch before Meaghan was through speaking. His eyes were wide, his lips taut, and this time he had the gun two inches clear of leather when Meaghan's barrel was tilted back, pointing squarely at the middle of his chest.

"Want to go on doing this all day, Art?"

Arty let the gun slide back into its holster, rammed his hands into his coat pockets, and shook his head. "You're fast," he said tonelessly.

"And I'm no gunfighter, Art. I'm just an average feller."

Arty laughed. "I've seen plenty average men with guns . . . they couldn't get in your shadow."

Meaghan looked disgusted. "You've seen cowmen, riders, town toughs. You've never seen men who handle guns for their health's sake, Art. They're the average, not backwoodsmen like in Chiloquin and Ute Valley. That's part of the idea I'm tryin' to get across to you, but you're too stubborn to catch on. You murder a man, this Sloan for instance . . . and you'll have men like me, average gunmen, after you every day of your life. You beat a couple of us and get to running with real gun hawks, and you wouldn't last a month. All right . . . you've learnt that lesson, I hope. Now this other thing . . . quit goin' around like you're going to bite the world. Not waving at Sarah, stuff like that. I know your pa and brother got a raw deal. Well, you and I are out to set that to rights legally . . . so shake off this attitude of a gunman out for a kill. Start acting human for a change."

Arty waited until Mike had finished, then turned his back on the lawman, stuck his left toe into the stirrup, and sprang into the saddle. He sat there ignoring Mike and reloading his pistol.

Mike mounted and cast a last look backward, down the gray day, to where the Lance cabin and barn showed through the wintriness. He led the way out.

They had ridden about three hundred yards farther when Mike heard Arty suck in a gust of breath. He was turning when a flat gunshot smashed the silence. His horse gave a huge leap and collapsed when he came down. Mike was dazed by the fall. A terrible burst of pain made him cry out. Somewhere behind him he heard a carbine open up. It was difficult to get his breath. He struggled mightily, felt the wound in his side re-open and blood flow, but finally air came into him in larger drafts, clearing his head. He shook the snow out of his eyes and raised his head. The dead horse was half across him.

"Lie still, Mike. Quit wiggling. I'll get you out in a minute. They'll shoot at you if you keep moving. Lie still!"

Mike relaxed, lay back, and gasped. The pain was moving up through his body. It settled in his chest, and each breath was agony. He took small, shallow gulps of air.

Arty crawled through the snow to him. His face was white and set, his blue eyes dark with excitement. "I can't stand up to haul him off you yet, Mike. How bad is it?"

"Broken ribs, I think. What happened?"

"I saw them just before one of them let fly. Four of 'em coming toward the Lance place."

"Four . . . ?"

"Yeah. It's probably them all right. They'd figure they got to do this. With us dead, there'd be no witnesses to Jase's murder." Mike ground his teeth in silence. Arty was looking to the east, puckering up his eyes. A few lazy snowflakes came down.

"They're off their horses. One's minding the animals."

"Where are the others?"

"Creepin' up."

"Then for the Lord's sake haul this horse off me."

"I can't. If I stand up, I'll get it."

"Scairt?" Mike asked sharply.

Arty's eyes dropped to the gray lips, the tortured eyes. He shook his head. "Not scairt, Mike," he said quietly. "If I get it, where's that leave you?"

"Then get rid of 'em, Art. I can't stand this much longer."

Arty studied Meaghan's face briefly, rose to one knee, and fired twice. He laid the gun across Mike's arm, and rose to his full height, grasped the dead horse's tail, and sank his feet into the snow, straining. The carcass moved. He strained to the limit of his strength. A bullet sang close. The carcass began to slide, and with a final, gasping pull Arty swung the animal's rear quarters clear. Three rapid shots forced him to drop down. He twisted his head as he fell.

"You able to move, Mike?"

"Yeah. Thanks. Get my carbine out of the boot."

Arty got the gun, slithered behind the dead horse, and shoved it across to Meaghan. The deputy marshal pushed himself upright with a stifled sob and laid the gun upon the warm carcass. They both fired together. A single reply came back. The snow began to fall a little heavier, obscuring vision.

Arty touched Mike's sleeve. "We've got to get back to the Lances. There's only two out there, Mike. Others're probably slipping around behind us."

"Get your horse and help me up."

Arty got the animal, picked Mike up bodily, and was surprised to find him so heavy. Mike spread his legs, felt the wet saddle under him, and kicked the left stirrup out. Arty toed in, landed behind the cantle as Mike was turning the horse. Three tearing shots came close. One jetted snow underfoot. The horse gave a startled bound and lit running. Mike was hanging on with both hands, head bobbing crazily on his chest. Arty sat sidling, shooting.

They were almost to the cabin when a pistol roared in front of them. Arty swore and swung to face the new menace. Mike was slipping sideways. Arty grasped his belt and held him. The snow-shadowed riders ahead were fanning out. Orange flames showed fleetingly through the snow before the reports came. Arty fired three times as fast as he could at one rider, saw the horse flinch, thumbed for another shot, and found his gun empty. He dropped it and dug for Meaghan's pistol. He was raising it to fire when a thunderous blast exploded far ahead somewhere. Beside the man he was aiming at a gigantic mushroom of snow erupted. The attacker's horse gave a mighty shy sideways, the man's pistol went off skyward, and Arty drew a long bead and squeezed a shot off. The man went off his horse, backward, struck the snow with silent impact. His companion was nowhere in sight.

Arty craned his neck to see behind them. There were horsemen back there, but much too far off to be dangerous. They showed dimly as the snowfall became heavier.

Again the prodigious musket up ahead exploded, and this time Arty's panicked horse flinched. He was reaching around Mike for the reins when he saw the dim, short figure, and recognized John Lance.

V

The assassins did not follow them into the yard, but, in case they should, John Lance walked back out a way and stood there, short, thick, swathed in a thick horse-hide coat, and holding his buffalo rifle across his body. Arty got Mike Meaghan down from the saddle and lugged him inside. Sarah's face was ashen, her eyes large and dry-looking. Straightening up from the cot, Arty said: "Busted ribs . . . maybe more. His horse fell on him."

He went back outside, snagged the reins of his shaking horse, led him to the barn, and dropped the bar behind him in a tie stall. The hush of heavily falling snow pressed silence in upon him. It was as though the world ended completely just beyond the doorway.

Back inside the cabin, he removed his hat and coat. John Lance was swabbing dampness out of the burly rifle. He looked up but didn't speak when Arty returned.

"Know how to roll a cigarette, Art?"

Arty turned toward the cot. Mike's hat, coat, and shirt were lying in a soggy heap beside the cot. His underwear had been peeled back and a tight white girdle-like bandage was around his upper body.

Arty shook his head, drawing up a chair. "Never learnt. Paw didn't hold with smoking."

"That's best," Mike said philosophically. His face was feverishly red. "But I don't expect to be around long enough for tobacco to kill me . . . not at this rate."

"Sarah bandage you?"

"Yeah. Where'd they go?"

"I don't know. I guess the snow got too bad."

Mike's glance grew ironic. "I'm not that believing," he said. "This'll be the best chance they'll get to finish us. Right here . . . snowed in."

"I think I got one of them. It was just before we got back."

"That so? Makes three left then, doesn't it?" Mike let his gaze wander as far as John Lance's buffalo gun. "Odds're the same though . . . were four to two, and now they're three to one and a half." He nodded toward Lance, who turned his head, leaned the big-bored musket against the wall, and faced them.

"I didn't shoot to kill, Deputy. That's against my principles."

Mike seemed neither surprised nor annoyed. "Then I expect the odds're more in their favor than ever, Arty. Three to one." He grinned crookedly. "Of course, if they get inside, I can account for myself from right here."

Sarah came in with two large cups of steaming beef broth. She bent, handed Mike one, offered the other to Arty. He set his down quickly because the handle was piping hot.

"They can't stay out there, can they? she asked. "It's cold, and, besides, they're exposed to us."

Arty tried the broth. It wasn't as hot as the cup was. He sipped it. "All they got to do is leave one man guarding," he said. "We can't go anywhere. When the storm lifts. . . ."

"If you got one," Mike said, "I expect they'll hang around long enough to make some kind of an effort."

John Lance got up, stood wide-legged. His face was molded into lines of anguish and dread. Seeing his expression, Arty felt self-conscious. He wished there had been another place they could have gone. He finished the broth, cleared his throat.

"Mister Lance, I'll go for help if you think you and Mike can hold on. I'm plumb sorry we had to come back here and bring all this trouble."

"It's Providence, Arty," Lance said quietly, but the worry lingered in his expression.

Arty knotted his fists. Providence! He stood up, picked up a blanket, and went to the front window, hung it over the glass, and immediately the weak light was gone. "Light the lamp, Sarah."

John Lance took his cue, went through the back of the house putting blankets over windows. When he returned, Sarah had the light going. It seemed warm, friendly, and snug. Sarah was sitting erectly beside the cot. Neither she nor Mike Meaghan noticed Lance's return. He looked at their faces, saw their alert, expectant expressions, and went closer. "What is it?"

Sarah didn't speak. Mike said: "Art's gone to the barn."

Lance moved swiftly, caught up his buffalo gun, and went into the kitchen, sought an edge of darkness near the door, knelt there with the panel opened a fraction and icy cold stinging his face.

Arty was lost in the snow before he'd gotten twenty feet from the house. He couldn't see either building. When the barn loomed up, it was a great roll of snow with only occasional patches of siding showing. He entered its ghostly, dark interior and stood back, listening. Nothing. The grip of silence held even the animals.

It took time for his eyes to become accustomed to the gloom. After a while he caught up the chain, slipped it around his horse's neck, produced a lock from his pocket, and snapped it through the links. Then he stood there straining to hear, knowing how futile such effort was.

He went to the loft ladder and climbed it. Overhead, it was a trifle lighter, but not much. A scented richness filled his nostrils. He climbed higher, probing. Finally he stood upright by the ladder and rested his fingers upon his pistol butt. The barn was a frightening place. There was life in it, animal life, lungs that breathed, eyes that searched, muscles that moved. He could feel the emanations in the obscurity all around him. What he wanted to know and couldn't feel was whether the life was purely animal, or if there was human life in there as well.

After a time he took up a pitchfork in his left hand and moved across the loft, skirting its mounded hay. Down below a horse nickered, a cow struggled to her feet and blew out a repressed grunt. Arty relaxed a trifle. Probably no strange human scents around or the animals would have known it.

He went to the far side of the loft and pushed hay down into the mangers below. Animals stirred down there—dark shapes of horses and tall, squarer shapes of cattle. The heat of their furred bodies rose up pungently to him. He went back around the loft, was hanging the fork upon its nails when he heard his own horse move, nicker softly. He froze.

The horse moved again. There was a sound of the chain brushing wood. The animal snorted softly, nervously. Arty took a quick step away from the square opening above the ladder, and went down to one knee. Along the back of his neck hair bristled.

The hush bore down chokingly, closer, heavier. He felt perspiration break out upon his forehead, and it was cold. His pistol butt was cold, too, when he lifted the gun slowly, held it back against his body, pointing downward.

Uncertainty was dispelled when he heard the unmistakable crunch of boot steps just beyond the door. When they ceased, he knew the man was over the threshold, inside, standing motionlessly as Arty had done, waiting for his eyes to adjust. Quite suddenly a slab of wet snow made a grating, sliding sound as it broke loose and slid off the barn roof. Arty went lower in that moment of smothered sound, lay with only his head and gun hand inched out over the ladder's opening to the loft.

He couldn't see the person down below. His horse began to eat again, with rhythmic cadence, accepting the presence of a strange human smell. On the far side of the barn one of Lance's calves bawled abruptly.

The shadows gave up a part of their density. Arty saw movement, watched the man go toward his horse. He was holding a pistol in his hand. The horse moved as a strange hand went up its withers, found the chain, felt the lock, and let the chain drop away from his fingers.

The man stood by the horse a long time. When he finally moved again, it was back toward the doorway. He stopped several feet away, stood still as though listening, then he holstered his gun and knelt. Arty thought he was peering toward the cabin. Realization didn't come until he heard the sounds of fingers crushing dry hay. Then he understood. When the man flicked a match, he knew.

Edging the gun out farther, Arty cocked and fired in one motion. The match went out as though drowned in roiled air. The man gave an inarticulate yell and leaped sideways, legs like steel springs. Arty threw himself forward through the opening. He landed on bent legs as the man fired upward, saw the flash, and fired at it. The man bounded away with a rush of scratchy breath mixed with the gunshot's echo.

There were other sounds. Arty's horse was dancing nervously in his stall. Somewhere around the far side of the barn animals could be heard stampeding out into the snow, snorting and bawling in panic.

Arty stooped, picked up a rotting piece of leather, and threw it. The hidden gunman didn't fire, so Arty moved a little, testing each footfall before easing his weight down. Something creaked down in the darkness where a log partition separated the outside mangers from the part of the barn when Arty was. He swiveled his gun, waiting. The sound wasn't repeated. He surmised the stranger was trying to get over the partition, to the whiteness of open country on the far side of the overhang.

Moving an inch at a time, he went closer. Farther down, the barn darkness lay in dense layers. He felt a stone with his foot, threw it overhand, heard it land beyond the partition, and waited. Then he heart a sound, a whispering rush as though a body were being levered over something. He fired twice, rapidly, hunched down, and waited. There was a solid dull sound, as though the man had completed his climb over the partition. Then silence.

Arty went down on hands and knees, crept to the partition, and ran one hand over its smooth, rounded height, feeling for the top. He had to stand up to find it. There were no cracks he could peer through and he wouldn't straighten up to his full height to look over.

Seconds fled by, became minutes, finally becoming a half hour. Arty's legs pained from the strain of remaining crooked, straining. Logic told him the stranger had escaped, for beyond the partition lay nothing but trampled snow and an overhang that jutted ten or twelve feet back from open mangers.

He reloaded his gun, moved along the partition until he met its juncture with the east wall of the barn and there, where a sway-backed top log was, thrust the gun over first and followed it with his head. No shot came.

The hay he'd forked down was strewn about where Lance's livestock had carried it in their stampede after his first shot. The ground was like thick soup. Beyond, where the overhang's slope ended, were ridges of snow. Beyond stood animals, awaiting sufficient courage to return to the manger. He stood up full height and leaned upon the log. It was still snowing heavily, and while the day was little more than half spent, there was a lowering duskiness, more gray than black, a short distance beyond the barn.

He raised himself with both hands, dropped down into the strong-smelling mud, waited a moment, then walked northward along the barrier. Halfway up it he stopped in mid-stride. A man was lying up against the partition, unmoving, one side of his face in the filth.

Arty's heart pounded in his ears. He poked the man with his foot, bent far over and grasped his hair, lifted his face clear of the mud and turned it upward. The man's eyes were closed—that was enough. He holstered his gun, reached for a better grasp, and hauled the man upright, boosted him over the partition, balanced him there, crossed over himself, and got the stranger across one shoulder.

Before he went back out into the white silence, he palmed

the pistol again, keeping his thumb over the hammer. As soon as he was clear of the barn, the snow engulfed him. Moving steadily in the direction of the unseen cabin, he drew assurance from the knowledge that the remaining assassins wouldn't see him any sooner than he'd see them. None materialized, and he rapped sharply upon the partly opened doorway with his pistol barrel. John Lance was suddenly standing in the open with his buffalo rifle. The older man's eyes were wide. He stepped back as Arty stumped past, barred the door, and put aside his musket as Arty eased the stranger down upon the kitchen floor.

Sarah was there, like a statue. Horror showed in her eyes. John Lance went down beside Arty, called for a towel, which Sarah handed him, and began to wipe the man's face.

"Get warm water, Sarah."

Arty unbuttoned the man's coat, searched him, found a wallet, an empty holster, a bullet-studded shell belt, and some odds and ends. While Lance was opening the stranger's clothing, Sarah was stoking up the stove beneath a pan of water. Arty went through the kitchen to the little parlor where Mike Meaghan's quizzical eyes met him.

"What's going on out there, Art?"

"I brought some feller back. He came into the barn when I was in there. Started to build a fire inside. I shot the fire out and he ran. I thought he'd gotten away. When I looked beyond the partition, there he was. I got him with a lucky shot."

"Dead?"

Arty dumped the stranger's possession in Mike's lap. "Naw, his eyes were closed when I looked at him close. He may be near to it, but he isn't dead yet."

"What's this stuff . . . come off him?" Mike asked.

"Yeah."

Mike picked up the wallet first, spoke without looking up. "Do you know him?"

"Never saw him before in my life. Plumb stranger to me, Mike."

"See if he's going to make it, Art. I'd like to talk to him."

Arty left Mike rummaging through the stranger's wallet. Back in the kitchen, John and Sarah had the man stripped down to the waist. There was an ugly little purple hole under one collar bone, and where John had washed away the filth on the right side of the man's face, there was a deep, angry groove through the flesh. The top half of the stranger's ear was shot away. This wound bled copiously.

"Where did you find him, Arty?" John Lance asked without ceasing his attempts to staunch the scarlet freshet. John told them what had happened, and Lance nodded. "Yes," he said firmly, "I thought of that . . . firing the barn or the cabin. That's what would be the best way to drive us outside. In summer we wouldn't have lasted this long. The Lord's Providence, Arty."

"Yeah. Is his skull busted?"

"No, but I think his collar bone is."

Arty shrugged. "That won't kill him," he said. "If the light'd been a little. . . ." He let it trail off and die when Sarah shot him a still look.

They made the wounded man comfortable on the floor near Mike Meaghan. Nothing else happened the first day of their siege, and when nightfall came Mike said he'd remain awake until midnight, after which John Lance could take over the vigil.

It was late the next morning when the wounded man opened his eyes, groaned, felt clumsily for his head. Sarah gave him a cup of snow water. He drank it greedily. She got him another. When he rolled his eyes to her face, he saw Arty and John Lance standing behind her. The stranger swallowed the last gulps with difficulty. It was Mike who broke the silence.

"Had enough, Joe?"

The stranger looked toward the cot, met the saturnine gaze

of the lawman, said nothing, and let his head go back against the pillow made of a rolled up blanket.

"What relation are you to Pete Cuneo, Joe?"

"Half-brother. How bad I got it?"

"Not bad enough," Arty said brusquely.

The wounded man's eyes closed briefly, opened. "Head sure hurts."

"You've got a bad wound over your ear," John Lance said. "You were also shot in the shoulder. We thought your collar bone was broken but it wasn't."

"Am I in Lance's cabin?"

"You are."

Mike leaned forward a little on his cot. "Let's hear your story, Joe. We've got your wallet, so we've figured some of it out." When there was no reply, Mike said: "Talk, feller."

Arty moved around Sarah, nudged the man with his boot toe. The pain-filled eyes went up, saw the coldness in Arty's eyes, and blinked.

"I come when I heard what happened to Pete. He was my half-brother."

"You said that."

"My cousin Jack tol' me about this Jase Swift . . . how he killed Pete. We went along an' met some of Pete's friends. There was this feller, Sloan . . . said he would either kill both the Swift boys or let the law have the one that was an outlaw, and then take the cattle an' burn the ranch of the other one." Joe Cuneo went silent, closed his eyes. When Arty toed him again and he opened his eyes, they were swimmingly wet.

"Go on."

"I . . . after they took Jack to jail, this Sloan come around with some others. He said he knew about where Jase Swift would be."

"Did you go with him to the cabin?" Arty asked softly.

Mike looked up quickly. "Shut up, Art. Keep talking, Cuneo."

"Yeah, I went. I was supposed to guard the trail so this Swift couldn't get away. When I heard the yelling and shooting, I run back into the trees behind the cabin. They were pulling him up."

"I wish," Arty said with cold ferocity, "I'd known this out in the barn."

Cuneo's wet eyes moved to Arty's face. "You're the one shot me?"

"Yeah. I want another chance. I'll promise you next. . . ."

"Art! Cut that out!" Mike looked savage. "All right, Cuneo, how many are left and what are their names?"

"Left? I don't know. I run off back at that cabin when I heard all the shooting down by the trail. I met Sloan and that feller named Balester when I got back. They run off afoot, Sloan told me. There was my other cousin, Charley, but someone got him this morning."

"So there's Sloan, another Balester, and you. Is that all?"

"Yes. Maybe not me . . . I think I'll die. I feel awful."

"You won't die," Mike said. "There may come a day when you'll wish you had, but you aren't going to die from those scratches." Mike looked thoughtfully at Arty. "Two to two," he said. "Better odds." Arty turned away, went out into the kitchen, and drew a dipperful of water, drank it, replaced the dipper, and was standing there when Sarah came up. There was a pain and ferocity in his face that shocked her.

"Help me get dinner," she said, moving aimlessly in the room. Arty didn't move away from the little stand holding the water bucket.

She poked up the embers in the stove, got stove lengths from the woodbox, stoked them, and used the lid lifter to replace the circular covers. Long practice guided her hands in the chore of preparing a meal. When she had things cooking, she looked at Arty's long, tall back. She went close and in a very matter-of-fact way told him to set the table. He didn't respond, so she went around and faced him.

"This is none of my choosing, Arty. I don't see why I should be penalized for it . . . work all the time, cooking and nursing. You could help a little."

It worked. He looked down into her face, turned, and began to lay out the eating utensils for three. When the meal was ready, Sarah made up two additional plates and handed them to him. "One for Mike, one for the other man."

He went into the parlor, handed Mike his plate, turned, and looked at the ashen lips, the closed dark eyes, and swollen, lop-sided head of Joe Cuneo. Without arousing the wounded man, he bent, put his plate beside the pallet, straightened up, and turned his back. John Lance watched the tableau, got out of his chair, and knelt by Cuneo, roused him, and spooned food into his mouth.

Mike, eating with a healthy appetite, looked up as Arty was turning away. "Sit down, Art." He swabbed at thick gravy with a soggy piece of bread. "Come on, sit down here."

When Arty was seated, Mike finished eating, put the plate aside, and felt around for his tobacco sack. He took time to manufacture the cigarette, light it, and exhale a gust of gray smoke.

"I think they're gone, Art."

"Or frozen stiff," Arty said.

"Then we've got to think about getting some help."

"Help?"

"Yeah. I can't ride and fight, too. Not now. And sure as shoot-ing, Art, as soon as we get a few miles out, they'll show up."

"What good'll it do them now?"

Mike looked around with raised eyebrows. "Good? We're still

the only witnesses to murder."

"I wasn't thinking like that, Mike. By now they know we got this skunk, Cuneo. If he didn't come back to them and they haven't found him lyin' out there by the barn, they'll figure we got him alive. They'll know we've got talk out of him in front of Sarah and her paw."

Mike looked fixedly at Arty. "Sure," he said. "Why didn't I think of that? Must be foggy-headed from getting knocked around. Sure, they'll know there's more'n two of us who know about Jason's killing. So?"

"So, they won't keep tryin' to get us."

"No? Then what?"

"It's storming like blazes out. Regular blizzard. We can't go very far, and they know that, too. So they'll go back home, pack up, and beat it. They'll use the storm to get lots of miles between us and them, Mike. That's just plain common sense. By the time we can get out of here, they'll be a thousand miles away."

"Well," Mike said, "a few hundred miles away, anyway."

Arty stood up, shrugged. "If this lasts another couple days, it'll be more'n a thousand."

Mike sucked on his cigarette. "How bad is it outside?"

"About two feet thick on the level."

Mike grunted, smashed out the cigarette in a tin cup, glanced past Arty where John Lance was wiping Cuneo's mouth after feeding him. "Cuneo, what did Sloan and Balester have planned?"

"Planned? Whatcha mean . . . planned?"

"About fighting us, and afterward."

"They sent me to fire the barn. Figured you fellers'd run out when you seen the flames. They were going to lie out back and pot you when the fire showed you up."

"And after that?"

"Nothing. Nothing I know of."

"What'd they say about leaving the country?"

"Never said anything like that around me."

"Well," Mike persisted, "what d'you think they'll do now, knowing we got you?"

Cuneo moved his head a little, rocking it slightly. "I don't know, don't care. Maybe they'll wait till the storm's over and try again. I don't know."

Sarah came to the kitchen door, called Arty and her father. They went to eat. It was a silent, strained meal, and Arty felt recurrent discomfort over bringing his fight to the Lances. He wanted to say something, but the proper words eluded him, so he kept his head down and picked at his food.

When the meal was over, John Lance took the old horse-hide coat from a nail near the kitchen door. "I'll go check the animals," he said.

Arty got up quickly. "I'll do it. Be better if you sort of looked after Mike."

"And the Cuneo lad," Lance said, looking steadily at Arty.

Sarah got his hat and coat; he shrugged into them, passed her father, and went outside. The snow had stopped. It lay several feet thick, and wet. The stillness was as heavy as ever. He stood back by the cabin for a while, satisfying himself Sloan and Balester weren't waiting. It didn't seem likely they would be. After he'd crossed the yard and entered the barn, his pants legs were soaking wet above the tops of his boots. He stopped to listen a moment, heard nothing, and stomped his feet, kicked off the snow, and felt the chill as he moved toward his horse. A recurrence of his earlier tenseness in the gloomy barn swept over him. He fed the horse and stood beside him waiting for something, anything. When it came it was from the Lance animals across the log partition. He went up and peered over at them, at the ground and beyond, where grayness lay above the opalescent snow. There was nothing to see.

He went up to the loft ladder, climbed it, skirted the hay, and forked the far side manger full, hung the fork up again, and was peering down into the shadows below when he saw the faint, pale blur of movement.

"Arty? Are you up there?"

His knees felt like glue. "What'd you come out for, Sarah?"

"To talk to you."

She swept up the ladder with sure movements. He bent, caught her elbow, and pulled her gently to firm footing. "You should've stayed inside," he said.

"It's safe enough."

He bent a close glance upon her face. "How do you know? There was one of them in here before."

"I feel it, Arty. If they aren't under cover in here, then they're gone. It's too bitter cold for anyone to be waiting around outside very long." She moved away from him, looked at the mounded hay, and heard the animals crunching below. "Besides, they'd be hungry," she added with female practicality, and turned to look at him. "Come here."

He went. She sat down in the hay and pulled him down beside her. "Arty, you killed a man up in the mountains, didn't you?"

"Sure. You know that."

"So does my father," she said, watching his face in an unblinking, steady way.

He twisted to face her, pushed the hay around to make it more comfortable. "Well, what else could I do?"

She didn't answer right away. "You said you loved me, Arty." He stiffened. She reached up and touched his face. "Don't," she said softly. "Don't say something bad, Arty."

"What do you mean?"

"Like you wanted to kill him. Like you're glad you did it."

"I did want to and I am glad. He was one of those hung Jase,

Sarah. I'd have killed more if I'd had a chance. All of them."

"Do you want to marry me, Arty?"

Color flooded into his face. "Yes, Sarah, I want to," he said simply. "I want to a lot."

"That killing. . . ."

"I know what you're fixing to say, Sarah. Your paw won't approve of me as your husband because of that killing. Well, I thought of that when I was riding back from the cabin with Jase and that lawman. Sarah, if we were all God-fearin' folks like your paw, it'd be fine. Wouldn't be any call to shoot men. But we all aren't. They didn't give Jase half a chance. Shot him in the back, and, when he was dying, they strung him up. Is that right?"

"No," she said, hiding a shudder.

" 'Course it isn't. I'm sorry your paw doesn't see it like that."

"He does, Arty. He doesn't approve of what they did. Only he won't approve of what you did, either."

"Did he say so?"

"No, but I know him. I know what he thinks, and I saw the way he kept staring at the wall when Mister Meaghan told him what happened up there."

"But that feller was running for his carbine. If I'd held off, he'd've shot me."

Sarah was silent. Arty picked up a straw, carefully peeled away the husk, stared at it, then threw it away. A foreboding hopelessness filled him. He looked down at her. Her eyes were large and dark. He wanted to say something convincing, something full of irrefutable logic. There were no words to fit. He made a wide motion with his hands.

"I don't understand, Sarah. I can't think of anything more to say about it. He'd've shot me, so I shot him first."

"Arty, when this is all over, when things are better for you, will you put up your gun?"

He considered it, felt around for the right answer, and his instinctive caution intervened. "I dassn't, Sarah. An unarmed man's a sitting duck for anyone wants to take a pot shot at him."

"An unarmed man's safer than an armed one," she said. "No one would dare shoot him."

Arty looked at her incredulously. "That's not so, Sarah. I'm surprised at you. When men're out to get other men, they'll get 'em by fair means or foul. Those fellers never gave my paw a chance . . . they shot Jase in the back. They'd do the same to me."

"No," she replied, "not after this is all over."

He frowned at her, drew back a little. "You're asking me to get shot, Sarah, that's what you're doing."

She said nothing, fought against the gathering storm in him with silence. She drew closer to him, and felt him relax beside her. Deep down, his stubbornness worried her. "Arty, it doesn't matter. Maybe you're right. I was thinking of Pa."

"Well, don't," he said shortly. "I'd do whatever I ought where he's concerned, you know that, but it's us, Sarah. You said you didn't want to be a widow one time, remember? Then quit talking about me putting my guns away. The best insurance a man can have in Colorado is around his middle an' in his saddle boot. I'm not going to kill anyone unless they come shooting, Sarah. But if they do, by golly, I don't want to have to try an' outrun bullets, because it can't be done."

She cradled his head against her shoulder. "I guess it's just got to be this way, doesn't it?" she said.

"Yes, I expect so. I wish it didn't. I wish your paw'd understand." He thought of something and pulled up a little so that he could see the oval paleness of her face in the gloom. "Sarah, he ran out there with that buffalo gun. He was helping us. What about that?"

"He didn't shoot to hit anyone."

Arty nodded, more perplexed than ever. "Yeah, that's no way to use a gun, though. Either you aim to hurt or you don't aim at all. My paw always taught me that. Draw it to kill or don't draw it at all." He sat back, stared at nothing. "Your paw's hard to understand. Guess I'll never understand him in some ways."

"He won't oppose our marriage, I know that, Arty. He'll just wish you hadn't killed that man."

Arty grunted but said nothing.

"Kiss me, Arty. We'd better get back. They'll be worrying."

He kissed her, then they stood up and he helped her to the ladder, waited until she was down, and began his own descent. "Let me go first," he said, stepping around her at the door. "Golly, it's darker'n the inside of a well. We must've been out here for an hour."

She sighed. "I guess."

They went across the yard and were immediately struck by the unusual warmth of the night. With his hand on the latch, Arty said: "Chinook coming sure as you're a foot tall." He sounded warmed by the prospect.

When they came in the kitchen, John Lance was looking at them from the parlor doorway. He said nothing and after a moment disappeared from view. They heard Mike Meaghan ask Lance if they were back. Sarah's father answered shortly that they were. Sarah looked embarrassed. She turned away from Arty, and approached the stove. He removed coat and hat, hung them on nails, and crossed the kitchen to the parlor.

Mike was looking at him from the cot. Joe Cuneo was as still as death on his pallet, lost in a world of pain. He didn't even open his eyes. John Lance was tinkering with the stove damper, his back to Arty.

Mike said: "Sit down, Art. I want to talk to you."

Arty sat. "There's a Chinook coming," he said.

"I know. I can smell it. That's what I want to talk about. It may be what we're waiting for." Mike's fingers began slowly to twist up a cigarette. He was thinking. "I've got a notion you might be right about those fellers running off." He lit, exhaled. "That'd be all right 'cause I'd eventually get 'em. Only right now I'd like to stop them before they run, if possible."

John Lance had his back to the stove, listening, watching them both.

Mike went on: "If they haven't run yet, this Chinook'll help us. You saddle up and ride for Chiloquin. Get Sheriff Whitney. Tell him to get a posse and cut those fellers off. We know their names and he'll know about where to find them. I'm gambling he will anyway." The sharp eyes swung to Arty's face, stayed there. "What do you think?"

"If they aren't already gone," Arty said.

"Yeah. Well, we got to take that chance. Anyway, you ready to try it?"

"Sure. Right now?"

"Yes, right now. It's pretty dark out, isn't it?"

"Like the inside of a boot."

"Good." Meaghan looked at John Lance. "You could sort of cover for him until he's out of sight if you would."

"I will," Lance said, without moving.

Arty stood up, hesitated. "Suppose we're wrong . . . suppose they're still around, or maybe come back after I'm gone. What then? They might have more friends."

Mike looked at his cigarette. "Chance we got to take," he said evenly. "But I don't think they'll come back. I think like you said. They know we got Cuneo . . . they've figured he's talked . . . they'll be fixing to leave the country." The marshal's gaze swung to Arty's face. He held out one closed fist. "Here, put this on. It won't help much with Balester and Sloan, but it will with Sheriff Whitney."

Arty reached out and felt the warm steel fall against his palm. It was a deputy U.S. marshal's badge. He blinked at it, wrinkled his forehead at Meaghan. "I got no right to wear this."

"Raise your right hand."

Art complied, and Meaghan rolled off a memorized oath, a pledge to uphold the law—apprehend lawbreakers when possible—defend the United States Constitution—pursue his duties as a lawman with diligence, impartiality, and perseverance. Arty let his arm drop, and Meaghan watched his face a moment before he spoke again.

"Put it on. Don't stand there like a wooden Indian."

Arty pinned the shield to his shirt, felt its weight tug at the cloth, and looked down oddly at it. "You sure this is all right?" he asked.

"Right as rain. I got the power to deputize men, Art. There's one thing wasn't in the oath I want your word about."

"Yeah," Arty grunted. "I know."

"Do you? Will you promise me not to use your gun against your brother's killers unless you do it in self-defense? By that I mean don't call on 'em to draw. Don't bait 'em into fighting you. Take them alive if possible . . . dead only if you can't get them any other way. Promise?"

Arty was conscious of John Lance standing back by the stove behind him. He knew instinctively that Sarah was in the kitchen doorway. "I promise," he said.

Meaghan didn't smile. He nodded his head and shot Lance a look. "Help him get under way, will you?"

They were going toward the kitchen when Meaghan said: "Good luck, Art." He was holding out his hand.

Arty went back, shook the outstretched hand, and smiled. "Don't worry, lawman, I'll do it your way . . . if I can."

"You can, lawman."

Sarah's father was clumping through the snow toward the

barn when Arty stood framed in the doorway leading outside. Sarah caught him there, held up a small packet. "Food, Arty," she said, and kissed him. "Be careful, and remember we'll be waiting for you."

"*We?*"

"Me then . . . I'll be waiting for you."

He touched her face gently, then went out into the night.

The warmth was even more noticeable than when he'd last walked through it. Underfoot, snow was melting. It no longer held up his weight even a little. Each footfall sank through and struck soggy, hard ground underneath.

At the barn John Lance had his horse saddled. Arty removed the log chain and bridled, led the horse outside and turned him. Lance shifted the buffalo rifle from his right hand to his left. "Keep an eye peeled, son," he said. "I think like you do. They're gone, but I won't bet they won't come back."

Arty looked at the massive old rifle. "Anyone'd face that cannon's crazy," he said, and grinned, looking down into the older man's face. "Mister Lance, I'd like to talk with you."

"When you come back, Arty. Now remember, stay to the ridges when you can . . . don't ride near no brush or trees, and, if you see anyone, try and see 'em first."

Arty shook Lance's hand and swung up. Lance said: "Hurry, Arty. Make it as fast as you can. If you can't come back right off, at least have the sheriff send some men back *pronto.* Understand?"

"I will."

In case anyone was lying out there watching, he rode diagonally across the yard in order to hit the range a good distance south of the cabin.

The night was pitch dark. The warmth helped a good deal but the darkness hindered him a lot, too. He knew the country well enough, but the snow had changed it as far as making time was concerned. The north side of every hummock had deep drifts. South slopes were almost clean of snow.

But the farther he rode the less he feared his enemies. In all that dark void there was no movement, no sign of life of any kind. He found some fresh horse tracks once, about seven miles from the Lance place, but, when he got down to inspect them closely, he found they had been made by unshod horses.

Feeling secure, he began to zigzag back and forth across the white world looking for other tracks. It was three miles farther out that he saw the first set of them. He followed along beside the tracks until they joined another set. Both sets of tracks milled as though the riders had sat there talking for quite a while before they struck out to the north together.

He figured that, if they were Sloan's and Balester's tracks, at least they were heading northward, not westward. They weren't going toward the Lance place. That was reassuring. He urged his horse eastward again, toward town, thinking the killers had probably headed for a place where they could warm up.

By the time he got to Chiloquin dawn was near. There was a bloody smear in the east along the horizon. All around it was a clear, pale grayness. He heard the first whispers of wind as he rode down the deserted roadway. They came from the northwest, moaned softly beneath eaves, smelled strongly of pine and warmth. He tied up outside the sheriff's office, sniffing. The Chinook would hit very soon.

Sheriff Whitney's night man was drowsing, his feet cocked up on the desk, the little iron stove popping merrily, and the room insufferably hot. Arty recognized the man's watery eyes, feral features. He closed the door and struck the sprawling feet with his gloved hands.

"Wake up!"

The man opened his eyes wide but otherwise didn't move. At sight of Arty he blinked, blinked again, then began to rub his eyes vigorously.

"When's the sheriff due down here?"

"Hour," the night man said. "Maybe hour 'n' half. Why?"

"That's too late. Go get him."

"What?"

"You go get him," Arty said again. When the deputy made no move, Arty reached out, grasped his ankles, swung them off the desk. "Now, not a year from now. Move!"

"Say," the night man said, offended. "Who the . . . ?"

Arty caught a handful of shirt and wrenched. The deputy came up out of the chair like a puppet. "Go get him and don't stop running till you're back here with him." He flung the man toward the door. "I owe you that, mister. I owe you more . . . maybe you'll get the rest of it later on. Right now, get!"

The deputy left without his hat or coat. Arty went over by the stove, unbuttoned his coat, and clasped his hands behind his back. Heat burrowed through his clothing into his flesh, into muscles, into the marrow of his bones. It was a blissful sensation.

He had no idea how long he stood like that, but he finally had to walk around the office, for sleep was threatening to overcome him. He was walking back and forth when the deputy returned with a hastily clad, puffy-faced, and unshaven sheriff.

"Swift, I thought it was you from the description. What do you want?"

Arty spoke clearly and rapidly. When he'd finished, he held his coat open. The deputy marshal's badge shone. "That's all of it. You hustle the men . . . I'll wait here."

VI

Gordon Whitney was a methodical man—slow in movement, slow in thought. He stood rock-like, appraising Arty. Finally he said: "You sure that's how you got that badge?"

"I'm sure enough," Arty answered cryptically, "and I don't aim to stand around here all morning waiting for you to do something. Meaghan, Sarah, and John Lance are out there. If you don't get up a posse, I will."

"You will? How?"

Arty touched the badge. "As a deputy United States marshal, that's how."

Whitney fell silent, ruminating. Finally he said: "All right, Swift. One thing . . . we'll be together. If this is some scheme you've cooked up, you'll regret it."

"I'll be around," Arty said, "just like I've always been around, for rawhidings, blame, trouble. Wish I could say as much for Chiloquin's law."

The sheriff eyed Arty silently a moment longer. "Newt," he said calmly, "go see who you can round up. It's kind of early. . . ."

The night deputy left, and Arty watched the sheriff sluice out a tin cup, peer into it critically, go to the stove, and pour coffee from a small black pot simmering there. As he drank, Sheriff Whitney kept his eyes on Arty, whose impatience was very evident. When he'd finished the coffee Whitney rinsed the cup, hung it upon a nail, and dropped down behind his desk, spoke without looking up.

"What're the names of the men involved in your brother's killing?"

"Murder, not killing. The deputy marshal was witness to that."

"All right," Whitney said wearily, "murder."

Arty ticked off the names of those he knew. Men like Joe Cuneo he identified by appearance, by the glimpses he'd had of them.

Whitney looked up from writing. "Only two left now?" he asked.

"As far as we know, yes. Ted Sloan and Balester."

"Know which Balester it is?"

"No. This Joe Cuneo told us his name was Balester. I didn't ask his first name."

Whitney finished writing, stood up, looked down at his shell belt, ran spatulate fingers over the worn butt of his pistol and grunted. "Care for some coffee?"

"No. How long's this going to take?"

The sheriff looked mildly annoyed. "You can't roust folks out of bed at four-thirty in the morning and expect them to be armed and ready to ride, Swift. Calm down."

"With those people out there in that cabin?"

"Well, you said yourself you figured Sloan and this Balester'd be hightailing it. Meaghan and the Lances are probably safer'n you are."

"Then get at least a couple of riders down the south road, Sheriff. For all we know, Sloan and Balester've already gone past."

"Sure," the sheriff said, pouring another cup of coffee. "The first ones show up I'll send downcountry."

When the deputy returned, breathless, he had four men with him. Sheriff Whitney immediately sent two southward, two northward with orders to arrest Ted Sloan and Balester on sight, and to hold any others they found who couldn't give a sound reason for being out so early. Arty was amazed at the efficient way Whitney swore in and instructed his men.

When the posse had gone, the sheriff gestured toward the stove, and his deputy went to get coffee. While he was sipping it, Whitney said: "How many more'd you get, Newt?"

"Six. They'll be along directly. What's this all about?"

Whitney told him, looking across at Arty for confirmation. Arty nodded without speaking. He was beginning to fidget when five men entered the office, tousle-headed and buckling guns around their middles. Several were scowling.

Sheriff Whitney stood up, looked at the men, and asked if they had all gotten their horses. Answered affirmatively in a variety of ways, he then ordered his deputy to come along. Arty was the last one out the door. Off in the north a peculiar whiteness lay like high fog. The Chinook's steady blowing, not hard or unpleasant, was keeping up a steady moaning sound. It was warm and getting warmer.

"Swift, what d'you think of going to the Sloan place first?"

Arty had already thought that out hours before. He shook his head. "If Balester's with Sloan that would be fine, but, in order to cover all bets, let's split up . . . half of us go to Sloan's, half of us go to the old Balester place."

Sheriff Whitney dropped into one of his appraising silences. He finally frowned at Arty. "To play safe," he said, "suppose you and me 'n' one other go together. Newt can take the rest."

"Any way you want to do it . . . just so long as we get going. Only I think you'd better send at least three men to the Lances."

"Heck," the sheriff said, "there's only seven of us."

"Eight. I'm number eight. Send three to Lance's, three to Balester's . . . you and me'll go to Sloan's."

Whitney considered this for several seconds, then agreed. He had started to assign the men when Arty cut in, addressing those that were to go to the relief of the Lance Ranch. Each word he used was sharp, rattling-fast, and clear. He told them to be careful of ambushes, to be sure and make known who they were before approaching the cabin. When he was finished, the sheriff just shrugged. "Go on," he said. "You've got it all."

"And stay there," Arty added. "Wait there until we come along."

The sheriff then sent two more men to the Balester place, and, as the riders whirled away from the hitch rail, he turned and gazed stolidly at Arty. "You ready?" he asked.

Arty went to his horse, swung up, and watched the heavier man grunt up the side of his own horse, straddle it, and turn. They rode southward past a few early risers who stared after them curiously. Below town Arty cut southwest, with Gordon Whitney beside him.

As they rode, the sheriff asked innumerable questions. By the time the sun was up, the warm wind soughing with steady warmth that shrank snowbanks as if by magic, he had the entire story pieced together. He wagged his head back and forth.

"I don't understand it, Swift. I can't for the life of me understand it."

"I don't care whether you do or not," Arty said.

Sheriff Whitney looked quickly at the hard, smooth profile. "Now listen," he said. "I been sheriff here a long time, boy. I seen a lot in my time."

"I expect you have . . . from a distance. You sure never burned up no trails when we told you about our shot critters and run-off horses."

"That's where you're wrong. I went out there twice and hid out, watching. I didn't see anything. I even had Newt camp up in the hills, back of your place, for three days one time."

"That accounts for that," Arty said waspishly. "He wouldn't see anything if it was right in front of him."

Whitney spat, wiped his mouth. "Maybe you'd like to try," he said. "I need another deputy."

"What you need," Arty said, "is a replacement . . . not a new deputy."

Whitney mottled with angry color. He was turning his angry face when Arty sucked in a gust of breath. The sheriff swiveled his eyes enough to follow the younger man's gaze. There was a man on a leggy buckskin horse sitting atop a sloping knoll ahead of them. Whitney squinted, spoke more to himself than to Arty. "Who the heck's that?"

Arty lifted his reins without answering.

"Hold it," Whitney said. "Don't hurry. If he's someone we want, he'll be scairt if you run at him."

Arty lowered his rein hand reluctantly. They plodded along side-by-side.

The distant rider watched them a while longer, then disappeared beyond the whaleback hummock, and Arty swore, with feeling. "If that wasn't Ted Sloan, it was one of his family. The ranch's just over that hill."

"I know where the Sloan Ranch is."

"Then let's get moving. At this rate they'll be gone before we're close enough to stop them."

"Just simmer down," the sheriff said. "We're going to feel our way. I'll tell you frankly I'm skeptical. Don't figure to rush up and commence a war, before I know whether it's worth fighting or not."

Arty pointed to the southern end of the hummock. "I'm going down there. You come in from the north. That way we'll know what's going on above and below the ranch . . . maybe stop someone from running off." He kicked his horse out. Whitney's mouth opened to protest. No sound came. He growled and turned his horse to the north with evident reluctance.

When Arty cleared the lower end of the hill, he saw three saddled horses tied to stud rings in the side of the Sloan barn. Two were drowsing in the unusual warmth, but the third animal, obviously recently ridden, had his head up, ears alert.

The house was old, disreputable, and lifeless-looking. Arty slowed to a walk and studied it as he approached. When he glanced northward, he saw the distant figure of the sheriff.

Closer, the house seemed too still, too hushed. It was as though whoever might be inside was waiting. Arty removed his gloves, flexed his fingers, reined up, and stopped. No sound came from the house. He waited until Sheriff Whitney was nearer and went as close as an old tree, sat beneath its gnarled, twisted limbs.

Sheriff Whitney reined up beside him, leaned forward in the saddle. "One inside," he said. "We know that."

"Do we? How do we know he didn't keep right on going?"

Whitney didn't answer. After a moment's hesitancy he swung down, methodically looped his reins over a limb, and went stumping across the yard toward the house. A harsh voice halted him before he reached the sagging porch.

"That's far enough. What you want, Sheriff, you an' that whelp with you?"

Sheriff Whitney's head cocked a little to one side. He spread his legs and looked at the murky windows facing him. Back under the tree Arty eased his right hand back a little until he could feel the coldness of his gun.

"Want to talk," the sheriff said a trifle stiffly. "Is Ted in there?"

"He ain't."

"Well, whoever is come on out . . . I want to talk to you."

There was a second of silence, and then someone swore. "Sure, I'll talk to you, but get that Swift whelp out o' the yard. He's a killer an' so's his whole tribe. We don't talk to no one while he's a-settin' up there with his hand on his gun."

Arty's fingers closed around the pistol handle. He could see how Gordon Whitney's back was getting rigid. The sheriff was in an awkward spot, and his shifting position said very eloquently that he knew it.

"Listen, don't start any trouble in there," Whitney said evenly. "Just come outside."

"Nope. Get Swift off o' this place or you go with him, Sheriff."

Whitney's neck was reddening but his hands still hung loosely at his sides. When next he spoke, there was more anger than apprehension in his tone. "I didn't ride 'way out here to stand like a statue arguin'," he said. "Swift isn't going to do anything, so come out here."

"He sure ain't," a tight voice said. "First move an' he's dead." The voice raised a little. "Hear that, Swift?"

"I hear," Arty said. "I didn't come here for a fight or I wouldn't have come with the sheriff."

"Don't make a darn. You turn around and get off this ranch . . . *pronto.*"

Sheriff Whitney turned very slowly, facing Arty. He jerked his head sideways. "Go on, Arty. I'll catch up with you."

Arty studied the house, the windows, the sheriff's face that was red and grim-looking. He shrugged, reined around without speaking, and walked his horse back the way he'd come.

When the lift of swale appeared on his left side, he turned to go around it, shot a quick glance back toward the house, and saw a gangling man with a carbine standing defiantly by the open front door, talking to Sheriff Whitney. Some urgent sixth sense made him shift suddenly in the saddle, throw a glance around behind the hummock. A man was standing very quietly beside his horse, reins hanging from his arm, carbine up and aimed. Arty threw himself sideways when the gun went off. The shot sounded flat and clear.

Arty's horse shied violently. One stirrup swung up and caught over the saddle horn. Arty didn't notice; he was rolling toward the lowest rise of land. The carbine went off a second time. By then Arty was hidden from the would-be assassin.

With cold rage in his heart, he fisted his handgun, jerked his head over the lift of earth, saw the man whirling away, and fired. It was a wide miss. He steadied his hand and fired a second time. He came closer. His third shot dumped horse and rider; he had aimed at the larger target. The assassin got up drunkenly, swayed, then dropped beside his dead horse.

Arty heard someone shout behind him. He risked a look.

Sheriff Whitney was pounding his horse out of the yard in Arty's direction. Behind him the gangling man with the gun who had been on the porch had run out a little way from the house and was standing erect, raising his carbine. Arty threw a shot in his direction, hoping to divert him. The stratagem worked, for the man winced enough so that his own shot at Sheriff Whitney went wide. The sheriff came on, apparently unaware that his life had hung in the balance for a second.

Arty dropped flat when the man behind the dead horse fired. Dust and dirt sprayed upward in a geyser. When the assassin shot again, he was using a pistol; its report was louder, more thunderous.

Afraid the sheriff would bolt into view of the downed horseman, Arty began to wave him off. Whitney swept a little closer, than sat back, and his horse slid to a stiff-legged halt. He came out of the saddle ponderously. Arty hunched up, backed off, and made gestures indicating that Whitney should take his place behind the hummock's lowest flank. Whitney understood, came trotting up with his carbine in one big fist.

Arty got up, went farther along the hummock until he thought he was well behind the downed man, then trotted close to the eminence and lay flat, inching forward carefully until only the top of his head and eyes were exposed. He could see the bushwhacker hunched up close behind his horse. At that moment Whitney fired, and the man's attention was held long enough for Arty to draw a careful bead and tug off his last shot. The assassin gave a prodigious leap and rolled, writhing, behind the horse. Arty could hear his cries very clearly. He squirmed around, flipped open the gate of his pistol, punched out spent casings, and reloaded. The sound of running horses caught his attention.

Back by the house three horsemen were spreading out in a long lope, heading toward him. He could see the fourth man, the one afoot down by the house, trotting in an ungainly way, carbine thrust out before him.

Arty got upright and ran toward his horse. Sheriff Whitney was standing up, staring over to where the writhing man lay. Arty shouted at him, motioned toward the newcomers with his pistol, then caught his horse, jerked the carbine from the boot, knelt, and tracked the nearest man over his sights, and fired. The rider's horse plowed head-on into the ground, flipped over endwise, and catapulted the man upon his back in a frantic arc straight ahead.

Sheriff Whitney opened up on another rider, who immediately veered off, quirting his horse unmercifully in an attempt to reach the hummock's protection before he was downed.

The third attacker fired three fast shots. The last one ripped earth close enough to Whitney's nervous mount to stampede it. The horse fled toward Chiloquin with its head high and tail out.

Arty reached behind him for his own horse's rein, gripped it in his fist, and fired twice at the gangling man who was now kneeling out in the open, aiming. Neither of Arty's shots took effect, but they succeeded in disconcerting the attacker sufficiently so that, when he fired, the bullets sang high overhead. Then he leaped up and sprinted for cover. Arty tracked him, fired. The man collapsed in mid-stride; his carbine flew ten feet ahead of him.

Sheriff Whitney was yelling. Arty jumped up into a crouch, but there was no immediate danger near. The sheriff was crying out for Arty to mount up and find the remaining attacker who had fled behind the hill. Arty mounted, eased his horse out in a cautious walk. When the land began to rise, he felt too conspicuous, so dismounted and walked ahead of the horse.

Apparently the surviving horseman's idea had been to come around the hummock near where the writhing man lay, and flank both Sheriff Whitney and Arty. Arty first suspected this when he heard two fast shots, then a third shot. He whirled and saw Sheriff Whitney dropping his carbine, clawing frantically for his belt gun. Leaping astride, Arty spurred up the hummock and over its crest. He held the cocked carbine in one hand, but the fight was over. The last attacker lay face down.

Arty rode on down the slope, knelt by the wounded man, rolled him over, and peered into his face. He recognized him but had known him only by sight. Ted Sloan's youngest brother, a lad slightly younger than Arty was. The bullet that had crippled him had entered his side, ranged upward in some miraculous way, and had emerged through his armpit, breaking the arm at the shoulder. There was considerable bleeding.

Arty tore the youth's shirt, made a bandage of sorts, and was drying his hands upon the dead horse's side when Sheriff Whitney came stalking up, white and hot-eyed.

"You hurt?"

Arty shook his head, pointed at the man on the ground. "He is, though. There was one I shot the horse out from under . . . where'd he go?"

"I dunno." Sheriff Whitney looked at the wounded man. "I got to get another horse," he said irrelevantly.

Arty picked up the wounded boy, held him in front of him with one wiry arm around his chest below the armpits. "Come on, Sheriff . . . let's go to the house."

Whitney looked doubtfully at Arty's shield. "Those kind of skunks . . . I wouldn't rely on 'em not to shoot their own kin to kill me."

"Then stay down here and cover me," Arty said, and started forward afoot.

Sheriff Whitney hung back only until Arty's horse nudged him, then he mounted the animal and rode out around the hummock, head down in an aggressive way, pistol up and ready.

Arty hadn't gone twenty yards before the youth in his arms began to sob and roll his head from side to side. Arty tightened his hold. "Hold still or I'll put another one in you." It worked. The youth ground his teeth but made no more sounds or unnecessary movements. When Arty was halfway back across the yard, he saw the gangling man sitting on the ground with his carbine gripped tightly in both hands. The man was in plain view. Arty stopped, surprised. His pistol swung on him.

"Sheriff, go get that other one. I don't know why he's sitting like that. I don't think he got hit."

He waited while Whitney rode over and gestured with his gun. The man spoke through gritted teeth. "Can't get up. Ankle's broke. Fell on it."

"You get up anyway and throw that carbine aside. Come on, get up!"

The man was old. He used the carbine as a lever until he was standing, then cast a look of anguish at Whitney. "Can't drop it. Need it for a crutch."

Whitney got down, unloaded the carbine, and gave it back to the old man. "Now hobble toward the house, and, when you're close enough, call out an' tell 'em inside we'll kill both of you if anyone fires. Go on now, you old devil."

"Ain't no one inside 'ceptin' the women."

"Do like I say," Whitney said, taking the older man's arm in an iron grip, propelling him forward several feet.

Arty waited until the old man and his captor were ahead, then started forward again. The house was as still as before, but now it had a desolate air. At the porch Arty dropped the young Sloan into a wire hammock hung between two pieces of wagon tongue. He went to the door and gave it a savage kick. It flung inward, struck the wall with a resounding crash. Across the room, standing together and directly in the way of Arty's cocked pistol, were two older women and a girl in her early teens. They were rigid.

Sheriff Whitney tied Arty's horse to the porch upright and nudged the old man inside. He hobbled to a chair and sank down upon it with a small groan. The sheriff said—"I'll look through the house."—and started away.

The first thing Arty did was to go to the water bucket, drink two full dippers. Then he uncocked his pistol and let it dangle from his fist. "Go sit down," he said to the women. "Keep your hands atop the table." They complied. He moved around to face the old man, whose head hung low.

"Who sent that feller to dry-gulch me?"

No answer.

Arty bent from the waist, caught the old man's shirt front, and pulled.

"Ted did. Ted . . . not me."

"Where's Ted?"

"Gone."

"You lying old. . . ."

"No," a drab woman said. "He's gone. Pa's telling the truth. He told them what to do to keep you 'n' the lawman from gettin' too close. Then he went to the barn and rode off."

Arty released the old man, looked past the woman at the girl. Her face was devoid of any color. She was watching him with terror and fascination. "She lyin', miss?"

"No, sir. Uncle Ted left just when the fightin' started."

Arty snorted. "Brave Ted Sloan. Brave enough to kill an old man, shoot another man in the back." He closed his lips against the fury in his throat, stood looking at them for a while, then leaned upon the wall. "All right, I believe you. Only a Sloan'd be that cowardly. Five to two and he ran. Where'd he go?"

"He didn't say where he was goin'," the drab woman said.

"Who're you? What kin you to him?"

"I'm his mother." She nodded at the old man. "He's Ted's father. This here's his sister, and that's his niece."

"Who was with him?"

"That other feller . . . cousin to Jack Balester down at Raton."

"What were they doing here?"

"Getting ready to leave."

"For where?"

"Raton, I think. They didn't say."

"What kept them around this long?"

"I don't know."

"Lady," Arty said, "you're lying. You know what kept them around. They had two more men to murder over at Lance's place."

"We don't know anything about that."

"Don't you?" Arty asked. "Want to hear about it?"

"No."

"Want to hear about how four of 'em, Ted included, shot Amos Swift to death? How they slipped up behind Jase Swift and shot him in the back?"

"No."

The younger woman glared. "Leave her alone, you dirty killer."

Arty's gaze shifted. "I ought to make the herd of you sit here and listen to how your kinsman bushwhacks old men and those he's scairt to face."

"The snow kept them from going before," the little girl volunteered, trying mightily to stem the flood tide of hatred that was filling the room.

Arty stared at the child and let his breath out slowly. "All right," he said tiredly. "You know what a rotten whelp Ted is. We'll let that go for now." Sheriff Whitney came stalking into the room as Arty went on. "Too bad they let the snow slow 'em down, because now they're going to get caught sure as God made green apples. I figured they'd be miles away by now."

"No," Ted Sloan's mother said dispassionately. "You killed Charley. Ted was ready to leave before you did that. He said he'd wait for another chance at you after that."

"That was the biggest mistake of his life," the sheriff said. "He won't get far."

Arty looked around at him. "Why? Because you got the roads blocked?"

"Yes."

"Will that keep them from riding for the Lances?" Arty looked acidly displeased. "And now there's three of them again, I'll bet you a fat horse. There's Sloan, Balester, and whoever that other feller was I shot the horse from under. He's gone, you know."

The sheriff pondered, turned stiffly toward the seated people. "Who was that . . . another of your tribe?"

"That was Will Bailey, Ted's cousin on my side o' the family."

"Well, well," Sheriff Whitney said caustically. "More kinsfolk than ticks on a fat cow, haven't you? Is Bailey going to try to find Ted?"

"I suppose so," the mother said.

Arty, thinking back to the tied and saddled horses, said: "What was going on here when we rode up?" The woman didn't reply. Arty stepped away from the wall, gripped the old man's arm, and shook it. "What was going on here?"

"They were eatin'," the old man said. "I got to get to a doctor."

"That's tough," Arty said without mercy. "Except that you're a bunch of pea-poor shots, we'd need doctors . . . or undertakers. What were they planning while they were eating?"

"Nothing."

A vicious shake of the arm. The youngest Sloan woman leaped up. Sheriff Whitney put a big hand on her shoulder and leaned. She struggled. He leaned harder, and she collapsed into the chair. To the old man he said: "Better answer, Sloan, if you don't want your fangs shook loose."

Sloan answered. "They were talking about going back, now that a Chinook's here, and firing the Lance cabin. Ted and Balester, that is."

"How about Bailey?"

"He just rode in this morning, real early."

"But Ted planned on taking him along, didn't he?"

"Yes."

Arty let the old man's arm drop. He shot the sheriff a look. "Go find a horse and saddle and let's go. That's probably where they've gone."

The sheriff went out the door, across the porch, and swung east toward the barn and corrals. Arty rummaged the house for guns and bullets, found plenty of both, and, while he waited for Whitney to return, systematically smashed each rifle butt against the side of the house, removed each pistol cylinder, and threw them as far as he could outside, then stuffed bullets into his coat pockets until they bulged. The oldest woman hadn't looked at him since she'd been ordered to sit down at the table. The little girl's eyes never left his face. The younger woman looked up infrequently. There was mixed hatred and dread in her face.

"Can you womenfolk harness a team?" Arty asked from the doorway where he'd seen Whitney leading up a saddled horse.

The little girl nodded.

"Good . . . better hitch one to your wagon and take this old snake to Chiloquin to the doctor." He went to his horse, mounted, and started out of the yard.

Sheriff Whitney caught up with him, looked blankly at the stuffed pockets. "You plunder 'em, Swift?"

"Yeah. Of guns and ammunition. I broke their guns and took all their bullets."

"Oh. Well, say, spare me a handful of each, will you?"

They rode at a jog through the steady warmth of the Chinook. After Whitney had reloaded his guns and stuffed his shell belt full again, he said: "Of all the treacherous families I ever run across, those Sloans. . . ."

"What'd you expect, a kiss?"

"Now then, listen. . . ."

"*You* listen. I told you everything that's happened so far, you old fool, and you didn't believe half of it right up until I saved your bacon back there."

"Saved what? Whose bacon did you save?"

"Yours. When you were running toward me, old man Sloan was set to shoot you in the back. I threw a high one that dropped near enough to upset his aim."

Sheriff Whitney blinked. "I didn't see that."

Arty looked around. "You wouldn't have if it'd connected, either, but that's not the point. Do you believe what I've told you now?"

"Well, now I do, yes."

Sheriff Whitney rumbled along, shaking his head. When they had covered several miles, he hollered out for Arty to slow down or their horses wouldn't hold out.

"What's the sense of this, anyway? There's three good men up there. Besides, Meaghan's in the house with 'em."

"Flat on his back, just about," Arty said, but he reined down to a kidney-slamming trot, and kept it up until Sheriff Whitney refused even to try to maintain the killing pace. Finally, out of feeling for their horses, Arty slowed.

They didn't stop for a breather, however, and, when the sun was directly overhead, they had covered more than half the distance to the Lance place. The ground underfoot was sheeted with icy mud. Run-off rivulets boiled where the land dipped. Overhead, clouds scudded in a wind-whipped way. The sun, lacking warmth, was brilliant enough to make them squint. When it began its long, effortless slide toward the horizon, Arty booted his mount into a slow lope, held him to it for an hour. Sheriff Whitney rode in iron silence. When Arty slackened off to a trot, however, the sheriff swore.

"Walk or lope," he said, exasperated. "Trotting'll kill a man."

Arty kept on as though he hadn't heard. His eyes were glued to the distance. Sheriff Whitney dropped steadily to the rear. Finally he loped until he caught up. He argued against the pace Arty had set. Arty didn't reply, but, when his horse stumbled, he made him walk. They rode like that until the sun was far off the meridian, then Arty made a triumphant sound in his throat.

"There they are." He pointed.

The sheriff shaded his eyes from the glare. "Three riders all right," he said, dropping his hand and swinging his head from side to side. "No way for us to get around them, though."

"We don't want to get around them," Arty said. "Just give them lots of time to get close to the cabin. They'll be between your three men, Mike Meaghan, Lance's buffalo cannon, and us. If they try to ride back this way, we'll get 'em. If they. . . ."

"I know. If they go ahead, my men'll get 'em. All right."

They slowed until the distant specks were nearly lost in the sweep of dirty white land. They rode steadily and silently, watching Sloan, Balester, and Bailey until they dipped from sight over a rise. Then Arty kicked his horse out. The sheriff groaned but kept up.

At the lip of the swell Arty dismounted, stood back watching. He didn't move for a long time, until the unsuspecting riders were dim in the distance.

When he and the sheriff started down the slope, Whitney said: "The Lance place never seemed this far before. I hope those fellers I sent up there don't get caught off guard."

Arty shot him a look. "What kind of posse men do you pick, anyway?"

"It's been known to happen," Whitney said, "to the best posses. Trouble is, as I see it, my boys might not expect anyone to come slipping up. If there was no one there when they got there, you see. . . ."

"I see this," Arty interrupted. "They've stopped."

The three riders were sitting motionlessly a long way ahead. It was difficult to tell whether they were looking ahead toward the Lance place or down their back trail to where Arty and Gordon Whitney were plodding along. Arty pursed his lips.

"I don't think they've seen anything up ahead."

"Why?"

"Well, from where they are, you can't see the Lance place. Not his buildings anyway."

"Then they must be watching us."

Arty nodded and reined south a little. "Do like I'm doing," he said. "They may think we're just riders if we're not heading in their direction."

But Sheriff Whitney had doubts. "If that's Ted Sloan up there," he said dourly, "you aren't going to throw him off that easy. I know that feller . . . he's plenty smart."

Arty kept going as though he weren't interested in the three men. Sheriff Whitney brought a flat plug of chewing tobacco out of a pocket and worried off a corner of it, pocketed the plug, and tongued the sliver up into his cheek, ruminated briefly, and spat. "This might be pretty savvy at that, going out around them like this."

"I don't want to get ahead of them. I told you that."

The sheriff grinned wolfishly. "You got no choice now, kid. If they sit there long enough, we're bound to pass 'em far southward."

The renegades were still too far off for Arty to see which way their faces were turned, but after a half-hour's riding he could make them out. They were watching Arty and the sheriff.

Arty swore but made no move to alter his course or slacken it. "Maybe you're right," he said. "If so, it'll be the first time. Maybe we'll have to go around them to the south."

"Listen, Swift," the sheriff said stiffly, "I've taken about all that kind of talk from you I think I got to."

"No you haven't," Arty said, turning on the sheriff. "You haven't begun to."

"Maybe you saved my life. I didn't see it happen, but maybe you did. That doesn't give you no cause to keep. . . ."

"If you know any real good tricks," Arty interrupted, "you'd better get ready to use them, Sheriff. They're riding south to cut us off."

Whitney's ire trailed off into silence. He chewed methodically and squinted up to where the three horsemen were loping across their path. "That's fine." There was the trace of humor in his words. "I want to arrest 'em, anyway."

"What grounds?"

"Grounds? Why, that attack on us back at the Sloan place."

"Only Bailey was in on that."

"Well, on suspicion then," Whitney said stoutly.

Arty's lips curled. "I don't think they're going to hold still for that, Sheriff, not now. Not after killing Jase and shooting a deputy U.S. marshal. I think they've got just two things in mind . . . me, and getting out of the country . . . in that order."

"You could slope," Whitney said. "They can't have recognized you yet, Arty."

"That's not very good thinking," Arty said bluntly. "There were two of us at their home place. There are still two of us, and we're still behind them. I expect that's what they were puzzling over when they were sitting there so long, watching us. Trying to make up their minds how we escaped being murdered by the old man and the others, after Bailey ran out." Arty's cold smile lingered. "They won't know. That's why they're riding to cut us off . . . to take a look and make sure."

The sheriff spat amber. "I wish those fellers I sent to Lance's were close enough to hear shooting. I'd let fly a couple times."

The three riders far ahead had slowed their horses to a fast walk. As long as Arty and Sheriff Whitney kept their course, they would all meet about three quarters of a mile ahead.

"I don't think much of riding within carbine range of them," Arty said. "This isn't like back at the Sloans'. There was a little cover there. Odds are in their favor."

"You got no choice. You said that yourself."

"No, but we can open the ball, instead of waiting for them to do it." Arty drew out his carbine, and the sheriff looked at him.

"It'd take a howitzer to reach that far, Arty."

"I know." Arty balanced the gun across his thighs. "See that notch up ahead where they were when they first saw us?"

"Yeah."

"I'm going to open up and run for that as soon's I'm close enough to dump about five fast ones at 'em. Maybe I'll make it if the shots come close enough to scatter 'em a little."

"That'll put you in front of 'em."

Arty looked disgusted. "That's one thing," he said, "we can't help now, but if they come after us, which they'll sure as the devil do after I shoot at them, maybe we can stay upright long enough to lead them to the Lances. The noise ought to rouse up your sleeping posse men."

Whitney bent, drew out his carbine, and chewed. He lay it athwart his saddle forks, spat, and estimated the distance. "Won't be long now," he said.

They kept on going until the three riders drew up, facing them. They had spread out, and even at that distance their naked guns could be seen sparkling under the sunlight.

Without speaking, Arty raised the carbine, held it a mite high, and levered off two shots. He lowered the gun, looked at the electrified renegades, then levered off three more shots. Sheriff Whitney added to the turmoil by firing his carbine several times. The men they were aiming at had reacted differently. Two had dismounted, were on the offside of their mounts with their own carbines across the saddle seats. The third man was fighting a pitching, panicked horse.

"Let's go!"

Arty led out. Sheriff Whitney drummed along a length behind. He was swinging his carbine as if it were a quirt. They had gone a quarter of a mile before the attacked men recovered sufficiently to remount and take up the pursuit. The distant popping of their guns sounded deceptively remote and harmless.

What Arty couldn't have anticipated happened. Two of their pursuers were mounted upon exceptionally fleet animals. They left the third renegade far behind in the first half mile, gained steadily upon Arty and the sheriff, who couldn't make a direct run but had to keep angling in order to remain upon the fringe of carbine range. Over the noise of the wind, the drum roll of running horses, the sheriff called out: "We aren't going to make it, Arty! They're going to intercept us!"

He got no answer. Arty rode tall in the saddle. He held his reins lightly, threw up the carbine and emptied it, lowered it, and pushed fresh cartridges into it as he rocked along. Three times he emptied it and shouted for Whitney to keep up the firing while he reloaded.

Riding like that, at a dead run, one fired until the other reloaded. Finally, when Arty held out another box of shells to the sheriff, Whitney put into words his elation that Arty had taken all the ammunition from the Sloan place.

In the face of their steady, unending gunfire one of the

renegades veered off. He had to reload. His companion plunged ahead until he, too, was compelled to give way before the uninterrupted fusillade. The first man to ride off, jumped from his horse and knelt. Arty began to work his reins, making his horse change leads and course at the same time. He held his breath when the man fired, watched him lever up another shell, and yelled at Whitney to concentrate on the dismounted man. They were both firing at him then. The renegade finally gave up, leaped into his saddle, and whirled to put more distance between himself and the unusual, completely unexpected firepower of the lawmen.

As they milled, the third renegade came up and flung off his horse, knelt, and fired. The first shot was close. Arty could hear it sing overhead. He risked a glance westward. The Lance cabin and barn were barely discernible far ahead. The gunman's second shot brought a bellow from Sheriff Whitney. Arty turned to look. The lawman was riding bareheaded, his hair tumbling every which way in the wind. That second shot had carried the sheriff's hat away.

"Get him!" Arty shouted. "Keep shooting! That one's a marksman."

They emptied their guns at the kneeling man with no apparent effect, the back of a running horse being the most difficult shooting position in the world. Reloading, Arty's fingers fumbled badly; he spilled shells and swore. All three of the renegades were now kneeling and firing. Sheriff Whitney opened up again, levering shells up as fast as he could tug the trigger. When Arty was ready, the sheriff was lowering his carbine.

That was when it happened.

They could see red flashes, dirty puffs of smoke from all three guns. Suddenly the renegades stopped firing. Arty could see that two of them had lowered their weapons, but the last man to come up was tracking them with his gun barrel. Arty began a frantic zigzagging. Sheriff Whitney was just beginning to switch his reins when Arty saw the renegade's gunfire. There was a gasp behind him. He swung just as Sheriff Whitney went down in a sprawl of hoofs and leather, his carbine flying straight ahead.

VII

Arty reined up hard, slewed his horse as a triumphant shout went up from the watching renegades. Sheriff Whitney was struggling to rise. He would get part way up, then fall back. Arty swung in low, with his weight thrown on the horse's off-side. He caught Whitney by the shoulder, straightened his leg in the stirrup for leverage and heaved with all his strength. His horse staggered, but Whitney, dazed, had presence enough of mind to spring upward. He clawed at Arty's coat with hooked fingers that bit down through the sheepskin.

Arty was veering the horse when Whitney caught him around the middle, righted himself behind the cantle. His breath was upon Arty's neck. He tried to say something, but the Chinook and the strained huskiness of his voice made the words indistinguishable.

The outlaws were racing toward them. Arty laid the reins against his horse's neck and sent the beast to the north. There was a break in the land that way. Gunfire erupted behind them.

"You all right?"

"Will be!" the sheriff shouted back. "Shook the stuffin' loose in me."

"What happened?"

"He hit my horse." The sheriff was twisting, raising his pistol. "I don't think we'll get far now," he said, sounding more like himself. "Them first two got awful fast animals."

Arty's horse was laboring heavily. The double load, plus his long, grueling ride earlier, was telling on him. Arty wanted to favor him but dared not. Through slitted eyes he gauged the distance to the arroyo, doubted they would make it, drew his carbine out, and fired it rapidly until it was empty, in an effort to slow the pursuit a little.

Sheriff Whitney reached for Arty's carbine. "Let me have that . . . you just keep this horse goin'."

They rode two hundred yards, and Arty saw the broken lip of land looming up. Behind him the sheriff had reloaded the carbine, and was levering regularly spaced shots at the riders closing in. They were close to the arroyo when Arty heard a pistol fired behind them. He twisted to look; the renegades were close enough for handguns, all right. Arty's breath came in tight gasps. His horse stumbled, recovered, but was slowing badly, his lungs pumping with a bubbling sound.

Knowing they wouldn't make the arroyo, Arty yelled to the sheriff: "Get ready to unload! I'm going to haul up here. As soon as you hit the ground, run for that cutbank up ahead. There's a deep gully down the far side . . . brush down there, some trees. Understand?"

"Yeah, I'm ready."

Arty waited until the slowing horse stumbled again, lurched clumsily in his effort to recover, then hauled back on the reins, and, before the animal had fully stopped, Sheriff Whitney slid off. He levered off two shots while Arty was swinging clear, then they both ran for the uppermost tip of the arroyo.

Gunshots scattered earth behind them. One shot went overhead, too close for comfort, and Whitney swore as he slid to the very edge of the gully, drew in a big lungful of air, and threw himself over the steep side.

Arty was already going down the muddy slope, stiff-legged, fighting to maintain his equilibrium. Brush and trees swept past, and then he was on the bottom. There were crusts of dirty snow there to break through, slowing his momentum. Sheriff

Whitney fell the last thirty feet of his slide, rolling end over end until he struck the snow. He came up spitting and shaking his bare head, still clutching the carbine.

Arty pressed close to the nearly vertical cutbank and waited, eyes slitted, looking up. He could hear the men up above but they didn't come as far as the lip of land. Arty was disappointed.

The sheriff was stomping mud off his trousers when they both heard someone up above call out in an excited way: "That first one was young Swift! I got a good look at him!" There was a sound of men running afoot, jingling spurs, thudding boots. Arty called to the lawman, motioned for him to get closer to the wall of soft earth. Whitney stumbled through the snow, pressed close to the mud, and raised the carbine. They remained like that for several minutes. No one appeared overhead, and the sounds above ceased. Whitney looked questioningly at Arty without speaking. The younger man scowled.

Back from the earth wall were trees, brush, a little run-off creek boiling with dirty water. Arty jerked his head in that direction. They made a run for it but no shots came after them.

"You know this place?" Sheriff Whitney asked when they were concealed in the wild growth and shadows.

"Yes, I know it. It slopes up gently toward the Lance place. They could ride around there and come down in here, but eastward it ends in a pretty rough patch of chaparral growin' on a steep slope. Behind us there's a lot of underbrush. Men on horseback'd never get through that way."

"But they could from the west?"

Arty nodded, listening. There wasn't a sound. Even the Chinook breeze had stopped.

"We got to maneuver around," the sheriff said, "so we're able to cover that opening to the west, Arty." He started to move. The younger man reached out and restrained him with one hand.

"Listen."

They had to sit there a long time, but eventually the sound of riders came up above. Arty cocked his head. The men were going west. He smiled and nodded at the sheriff. "You're right. They're heading for the west slope. Come on."

They worked their way through the undergrowth as carefully as possible. The sun sank far enough toward the horizon to obscure the arroyo. It was cold down there, and, before they stopped creeping through the brush and trees, Sheriff Whitney was shivering. His muddy clothing was becoming stiff.

"Here," Arty said, sinking low in the tangle of brush and gloom. "See through there? That clearing's where they'll come down."

Whitney raised the carbine. It shook in his hands. The face snugged against the stock was grayish, the lips turning blue. "I'm ready," Whitney said, "but, if we got to spend the night here, I'm going to freeze to death."

Arty looked at the suffering man, and felt a faint stirring of pity. "Guess you've had time to figure whether I was bulling you along or not," he said.

The sheriff's eyes wavered, dropped to Arty's face. "Son," he said, "I'll never doubt you again."

Arty was embarrassed. He flicked open the gate of his pistol, spun the cylinder, punched out spent casings, and reloaded from the bullets in his coat pockets. "You stay here," he said, rising. "I'm going north a little and see if I can spot them. I don't like this quiet."

The sheriff looked disturbed. "What could they be up to?"

"I don't know. That's what I aim to find out." He strained for sound and heard none, shook his head a little. "Wonder how come those men at Lance's haven't heard all this firing?"

"Must be because the wind was carrying it away," Whitney said.

Arty conceded it was entirely possible. He began to move off.

When he broke clear of the brush, there were some scattered pines, a juniper or two, several scraggly oaks. The part of the arroyo where they were was gloomily silent. He stood motionlessly for several minutes, watching for movement, listening for sound, and then he went from tree to tree toward higher ground. By the time he reached a buck run winding up the northern side, he was worried. When he got high enough to see, his worry increased. There was no sign at all of the renegades.

He crept higher, strained to look down toward the Lance place. Shadows were lengthening on the range, early evening was coming. He couldn't see a thing. There was a little consolation in the fact that he couldn't hear anything, either. The renegades, wherever they were, weren't attacking the Lances, either. He had started back down the buck run, heading for the brush barrier that cut him off from Sheriff Whitney, when he heard a single gunshot.

He plunged deeper into the thicket, hurrying, but when there was no other shot he slowed a little, peering up over the brush from time to time. There was nothing to see.

Just as he was breasting the last of the thicket, a pistol shot rang out up ahead, where he knew Whitney was. But again there was only one shot. Puzzled, wary, he drew his handgun and slipped forward with all the stealth of an Indian. When he saw Gordon Whitney, the sheriff was squatting in the fringe of chaparral that separated him from the open, gently lifting land that led out of the arroyo to the west.

Arty crept up close, made a little sound, and said his name. Whitney only swung his head. He was obviously watching something out in the clearing. When Arty was down beside him, he pointed through a break in the brush. A big, tawny cougar was lying on its side out there, as though asleep.

"He was in the brush right here," Sheriff Whitney said. "He

got up and came right at me, snarling. I let him have one with the carbine an' he tumbled, got up, and lit out of here like a streak. When he was crossing the clearing, someone out there downed him for good with a pistol."

Arty sighed. "First time a cougar ever did me a favor. I was getting scairt . . . couldn't hear 'em or see 'em."

"They're up there to the right, Arty. Back in that brush."

"Waitin'," Arty said. "Just goin' to sit up there and wait for us to come out."

The sheriff rubbed one blue hand against his soggy pants. "I'd do the same," he said, "before I'd come down here across the open place." He blew on his hands and picked the carbine up again. "That cussed cougar like to frighten the tar out of me. First time I ever saw one make for a man."

"Must have a mate in here. Too late for cubs."

"Maybe. Maybe he had a bellyful of some hunter's strychnine, too, but he didn't act sick. Anyway, he sure didn't run like he was sick." Whitney peered through the brush at the dead animal. "Must be eight feet from nose to tip of his tail." He wagged his head again. "I'd rather face ten Ted Sloans than one of those things when it's on the prod."

Arty listened without heeding. He was studying the brush to their right and ahead. "Do you know about where that feller was when he fired?"

"About. I didn't let fly because I figured they'd all cut loose before I could get away. Besides, from up there they can see the brush move down here."

Arty nodded. "Pump one in up there where he shot from, Sheriff."

Whitney frowned. "They'll make it pretty hot if I do."

"Anything's better'n sitting down here all night waiting to freeze stiff," Arty said. "Go on . . . shoot."

Whitney's gun barrel moved a little along the brush patch off to the right; when he was satisfied, he fired. Both he and Arty could hear the slug tearing through the undergrowth. Apparently it was close, because an answering shot came, then another, finally four closely spaced, then more silence.

Arty drew upward a little and grinned at the sheriff. "Didn't bring any lead flood, did it? Give 'em another one, but this time don't drop flat." Arty raised his handgun, waiting. He bent a frown on the reluctant sheriff. "Go ahead . . . I'm ready."

When Whitney fired, he aimed in the same general direction. Arty was poised. When the first answering shot came back, he fired at the puff of dirty smoke, thumbed back the dog, and fired a second time, then again. His strategy had been elemental. He couldn't see the renegade, but he knew from his gunsmoke approximately where he was. He fired first at the position below the puff of smoke. Both other shots had been on either side of his original shot. He had blanketed the spot. His reward was a howl, some furiously wiggling brush, and a score of angry shots in return. He dropped flat in the mud beside the sheriff, who was staring at him with disapproval.

"See?"

"Yeah, but I got one. You heard him yell, didn't you?"

"If he yelled," the sheriff said bleakly, "he isn't dead, and if he isn't dead you didn't help us much, kid."

When the furious fusillade died away, Arty hunched forward, got up, and peered cautiously through the brush. There was no further sign of movement. He sat back, punched out empty casings, and reloaded. "They must have as much ammunition as we have," he said.

"Ammunition my foot," the sheriff said. "They got us bottled up neat as a whistle. Arty, we got to figure some way to get out of here. It's going to get to ten below tonight."

Arty nodded. "I've been thinking that, by now, those fellers of yours over at John's should have heard the shooting. The wind's gone down. It's clear and still out."

Whitney peered through the chaparral. "And it's gettin' dark," he said. "Couple hours from now they can cross that clearing and get right in here with us."

Arty looked up. The sun was streaking the sky with long, flaming streamers. He could picture it hovering over the mountains beyond Lance's place. With little conviction he said: "They'll be running as much risk as we will, Sheriff."

"Yeah? Three of them with horses against us two afoot? I'll tell you, Arty . . . you stay down here and I'll see if I can get over to the Lances."

"Afoot?"

The sheriff gripped the carbine tighter as he nodded. He squirmed around until he was on both knees, then leaned the carbine against the brush.

"Why don't I try it?" Arty asked.

"Because you're dryer'n I am, that's why. Even if I didn't freeze, I'd be shakin' so bad I couldn't shoot straight, sitting down here like this all night."

Arty nodded, watching the heavy features, seeing how they were pulled into a tight mask of cold and pain. "Take the carbine with you."

"I won't need it. Just my pistol's enough. It'll be dark soon now. If they see me, they'll have to be within pistol range to do it." Whitney was straightening up stiffly.

Arty twisted around and pointed northward. "Keep going straight through that brush, Sheriff. Don't cut right or left or you might get lost. It's about three hundred feet thick. When you come out where there's trees, pines, junipers, a few old oaks, turn west and keep going up the side hill. When you've gone about a quarter mile, you'll be atop the gully. From there it's straight as an arrow about two miles, maybe less, to the Lances'."

Without answering, the sheriff ducked low and began a waddling walk into the brush. Arty winced every time he heard limbs whip back. After that stopped, there was nothing but silence. He checked the carbine, shoved in fresh cartridges, reloaded his pistol, and shrugged down deeper into his sheepskin coat. The sun was gone all at once and night had come.

He left the place where they had made their stand. He worked his way back deeper into the brush, listening. Once he heard a horseshoe strike stone, but whether it was his loose horse or a ridden animal he had no way of knowing. The fact that no gunshot erupted made him think it was a ridden animal. He continued to retreat deeper down the little cañon, was almost to the eastern barrier, when, up where he and Whitney had been, someone fired a pistol. He stood still, listening. When no other sound came, he turned, grasped branches of brush, and began to work his way up the wall of the arroyo.

The moon came up, all silver and frozen-looking. The temperature dropped steadily. He got very close to the upper rim before he stopped, leaned into the brush, and let it support him. He was tired and hungry. Visibility was poor in spite of the moon. He could see no more than a hundred feet behind him. Beyond that distance things were shadowy.

With a powerful heave he gained the lip of the arroyo and lay there breathing heavily. He got up slowly, gripping the carbine, and waited a bit before he began to move away from the edge of the arroyo, traveling west.

He was striding along, wary but relaxed, within twenty feet of the arroyo's lip in the event he had to take cover again, when he heard a horse down below. He went flat, crawled to the rim, and peered down. There was a horseman down there, but he was leading his mount, not riding it. Leading it so that it was between the man and the tangled brush. Arty watched for several minutes, tried to understand how the renegades were working, then shrugged, got up again, and started walking.

Where he and Sheriff Whitney had abandoned his horse, Arty made a quartering excursion, but the animal had either been taken or had strayed away. It wasn't there. He resumed his former course and pushed on. Ahead was open country. If the killers found him out there. . . .

Then he saw the horses, dark and still beneath a dying fir tree, and his heart pounded so loud he thought everyone around must hear it. Three animals—his horse, and two of the outlaws' animals—were tethered.

With the elation of a man to whom a last minute reprieve has been awarded, he started toward the animals. He was crunching over the freezing ground, hurrying, when he saw a shadow move swiftly off to one side. There was an unmistakable glimmer of metal in the moonlight. Arty dropped as though shot, squirmed frantically toward the only cover around, a spindly growth of new chaparral about six inches high, and the gun went off twenty yards ahead of him.

The bullet sang low over the ground. Arty shouldered his own weapon as the man was levering, fired pointblank. The renegade jumped up as though an invisible hand had jerked a rope. He twisted in mid-air and broke at the waist just before he struck the ground. After that he made no move at all, and Arty leaped up and ran as fast as he could toward the excited horses. He wrenched one set of reins loose, swung the horse, toed into the stirrup, and shot a glance sideways at the downed man. His carbine was lying just beyond reach of one outstretched hand, his hat was beside him, and his face was twisted sideways with moonlight shining on it. He was dead.

As Arty hit the saddle, sank in the hooks, and leaned forward, he heard a horseman clattering up out of the arroyo. Farther away another man called out. The rider answered him.

The horse Arty had was faster than anything he had ever ridden in his life. Wind whipping past his face forced water out of his eyes, down his cheeks. He gave the beast full rein, gradually straightened up, and looked backward. Someone tried a long shot that was wide. Soon afterward he heard two riders thundering after him. He fired his carbine twice, but missed; the horsemen kept coming.

The stirrups were too short, so he had to ride jockey style, knees bent far more than was natural. After a time he kicked his feet loose and rode by leg grip alone. He was almost thrown out of the saddle a moment later when the horse snorted and gave a violent leap sideways. Arty had only a glimpse of the cause—a big black bear was glaring at him. He had no time to shoot because, aside from his preoccupation, the horse gave an extra burst of speed and swept forward with tremendous power.

By the time Arty had regained his balance, was gathering up the reins, the night erupted with gunshots, the roar of an angry bear, more gunshots, and finally several yells. He twisted enough to fire three carbine shots toward the sounds.

Up ahead quite suddenly a gun blossomed out of the night, and Arty ducked when the slug tore overhead, placed the report, and knew it was a pistol.

"Sheriff! Sheriff, it's me . . . Arty!"

A muffled roar came back, and dead ahead a figure rose up out of the darkness. Arty caught up the reins and drew back, but the panicked horse paid no heed. He sawed on the bit, finally looped one rein around the horn, and bent all his strength to pulling the horse's head part way around. Finally the beast responded enough to make a large circle and come in, much slower, near Sheriff Whitney. Arty fought him down to a standstill eventually, kicked the left stirrup out, and Gordon Whitney swung up behind the cantle with a loud grunt.

"Where are they?"

"There's a black bear back there a bit," Arty said. "That's the last I heard of 'em."

"How'd you get the horse . . . get out of the cañon?"

"Crawled up the far wall. Killed one they left with the horses, got this critter, and rode like the devil was behind me."

"He is," Sheriff Whitney said loudly. "I can hear him coming. How much farther to the Lances'?"

"Half mile. You see any sign of those men of yours up ahead?"

"Hide nor hair," the sheriff answered, and swore. "They sure must've heard all this commotion by now.

Arty was worried.

"They're gainin', boy."

Arty turned briefly, saw nothing, heard the roll of racing horses, and looked forward again. He thought he could make out a flickering light far ahead. He was peering intently at it when a whisking shadow up ahead darted in front of his trail. He had no time to raise the carbine before a second shadow materialized. This time he spat words at the sheriff and threw the gun to his shoulder. It was when a third rider showed briefly, then faded in with the others, that the sheriff caught his arm.

"Them's my boys . . . hold it!"

Arty lowered the carbine a trifle, and the sheriff called out. A man answered. The three men broke into a gallop and swung in beside Arty and Sheriff Whitney.

"What's up, Sheriff? What's the shootin' about back yonder?"

"There're couple fellers after us back there. One might be Ted Sloan." The posse men began to rein up, turn their horses in the trail. The sheriff shouted at them. "Come on! Don't stop to fight 'em here . . . head for the Lance place."

They rode in a tight group, and, while they could hear the pursuit, it was far too dark to see it. Arty strained to recognize the posse men but couldn't. He looked for the fading lamplight again, was surprised to see how much closer it was. He automatically began to draw inward on the reins, and this time the horse was content to obey. He slowed to an easy gallop.

"Nobody showed up around the cabin, Sheriff."

The sheriff made an inarticulate sound deep in his chest. "Don't expect they did," he said. "We been fightin' the passel of 'em since early this morning."

Arty turned his head. "How're the folks at the Lances'?"

"Fine. That winged deputy marshal's worried about you, and so's the girl. The old man's got a gun big enough to drive a team of mules into, and he's settin' on the porch waitin' for something to come along to shoot at."

"When did you first hear the shootin'?" the sheriff asked.

" 'Bout an hour ago."

"Well . . . never mind." The sheriff shook Arty's arm. "What now?"

"Have them go off to one side. We'll make the cabin now, all right. Have 'em go off where they can't be seen, and, when the whelps go past, close in behind 'em."

"Yeah," the sheriff said, "that's sense." He turned and yelled to the posse men, who drew off and faded into the night.

With the orange glow as his guide, Arty swept up to the yard and let out a shout of identity. Instantly the door flew open. He nudged the sheriff, who was slow getting down. "Tell 'em to close that door and put out that lamp, Sheriff." He continued around the house to the barn, flung the saddle off, stripped away the bridle, and left the animal loose. He ran swiftly across the yard to the rear of the cabin and was met in the doorway by a shadow that caught at him, held him close with astonishing strength.

"Arty. . . ."

He kissed her, held his arms tightly around her shoulders, the carbine sticking up past her head. "Sarah, everybody all right?"

"Yes." She released him, stepped back, and tried to see his

face. "Who is chasing you?"

"Two of 'em. I don't know for sure which two."

"But there are only two, aren't there?"

"There's three now . . . some kin of Sloan's named Bailey. He came in this morning, early." He brushed past her, heading for the darkened parlor.

"That you, Art?" Meaghan called.

He groped for the cot, gripped the hand that was being held out there. "Yes, it's me. We had a fight at Sloan's."

"The sheriff was just telling us. He said you got one at the arroyo where they bottled you two up."

"Yes, but there's still two of 'em left." Arty was turning away. "Where's the sheriff?"

"Out on the porch with Lance."

"I'll go out there. Things ought to open up pretty quick now."

"Go ahead," Meaghan said calmly, then raised his voice. "Sarah, lie down on the floor out there."

Arty went outside, his blood racing hotly. While his free hand was still upon the door latch, gunshots blew the night apart several hundred yards from the cabin. A man cried out in alarm and surprise. There was a regular drum roll of pistol shots, then Arty saw them. Both were riding twisted in their saddles.

The sheriff said: "Can't figure how we got behind 'em. Don't know it isn't us."

One of the renegades bent low; his horse exploded in a flash of speed and swept away from the other man. Arty ran down off the porch, raising his carbine.

The outlaw swung to look toward the cabin, apparently saw the man afoot waiting for him, and swerved his horse violently. Arty didn't fire but tracked the man with his gun barrel.

"Rein up! Throw down your gun and rein up!"

The outlaw fired a pistol; its tongue of flame lanced outward nearly a foot. Arty squeezed a shot, and off to one side two more shots exploded. The outlaw's gun flashed in the moonlight. His horse was doubling back when he fired. The man was a perfect target, erect and turning in the saddle. He got off two shots, both in Arty's direction. It was as though someone had kicked Arty's leg from under him. He went down in a sprawl, the carbine flying out of his grip. There was a wrenching stab of pain in the right leg. He rolled over, used both hands to push himself into a sitting position, flashed for his .45, and thumbed off shots as he brought the gun up. One of them found a home; the renegade reeled just as his horse came out of its bending turn, straightened out with a churning spurt of speed. He dropped his gun, made a wild effort to grab the horse's mane, missed, and fell hard.

Arty got up, groped for the carbine, used it as old man Sloan had used his, and began to hobble over to where the renegade lay upon his back. Sheriff Whitney beat him to the sprawled figure. John Lance came up in a few seconds.

Whitney gestured with his pistol. His voice sounded incredulous. "He's alive, Arty. I don't see how, but he is."

Arty worked his way closer, bent low, and peered. He grunted and holstered his pistol. "Sloan," he said grimly.

"Yeah, Ted Sloan." The sheriff knelt to see how badly the injured man was hit. Arty watched, speechless and bleak-looking.

John Lance bent down beside the sheriff. His head was lowered, his hands moved with dexterity, showing more experience than Whitney. The sheriff rocked back on his heels and looked at the rancher a moment, then let Lance finish the examination.

Looking at the injured man, Whitney said: "Recognize me, don't you, Sloan? Well, when you're up again, feller, I'm going to fix you up for a long time to come. You and your whole cussed rattlesnake tribe."

Arty lowered himself gingerly, using the carbine as a crutch. He growled at Sheriff Whitney. "Shut up for a while, why don't you? Better yet, go see what happened to the other one."

Whitney looked at Arty's face, sat there a moment, got up, brushed his knees, and turned away.

"Sloan, you know me? Arthur Swift. . . ."

The staring eyes flickered, stayed on Arty's face. Sloan could make no sound. A stingy trickle of blood, black and thick in the moonlight, lay over one side of his mouth.

"I didn't think I'd ever be sorry to see you die, Sloan. I guess a feller forgets a little when it comes out like this. I'm sort of sorry, Sloan. . . ."

The dying man's eyes warmed briefly as he struggled to say something. When his lips parted, blood came. He died.

John Lance went quietly to the house while Arty was still leaning upon the carbine, alone in the cold, still moon wash. When John returned, he had his Bible. Arty struggled upright, turned away.

The three posse men jogged into the yard with a fourth rider between them. His face was dirty and beard-stubbled, like wet putty where the moonlight touched it beneath his hat. At sight of Arty the men hauled up.

"Here's the other one."

Arty gazed at the man, saw no one he knew, and asked what his name was.

"Will Bailey. I'm cousin to the Sloans."

"Yeah, I know. They told us that after you ran out on them at the Sloan place."

"I didn't run out on no. . . ."

"Shut up, Bailey." In the silence John Lance's muted tones came softly. Arty flicked his head sideways a little. "Hear that?" he asked.

"Yeah. What of it?"

"Your cousin's dead, Bailey. That's John Lance readin' a prayer over him."

Bailey drew up his saddle, pulled his eyes away from Arty, and twisted forward and sideways to see past the posse men on his right.

John Lance's voice stopped. He was standing with his head thrown far back; the moonlight was glowing over him. Arty watched Bailey. The renegade froze, watching the tableau for a moment, then let out a long sigh and dropped back in his saddle again.

"Ted. . . ."

"Yeah," Arty said quietly, looking up. "Bailey, I'm going to do better by you than you did by me. Get down off that horse and get your gun." The renegade stared at Arty. "Go on, get down. You got a chance to outdraw me coming. Get down!"

"No."

"What d'you mean, *no?*"

"It's all over with, Swift. I never had anything special against you. It was your brother, mostly."

"They killed him, and my paw."

"And you killed Balester . . . Ted. It's all finished."

"Is it? With fellers like you still ridin' around?"

Bailey nodded. "I'm finished, too, I reckon. Came along just in time to get nailed."

Arty felt a tug on his sleeve, turned. Mike Meaghan was standing there with a thick shawl around his shoulders. His face was white, his eyes dry-looking but very steady. "Come on, Art . . . he's right. It's all over."

He pushed the younger man toward the cabin. Sarah was in the doorway. Her father was walking toward her, shoulders bowed.

Mike stopped. "The law's satisfied, Art, two ways." At Arty's silent look he went on: "Your law . . . an eye for an eye . . .

that's satisfied . . . fellers on both sides who started this thing are dead. The legal law's satisfied. There's Bailey as a prisoner, the witness, and me who can testify how things were." He paused a minute, sucked in a big breath of air. "Art, you kept your promise to me up there by the cabin and down here when I gave you the badge. I want another promise now."

"Yeah, I know you do," Arty said.

"Well?"

Arty nodded. "All right, Marshal, you got it. The feud's over."

Mike Meaghan put a hand around Arty's shoulder, and they started toward the door.

ABOUT THE AUTHOR

Lauran Paine who, under his own name and various pseudonyms has written over a thousand books, was born in Duluth, Minnesota. His family moved to California when he was at a young age and his apprenticeship as a Western writer came about through the years he spent in the livestock trade, rodeos, and even motion pictures where he served as an extra because of his expert horsemanship in several films starring movie cowboy Johnny Mack Brown. In the late 1930s, Paine trapped wild horses in northern Arizona and even, for a time, worked as a professional farrier. Paine came to know the Old West through the eyes of many who had been born in the previous century, and he learned that Western life had been very different from the way it was portrayed on the screen. "I knew men who had killed other men," he later recalled. "But they were the exceptions. Prior to and during the Depression, people were just too busy eking out an existence to indulge in Saturday-night brawls." He served in the U.S. Navy in the Second World War and began writing for Western pulp magazines following his discharge. It is interesting to note that all of his earliest novels (written under his own name and the pseudonym Mark Carrel) were published in the British market and he soon had as strong a following in that country as in the United States. Paine's Western fiction is characterized by strong plots, authenticity, an apparently effortless ability to construct situation and character, and a preference for building his stories upon a solid foundation of historical fact. *Adobe Empire* (1956), one of his best novels, is a fictionalized account of the last twenty years in the life of trader William Bent and, in an off-trail way, has a melancholy, bittersweet texture that is not easily forgotten. In later novels like *Cache Cañon* (Five Star Westerns, 1998) and *Halfmoon Ranch* (Five Star Westerns, 2007), he showed that the special magic and power of his stories and characters had only matured along with his basic themes of changing times, changing attitudes, learning from experience, respecting Nature, and the yearning for a simpler, more moderate way of life. His next Five Star Western will be *Lightning Strike*.